SAMANTHA SPINNER

SPINNER

AND THE

SPECTACULAR

SPECS

BOOKS BY RUSSELL GINNS

Samantha Spinner and the Super-Secret Plans

Samantha Spinner and the Spectacular Specs

Samantha Spinner and the Boy in the Ball

SAMANTHA SPINNER
AND THE
SPECTACULAR SPECS

RUSSELL GINNS

ILLUSTRATED BY BARBARA FISINGER

A VEARLING BOOK

Text copyright © 2019 by Russell Ginns
Cover art and interior illustrations copyright © 2019 by Barbara Fisinger

Image Credits: pp. 1 (top), 81 (left): Getty Images; p. 1 (bottom left and right): Kartapranata, Gunawan, "Borobudur Mandala." Wikimedia Commons. 17 December 2009, commons.wikimedia .org/wiki/File:Borobudur_Mandala.svg, and "Borobudur Cross Section." Wikimedia Commons. 6 November 2011, commons.wikimedia.org/wiki/File:Borobudur_Cross_Section_en.svg; pp. 81 (right), 90, 122, 170 (top), 291, 292: public domain; pp. 109 (left), 217: Shutterstock; p. 169: Bedaux, R., and Diaby and P. Maas, *L'Architecture de Ddjenne*, Snoeck-Ducaji & Zoon, January 1, 2009; p. 170 (bottom): Zamani Project; p. 388: EVOlution Graphics

All rights reserved. Published in the United States by Yearling, an imprint of Random House Children's Books, a division of Penguin Random House LLC, New York. Originally published in hardcover in the United States by Delacorte Press, an imprint of Random House Children's Books, New York, in 2019.

Yearling and the jumping horse design are registered trademarks of Penguin Random House LLC.

Visit us on the Web! rhcbooks.com

Educators and librarians, for a variety of teaching tools, visit us at RHTeachersLibrarians.com

The Library of Congress has cataloged the hardcover edition of this work as follows:
Names: Ginns, Russell, author.
Title: Samantha Spinner and the spectacular specs / Russell Ginns; illustrated by Barbara Fisinger.
Description: First edition. | New York: Delacorte Press [2019] |
Summary: "Uncle Paul is still missing. And Samantha just received a new gift from him: a pair of strange purple sunglasses. Are they another powerful present? A clue to his whereabouts? Or just a bad fashion choice? Samantha and Nipper need to figure it out fast, because here comes the SUN!" —Provided by publisher.
Identifiers: LCCN 2018028042 (print) | LCCN 2018034932 (ebook) |
ISBN 978-1-5247-2006-3 (el) | ISBN 978-1-5247-2004-9 (hardback)
Subjects: | CYAC: Adventure and adventurers—Fiction. | Brothers and sisters—Fiction. | Missing persons—Fiction. | Uncles—Fiction. | Family life—Fiction. | Mystery and detective stories. | BISAC: JUVENILE FICTION / Action & Adventure / General. | JUVENILE FICTION / Family / General (see also headings under Social Issues). | JUVENILE FICTION / Girls & Women.
Classification: LCC PZ7.G438943 (ebook) | LCC PZ7.G438943 Sam 2019 (print) | DDC [Fic]—dc23

ISBN 978-1-5247-2007-0 (pbk.)

Printed in the United States of America
10 9 8 7 6 5 4 3 2 1
First Yearling Edition 2019

TO KEN WESTERMAN

Teachers launch us on amazing adventures.
They broaden our horizons and expand our world
in ways we never expect.

Borobudur

Borobudur is the world's largest Buddhist temple. It was built in the fifteenth century in central Java, Indonesia.

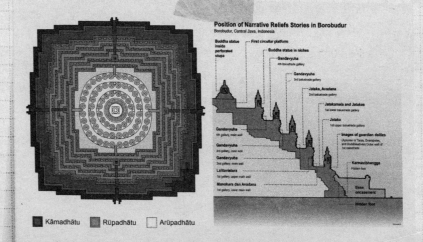

Position of Narrative Reliefs Stories in Borobudur
Borobudur, Central Java, Indonesia

Buddha statue inside perforated stupa · · · First circular platform
Buddha statue in niches
Gandavyuha
4th balustrade gallery
Gandavyuha
3rd balustrade gallery
Jataka, Avadana
2nd balustrade gallery
Jatakamala and Jatakas
1st lower balustrade gallery
Jataka
1st upper balustrade gallery
Images of guardian deities
(Aptunas or Taras, Dvarapalas, and Buddhisattvas) Outer wall of 1st balustrade

Gandavyuha
4th gallery, main wall
Gandavyuha
3rd gallery, main wall
Gandavyuha
2nd gallery, main wall
Karmavibhangga
Hidden foot
Lalitavistara
1st gallery, upper main wall
Manohara dan Avadana
1st gallery, lower main wall
Base encasement
Hidden foot

Kāmadhātu   Rūpadhātu   Arūpadhātu

The structure consists of nine platforms with a big dome on top. The lower six platforms are square. The top three platforms are circular and ringed with stone statues of the Buddha, each seated inside a small domed chamber called a *stupa*.

Borobudur is Indonesia's most visited tourist attraction. Millions of people climb the temple each year to marvel at its three thousand relief sculptures, its seventy-two stupas, and the panoramic view of forests and volcanoes.

* * *

One of the stupas isn't really stone. Look for the dome that's darker than all the others. If you take a closer look, you'll see that it's really an industrial-strength balloon filled with helium. Ropes tether it to the center of a shallow pit.

Push the balloon aside and hop into the bucket below. Your weight will pull the balloon down and you'll sink into a vast cavern . . . inside a volcano!

You'll drift down past razor-sharp stones and blazing-hot columns of steam. Keep your arms and legs inside the bucket at all times—if you lose your balance, you'll tumble into a river of hot lava.

CHAPTER ONE

A TAIL OF WOE

"Look here!" Samantha shouted from under the kitchen table. "Now!"

She shoved a chair out of the way with one foot to make room for her brother.

"What? Where?" said Nipper, bending down quickly.

He misjudged the height of the table and banged his head.

"That hurt," he said, rubbing his forehead and inching in beside her. "You forgot to say *duck.*"

"All right," she replied. " 'Duck.' Now look here."

Samantha removed the purple sunglasses Uncle Paul had given her. She put them on Nipper's face and pointed at a table leg.

"*PSST?*" Nipper asked.

"That's right," she answered, taking the glasses from him and putting them on again. Through the octagonal lenses, she saw four yellow letters glowing on the leg:

P

S

S

T

"And watch this," she told him.

She reached out and grabbed the leg where it met the table.

"Gotcha," said Samantha.

Click!

A section slid downward, revealing an opening. It hissed as a stream of air rushed into the hollow leg.

"Whoa," said Nipper. "A second secret pneumatic tube."

Samantha nodded. They had already found one pneumatic tube under the table when she'd gotten the glasses. She pointed at that hissing table leg on her right with one hand.

"Into Seattle," she said.

She pointed at this new opening with her other hand.

"Out of Seattle," she said, and let out a big, satisfied sigh.

At long last, this was a major breakthrough.

When Samantha's uncle Paul disappeared, he left presents for his nieces and nephew. Samantha's sister, Buffy, got $2,400,000,000. Samantha's brother, Nipper, got the New York Yankees. Samantha got an old rusty umbrella. Of course, it seemed terribly unfair—until Samantha started taking a closer look at things. She discovered that the umbrella was a super-secret map of the world! Samantha and her brother traveled to France, Italy, and Egypt, and defeated the RAIN—the Royal Academy of International Ninjas. They even rescued the *Mona Lisa*. But Uncle Paul was still missing.

Then a mysterious pair of sunglasses arrived with a note.

> *Watch out for the SUN.*
> —Horace

For Samantha, this was proof that Uncle Paul was alive.

She also had a sketch of an obelisk that she'd copied from a picture she found in the Temple of Horus in Egypt. When she discovered the obelisk was a monument in

New York City called Cleopatra's Needle, Samantha suspected that Uncle Paul was alive and also in New York.

Then a message came from her older sister. Buffy had written to tell the family that she had moved to Manhattan to work on a play with help from "the famous Broadway producer Horace Temple."

After that, Samantha *knew* that Uncle Paul was alive, in New York . . . and with Buffy Spinner.

Unfortunately, Samantha couldn't get there. The magtrain she'd found with the Super-Secret Plans didn't go to New York, or anywhere near it. Her parents promised they would visit New York after school ended in a month, and no amount of asking could make them go sooner.

So, since she couldn't explore New York, she explored Seattle with the purple glasses.

First, she'd used them to inspect her umbrella—the Super-Secret Plans. They didn't do anything special. She'd searched Uncle Paul's apartment above the garage, and around the house. Nothing. Everywhere she'd stared, things turned purple, but that was it.

When she went to the mailbox at the end of her street, she'd found her first clue. She stared at the outside of the box through the glasses and saw glowing yellow letters just like the ones on the legs of her kitchen table:

But that was a dead end, too. Next, she'd spent days searching the secret magnetic railway station beneath the mailbox. She'd found nothing. She'd doubled down and explored every wall, floor, and object in their house. Still no clues.

Why did Uncle Paul have to be so mysterious about everything? And why didn't he just come home?

Which had brought her back to the kitchen table, where she'd received the glasses in the first place.

"We're going to find Uncle Paul now," she told Nipper. "I'm sure of it."

Samantha took out a slip of paper and scrawled a note with a pen.

Paul/Horace:
Where are you?

She stuffed the note into the opening in the "out of Seattle" leg. A gust of air caught it, and it shot down and out of sight.

"Where do you think it went, Sam?" Nipper asked.

"I'm not positive," she answered. "But my guess is that—"

Crack!

Samantha looked over. A plastic sea salt grinder hit the kitchen floor and started to roll across the tiles.

Cra-tack!

A pepper mill dropped on the floor and shattered.

Samantha looked up. Their pug, Dennis, was walking along the kitchen counter, sniffing everything in his path.

"Uh-oh," said Nipper, pointing at the chair Samantha had shoved across the kitchen so she could inspect the table legs.

She looked at the chair, then back up at Dennis. He approached the open waffle iron.

"Watch out!" Samantha shouted.

"What? Duck?" asked Nipper.

"Not you," she replied, pointing to the counter.

"Dennis!" she shouted, even louder. "Get away from that!"

The dog turned quickly, bumping into the hot breakfast appliance.

Ka-snappp!

The waffle iron closed on his tail.

Dennis howled in pain.

CHAPTER TWO

POSTER BOY

"Try to keep our poor baby from moving, Jeremy," said Mrs. Spinner.

Nipper looked around. It took a minute to remember that his real name was Jeremy Bernard Spinner. People always called him Nipper because he used to bite people when he was a baby. He didn't do that much anymore, but everyone still called him Nipper. His mother only called him Jeremy when she was *really* angry.

He sat in the backseat of the car with Dennis whimpering in his lap.

"Stay still," he said. He held the pug's face to keep him from licking his wounded tail.

Dennis began to lick Nipper's hand instead.

"Hee-hee—stop that!" Nipper giggled, but he didn't let go of the dog's face.

Samantha sat up front with their mom. She had the sunglasses on, and Nipper could tell she was looking out the window for clues.

"It was careless and forgetful, moving the chair next to the counter," said Mrs. Spinner. "That dog waits for waffles all day long and— Are you listening to me?"

"I already said I was sorry, Mom," Samantha said, still staring out the window. "I needed something under the table. I didn't think it would be a big deal."

"Little things," her mom sighed, "can have big consequences."

Nipper was relieved that everything wasn't his fault for a change. It was a weird feeling.

They drove toward the drawbridge connecting Capitol Hill with North Seattle. Samantha continued staring out the window. Nipper could see that she was watching the blinking red light of the Space Needle. Then they were over the bridge and he lost sight of Downtown.

"Any sign of the SUN?" he whispered to her.

She looked back at him and shook her head. She took off the glasses and put them away in her purse.

"We'll be there in just a few more minutes," said Mrs. Spinner as they pulled into her reserved parking space at the North Seattle Animal Hospital.

As soon as the car stopped, Samantha got out and opened the door for Nipper. Nipper climbed out with Dennis in his arms.

"This way," said Mrs. Spinner. She waved them up the steps to her clinic on the second floor. At the top, she unlocked a door with words etched into frosted glass.

RODENT AND LIZARD WARD
DR. SUZETTE SPINNER, DVM

It was after hours, so the hall was dark. Mrs. Spinner flipped on the lights.

"Are you sure you know what you're doing, Mom?" Samantha asked, pointing to the sign as she followed her mother inside.

"I know how to care for all kinds of animals," she replied.

Nipper looked at his sister, then back at his mom. They were staring at each other.

"That includes dogs . . . and you two," Mrs. Spinner finished.

Nipper held out the pug.

"Okay," she said, heading to the far end of the waiting room. "You two wait here, and he'll be just fine in a few minutes."

She took Dennis and carried him through a metal door at the end of the room. It swung shut behind her, and Samantha and Nipper were alone.

It had been a long time since Nipper had visited their mom at work. It definitely looked like a grown-up kind of place. There were no toys, only magazines about golf and houses. He was playing with a box labeled "Powdered Nondairy Creamer" when a massive hardcover book with the title *Famous Art You Should Know from Around the World* caught his eye.

Nipper sat down on the floor and began flipping through the book from back to front.

"Page nine hundred sixty-seven is missing," he said. "Do you think one of Mom's patients ate it?"

"I doubt it," said Samantha, standing over him. "I can't imagine any situation where a lizard would bite a book. And it's not like you could teach a lizard to read or—"

Nipper had already lost interest in the giant art history book. He got up, walked across the room, and stared at a framed poster on the wall. It had a colorful illustration of a tropical island surrounded by clouds. Jagged mountain peaks and bubble-gum-colored beaches dotted the island, and sparkling rivers wound through lush forest valleys.

With dinosaurs!

Below the drawing, a poem read:

The Lost Island of Dinosaurs

In a mist-covered ocean
Far, far from home,
There's a mountainous island
Where dinosaurs roam.

While it sounds like a place
To amuse and delight you—
Watch out! Hungry creatures
Are waiting to bite you.

The rexes all roar
And the raptors attack,
While a lythronax wanders
In search of a snack.

If you climb up a tree
From the pink sandy beach,
The last thing you'll
Hear is a pterosaur screech.

A tar pit's a terrible
Thing to get trapped in.
It'll swallow you whole
And it won't need a napkin.

So be good, little children.
Remember that when you
Are not—there's a place that
Your parents might send you!

Nipper squinted at an illustration on one corner of the poster. A T. rex battled a triceratops. He looked at another corner. A maiasaur hovered over her nest of baby dinosaurs.

"Whoa, Nelly," he said slowly and quietly. "Where is this place?"

"What are you, five years old?" Samantha replied. "That's a silly poem to get little kids to behave."

Nipper held up both fists in front of her face and began to count his fingers.

"Five . . . six . . . seven . . ."

"And some eight-year-old boys, too," she said, cutting him off.

Nipper frowned.

Samantha leaned in and squinted at the poster.

"It's not a very good poem, either," she added. *"Trapped in? Napkin?* Is that supposed to be a rhyme?"

"Okay, okay, I get it," said Nipper.

Samantha walked away and Nipper read the poem again. At the bottom of the poster a ferocious dinosaur towered over treetops as it reared back on its hind legs, baring its deadly teeth.

Nipper mouthed the word *lythronax* silently to himself.

Something squeaked, and he turned.

Samantha was leaning over a small cage that rested on a shelf in the corner.

"Oh . . . so cute," she said breathlessly.

A furry animal gazed up at her. It looked a little bit like a rabbit, or maybe a huge mouse. It had a bushy tail, round pink ears, and a pointy, furry gray nose. A small tag was wrapped around one of the animal's front legs. Nipper walked over and tilted his head sideways to read it.

" '*Chinchilla lanigera*. Temuco, Chile,' " he said.

The animal stood up on its hind legs and stared at both of them with big round eyes. It wiggled its nose and made a soft chittering sound.

"I love chinchillas," said Samantha.

"Really? Since when?" Nipper asked.

The door to the back room swung open and their mom entered, carrying Dennis. She spotted them by the cage.

"You don't want a chinchilla, kids," she said. "They need a lot of special care. You have to give them dust baths."

Dennis wore a white plastic cone around his neck. He looked at them mournfully.

"It took a while to get this collar to fit just right," said Mrs. Spinner. "It was meant for a capybara.

"That should keep him away from his bandages for a month or so," their mom added.

Nipper noticed Dennis's tail, wrapped tight with white tape. The dog was busy looking left, right, up, and down, trying to see beyond the cone.

"What a nightmare," said Nipper.

His mom nodded and shot a glance at Samantha. Samantha gulped.

"Let's go," said Mrs. Spinner. She walked across the waiting room and out the door, the pug in her arms.

Nipper watched his sister as she followed Mrs. Spinner to the door. Samantha looked back longingly at the small metal cage. Then she turned and headed out.

Nipper looked down at a stack of brochures on the shelf beside the cage. He picked one up and opened it.

" 'Chinchillas Direct,' " he read out loud. " 'Delivery service.' "

In the past few weeks, Samantha had saved Nipper's life twice. First, she'd whacked a ninja in the face with a stale loaf of bread, protecting Nipper from being chopped into little pieces. Second, she'd used her umbrella to pin him to the floor of an Egyptian tomb, keeping him from being flushed into a bottomless pit. Samantha was turning out to be a cooler kind of eleven-year-old sister than he'd thought. Of course, he was still going to give her a lifetime of woe, wisecracks, and interruptions. And he would always need a test subject when he invented new booby traps. But first, she definitely deserved a special thank-you-for-not-letting-me-die-twice present.

"Are you coming?" his mother called from outside.

Nipper folded the brochure in half, tucked it into his pocket, and left the office.

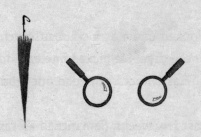

CHAPTER THREE

IT WASN'T FAIR

Buffy was in Manhattan, surrounded by luxury and city lights.

Samantha was in Seattle, surrounded by an annoying brother, an injured dog with a cone around his head, and rain. Not *the* RAIN—she'd taken care of them—just ordinary stuck-in-the-Pacific-Northwest rain.

Day after day, she'd overhear her mom or dad on the phone with Buffy. Buffy was decorating her fabulous three-level penthouse apartment. Buffy was hiring musicians and performers. Buffy was doing great. Buffy was having fun. Buffy. Buffy. Broadway. Buffy.

Every day, her older sister spent time with "Horace Temple" to work on her big musical play. Every night, she called her parents to talk and talk about *Secret of the*

Nile. Samantha overheard them discussing costumes, sets, red-carpet parties, menus for award banquets—it never ended. But she didn't hear a single super-secret clue.

Meanwhile, Uncle Paul (aka Horace Temple) was ignoring Samantha. He didn't answer the message she sent through the pneumatic tube. He didn't send any new messages. Her uncle had given her glasses, warned her to "watch out for the SUN," and clearly wanted her to know about Cleopatra's Needle. But what did it all mean? And as long as she was stuck in Seattle, what could she do about it anyway?

Samantha even reached out to Buffy. Unfortunately, when she asked about Horace Temple, her sister only said, "Horace says not to miss *opening night,*" and hung up the phone. Her sister was exactly as helpful as she expected her to be—not very helpful at all.

Samantha asked her parents every day and every night if they would send her to New York City. They told her—every day and every night—that she would have to wait until school was out. Then they would take a trip together to the East Coast.

But Samantha knew that she needed to get there *now*!

She walked into the kitchen. Her mother stood at the counter, sifting through the mail. Before Samantha could say anything, she heard her mother's voice.

"The answer is still no, Samantha," said Mrs. Spinner without even looking up.

Samantha sighed.

She heard a rattling sound and looked down. Dennis was trying to eat from his food dish as his cone bumped it along the floor. The pug stopped near Samantha's feet and looked up at her with a tragic expression on his face.

"I feel for you, pal," she told him. "It's awful to be trapped, trapped, trapped, isn't it?"

"You are so dramatic, Samantha," her mother told her. "You should audition for a role in your sister's play."

"Okay," said Samantha. "Then let me go to NYC."

"Plane tickets are two billion, four hundred million dollars," said Mrs. Spinner.

"Very funny, Mom," Samantha replied.

There had to be *something* she could do to get to New York. She let out a soft groan. She felt like power moping. Maybe it was time for her to return to her gloom journal and write sad entries about unfairness, misery, and gray, drizzly skies.

She closed her eyes and started to compose a poem.

Nelly McPepper met a terrible fate,
But we all can get trapped in a place that we hate.

"Well, look what came in the mail," said Mrs. Spinner.

Samantha opened her eyes. Her mother held out a neon-green postcard. Samantha could see a glittering gold unicorn and a mummy.

"'Pre-order your tickets to *Secret of the Nile,*'" her mother read. "Admit it, dear," she added. "Your sister is taking this very seriously."

"Seriously?" asked Samantha. "An Egyptian unicorn?"

She turned away from her mother and the postcard. She shut her eyes and went back to her poem.

I'm a gloomy sad egg. I'm a chicken of woe.
I have so much to do, but they won't let me . . .

Samantha stopped. She opened her eyes . . . and smiled. It was definitely time to do some writing, but not in her journal.

She walked quickly to her dad's office.

CHAPTER FOUR

A SPECIAL CASE

Samantha moved two lightbulbs out of the way and placed them gently on a corner of her father's desk, on top of a box labeled "Miniaturized Infrared Diodes." As Senior Lightbulb Tester for the American Institute of Lamps, her dad always had experimental gadgets and electronic equipment lying around. She adjusted the purple sunglasses on the top of her head and started typing on the computer.

"Dear Mr. von Bagelhouven," she said out loud.

"Bagelhouven? What's that?"

She turned around. It was Nipper.

"Good," she told him. "I was just about to look for you. I've come up with a way to— What's that in your hand?"

Her brother held out a small flat item.

"Here," he said. "I figure this might protect your specs."

Samantha took the object from him. It was a leather eyeglass case.

"Where did this come from?" she asked.

"Uncle Paul gave me some sunglasses last year," he said. "I took them to the beach and they washed out to sea while I was making a sandcastle."

Samantha opened the case and examined it. It had nice padding, but it was designed for small round glasses. Her octagonal lenses were too big. She put it down on her father's desk and turned back to the computer.

"The case is too small, but thanks anyway," she said. "Now look at this."

Nipper leaned in to see what she was typing.

You are invited to a SPECIAL performance of
SECRET OF THE NILE!
Don't miss this EXCLUSIVE one-night preview!
You will be AMAZED by what you see!

"I used a lot of extra capitalization and exclamation points," said Samantha. "It makes it seem Buffy-like, don't you think?"

"You're inviting someone to Buffy's play?" Nipper asked.

"Yeah," she said. "I know it's cruel. But I think this will get us to New York."

"Okay . . . and why this guy?" he asked.

"I did some research," she answered. "He's a theater critic who hates every play he ever sees."

"Okay . . . ," said Nipper, sounding confused. "Exactly how is this helping us find Uncle Paul?"

"Just watch what happens next," she answered, and hit *send*.

The doorbell rang.

"Wow! That was fast," said Nipper.

"Don't be silly," Samantha answered. "Go see who that is."

Nipper left. Samantha heard him answer the door. A minute later, he came back into the room carrying a large cardboard box. It had animal tracks printed on each side. Rows of holes, about the size of quarters, lined the top. Little twitching pink noses poked out from several of the holes. The package shook in Nipper's hands. The contents were moving . . . and squeaking.

" 'Chinchillas,' " he said, reading from the top of the box. " 'Twelve count.' "

CHAPTER FIVE

CHEEPERS BY THE DOZEN

Over the course of two days, twelve boxes arrived from Chinchillas Direct. Each one squeaked and buzzed like a crazy cardboard beehive. By the time Samantha came home from school on the third day, the Spinner house was overrun by chinchillas.

"Why did you do this?" asked Mrs. Spinner.

"It was a present for Sam," Nipper answered as he brushed a chinchilla away with one foot.

"Chinchillas Direct is a bulk rodent-delivery service," said Mrs. Spinner. "I sure wish more people paid attention."

Samantha thought her mother sounded unusually frustrated with Nipper. It certainly wasn't the first time he had done something that messed up the house. Or nearly destroyed all the furniture.

"Chinchillas are *crepuscular*," Mrs. Spinner added. "They're most active around dawn and twilight."

She set a bowl of pasta salad on the table and sat down.

Everyone began to eat, pretending not to hear the squeaks, the chirps, and the little claws scratching.

"I don't love chinchillas," said Samantha.

"Really? Since when?" Nipper asked.

He scooped up some pasta with his fork and was about to take a bite when a chinchilla hopped onto the table and scurried to the center of his plate. It stood up, looked at him, and made a chittering noise. Then it snatched the pasta off the end of the fork and scampered away.

"Gross," Samantha said.

"Well, Nipper did order a *gross* of chinchillas," said Mr. Spinner.

"Huh?" Nipper said.

"A dozen dozens is a gross," his father replied. "One hundred and forty-four."

Samantha ignored her father's math fact and her brother's grossness. It was impossible, however, to ignore twelve dozen chinchillas.

When she'd seen one in her mother's office, she'd thought it was cute. She liked the soft sound it made.

Now rodents were everywhere—squeaking, scratching, and chewing. Little gray hairs covered the furniture.

Samantha got up to help clear the table. Two chinchillas chased each other around and around the sink, so she set her plate on the counter.

Snap!

She looked above the refrigerator. Last fall, her dad had helped her build a tongue-depressor suspension bridge for the science fair. Now a pair of chinchillas gnawed the sticks, snapping them one by one. Her dad had been correct. You *could* take away half the supports and the structure would still stand.

She noticed a trail of droppings along the floor.

"This is *exceptionally* gross," said Samantha, watching her step as she headed out of the kitchen.

"Well, you know, Sam," Nipper called, "a dozen dozens is the same as—"

"I know!" she shouted, and headed up the stairs to her room.

Samantha sat down at her desk. Her notebook lay open to the sketch of Cleopatra's Needle. The note from Uncle Paul sat beside it. If she ever did get to New York, what would she find there?

Chinchilla noises began to fill the air.

"Just great," Samantha muttered.

She rubbed her forehead and tried to ignore the sounds. She looked again at the note.

" 'Watch out for the SUN,' " she read.

She heard a chirp and turned. A chinchilla inched slowly toward her purse, which was hanging on the desk chair.

"Oh no," she told the rodent, and grabbed the purse. "That's not for you."

She checked to make sure her purple sunglasses were still inside. Then she draped the straps over her shoulder.

"Any progress, Sam?" asked Nipper, walking into her room.

"Not really," she answered. "Come take a look at my sketch of Cleopatra's Needle."

The chinchilla hopped from her chair to her open journal.

"Just knock it on the floor," said Nipper.

"Nipper! Don't you dare," Samantha scolded. "They're defenseless rodents."

She gently nudged the animal off her book.

"Hey, look, Sam," said Nipper, pointing across the room. "A defenseless rodent is chewing on your Super-Secret Plans."

Samantha turned. A chinchilla sat inside the open, upside-down umbrella. It gripped a shred of red fabric between its teeth and tugged. She heard a ripping noise.

Samantha gasped. Then she lunged.

"No!" she shouted. She swatted the animal with one hand, knocking it from its perch inside the Super-Secret Plans. It skidded across the floor until it found its footing. Then it zipped through the bedroom doorway.

Samantha grabbed the umbrella. Trembling, she inspected it, running her finger along the fabric where the animal had attacked it. A fresh tear, about an inch long, sliced through the center.

Chirp!

Samantha snapped the umbrella closed and looked over at her desk. Another chinchilla stood on its hind legs. It held the note from Uncle Paul between its teeth.

"Stop!" she shrieked, and reached to grab it.

The animal turned and hopped from the desk to the chair to the floor. With the note still in its mouth, it scampered out the door.

"Stop, chinchilla! Give it back!" she yelled, and took off after it.

Swinging the umbrella like a sword, she chased the fuzzy clue stealer down the stairs.

"Give it back!"

The defenseless rodent ran for its life.

Samantha raced down the stairs and into the kitchen.

"Give it back! Give it! Give—"

She lurched to a stop. Her mother sat at the table.

The chinchilla zipped under the chair between her mother's feet.

"Oh, hi, dear," said Mrs. Spinner. "I was just about to call you and your brother."

On the table in front of her, a printout read:

ITINERARY

"Seattle to New York!" Samantha said breathlessly.

"Your sister bought tickets for you to come and help her this weekend," said her mom.

"This weekend!" Samantha repeated.

"It seems she's run into trouble with her play. Now she says she needs you. She says Horace is gone and—"

"Horace is gone!" Samantha interrupted.

"Who's Horace?" Nipper asked as he walked into the room.

"What's wrong with you?" Samantha said quickly. "Don't you remember we just sent a message to—"

"Samantha," her mother cut in. "You didn't have anything to do with this, did you?"

"Oh, no, Mom," Samantha answered, trying to look serious.

"Well . . . Buffy wants your help," said Mrs. Spinner. "So have a good time, but please try to be useful."

Samantha grabbed the purple sunglasses and put them on.

"Sure thing, Mom," she said, beaming. "Sometimes, brothers and sisters are what you need most of all."

"Maybe you really should audition for a part in that play," said her mother.

A squeak rose from beneath Mrs. Spinner. She looked down at the chinchilla, still hiding under the chair. She reached down and plucked the note from the rodent's mouth.

"Don't forget this," she said, holding up the note and reading it out loud. " 'Watch out for the SUN.' "

With the glasses on, Samantha caught a glimpse of the back of the paper.

It glowed yellow.

She'd never thought to look on the reverse side!

DNT TRST NT

CHAPTER SIX

ROUGH RIDERS

The trip to New York was long and miserable. Buffy had purchased double-triple super-economy-class tickets for Samantha and Nipper. They flew to Los Angeles, then changed planes and flew to Minneapolis, then to Boston, and finally to Newark. They sat at the very back of each plane in "cabins" that had been converted from bath-rooms. There were no windows, and though the seats were freshly upholstered, it didn't smell great.

They left Seattle, Washington, at midnight on Friday and were due to land in Newark, New Jersey, at eight p.m. Saturday, seventeen very long hours later. Saman-tha thought about the super-secret waterslide from Flor-ence to Paris. That ride had been bumpy, bruising, cold, and wet. It hadn't been half as unpleasant as this trip.

Somewhere between Minnesota and Massachusetts, the plane hit a patch of strong turbulence. Samantha's head bumped against the hand-sanitizer dispenser. It jostled her sunglasses and they fell on the floor. She picked them up quickly and inspected the octagonal purple lenses for any damage. She was finally on her way to New York City, and it would be a disaster if they broke now.

Samantha put them on and looked around her cabin one last time, hoping to find secret messages. There weren't any. She stowed the glasses in her purse. Then she sat back and tried to think.

Horace is gone. Was Horace Temple—Uncle Paul—really gone? Or was he hiding again? How was it possible that Buffy didn't recognize him? And was he near Buffy's place or Cleopatra's Needle? Was he inside the Needle? She had no idea what dangers they might face in New York.

She thought again about the umbrella, safe at home. After the chinchilla bite, she'd covered the tear with a strip of tape. Then she hid the umbrella under her bed, between the mattress and the box spring. No chinchilla would be able to lift the mattress to get to it. Samantha hoped the SUN couldn't get to it, either. Whatever "the SUN" was.

Of course, there was that last message from her uncle. *DNT TRST NT.* She and her uncle used to play the license plate game all the time. This was definitely a message without vowels.

"Don't trust . . . ," she puzzled out loud, "N . . . T."

Was she even halfway close?

"Nipper, are you awake?" she called to the other side of the wall.

"Yes," he said. "But it's hard to hear you over the sound of my seat. Every time we hit a bump, it flushes."

"Don't trust N T," she said, much louder than before. "Do you have any idea what N T stands for?"

"Possibly," he shouted back. "Maybe it means 'aunt.' 'Don't trust aunt.' Isn't Aunt Penny picking us up at the airport? I don't think we should trust her."

"Yes we should," Samantha said confidently.

They had known Aunt Penny their whole lives. She was glamorous, she was a little goofy . . . and she was one hundred percent Spinner. Their dad's older sister could definitely be trusted!

Why didn't Uncle Paul just say who it was? Once again, Paul Spinner hadn't made things very clear. Samantha took a deep breath and let it out slowly. It was okay. She was finally on her way to figuring it all out.

"We're visiting Cleopatra's Needle first thing in the morning," she called to Nipper.

Just then the plane began its descent. The engines outside their "cabin" walls roared, drowning out her words for the rest of the flight.

CHAPTER SEVEN

PENNY-PINCHING

Samantha stood behind Nipper as they rode the moving walkway through Newark International Airport. Framed posters passed by, advertising museums, hotels, and Broadway plays. Between *The Lion King* and the Metropolitan Museum of Art, a neon-green poster featured two hot-pink pyramids and a flying unicorn.

COMING SOON!
SECRET OF THE NILE

"Yuck!" said Nipper as they coasted along. "I'd rather be attacked by forty-eight ninjas than sit through something like that. It looks like a play that Buffy would make."

Samantha didn't bother to point out that it *was* the play their sister was making. She studied the garish ad. The unicorn floated above an obelisk. The poster receded into the distance before she could make out any more ridiculous details.

She faced forward and followed Nipper off the end of the belt. Automatic doors swung open. A woman with purple hair stood waiting with open arms, smiling from ear to ear. Aunt Penny.

"Oh . . . my . . . gosh!" she screamed, staring right at Samantha and Nipper. "Look at those two grown-up kids!"

She reached out and gave Samantha a pinch on her left cheek. It didn't hurt, really. Samantha expected it. Her aunt had always been a cheek pincher. When Aunt Penny turned to do the same to Nipper, he stepped sideways quickly and pulled Samantha into his place. Aunt Penny kept moving and pinched Samantha a second time. Samantha wasn't expecting that, and it was really annoying.

Aunt Penny used to be a professional shopper and treasure hunter in California. She helped everyone from museum directors to movie stars locate unusual, valuable, or just plain hard-to-find things. She helped a mystery writer buy a home that looked like a medieval castle. She tracked down a gold-plated salad spinner for a celebrity chef. She helped a candy museum curator locate the world's largest lollipop. One time, she spotted an original print of the Declaration of Independence in an old frame at a yard sale. She was a pro with her metal detector or your million dollars. If your mind was made up and there was something you really, truly wanted, Penelope Spinner was the person to call.

Then, two years ago, she retired.

"I'm done shopping," she told everyone. "The only treasure I'm looking for now is fun!"

She bought a purple car, dyed her hair to match, and hit the road in search of adventure across America. Some people—Samantha's parents included—said they thought she was still out treasure hunting. But if so, Aunt Penny kept it a secret.

Samantha thought that her aunt was a little bit crazy, and that most of the things she helped people find were a waste of time and money. But everyone said her aunt was a four-star treasure hunter. And it was always fun to see Aunt Penny.

Samantha still remembered the purple convertible parked in front of their house the last time her aunt had passed through Seattle. She got to stay up all night playing Word Whammy! with Aunt Penny and Uncle Paul.

"Puzzle," Samantha said, laying six cards on the table.

Uncle Paul studied his cards. Then he looked down at his pajamas and back at the table. He stole the P card from Samantha and added four cards of his own.

"Plaid," he said.

Aunt Penny stared at her brother. She studied his green plaid pajamas and bright orange flip-flops.

"Hideous," she said loudly.

Then she stole the I and D cards from him and added five of her own.

"One day, I'm going to help you buy some real pants and shoes," she mused.

"I doubt it," Uncle Paul said cheerfully. "Fashion is fleeting. Flannel is forever."

Penny cupped her hand around her mouth and leaned over to Samantha.

"And little brothers are endlessly annoying," she whispered.

Samantha usually sided with Uncle Paul, but that night, her aunt made a good point about little brothers.

After receiving a dozen hugs from their aunt, and their suitcases from the baggage carousel, Samantha and Nipper followed Aunt Penny to the parking garage. The little purple roadster took up half the space of an ordinary car.

"The trunk is full of fake Egyptian jewelry for your sister's play," Penny said. So they loaded their luggage into the front passenger seat.

Samantha and her brother squeezed into the back.

"Buffy will be so happy to see you two," their aunt told them as she drove. "She's been so upset since she used up most of her money. Now she has to watch every nickel and dime. It really breaks your heart."

Samantha couldn't tell if Aunt Penny was joking or serious. It was hard to imagine Buffy watching nickels and dimes, especially since she'd become a double billionaire.

"I'm here, out of retirement, just to help," Aunt Penny continued. "Your sister has created some very big shopping challenges for me."

The little car joined an endless stream of taxis, delivery trucks, and buses funneling into the Holland Tunnel.

"Sometimes, of course, brothers and sisters are what you need most of all," said Aunt Penny.

Samantha was so excited to see Manhattan that she forgot about the purple sunglasses. They stayed in her purse as she took in the sights and sounds of the city.

They headed up the West Side Highway. On their left was the Hudson River, and on their right, the glittering Manhattan skyline. A huge, glowing skyscraper towered high above the others.

"The Empire State Building," said Samantha.

"Is it always red, white, and blue?" asked Nipper.

"It's lit that way for Memorial Day," Aunt Penny told them.

To Samantha, all the shimmering buildings seemed

magical. And so did the streetlights, billboards, and flashing video screens. Soon they were speeding along Central Park West. The walls of the park appeared on their right. On their left were brightly lit apartment buildings in an endless row.

One especially tall building came into view. It was a red brick apartment complex, at least forty stories tall. On top perched a sparkling blue castle. It was trimmed in neon and had a glittering tower rising at each side. A giant mirrored disco ball spun atop one tower. The other tower sported a unicorn flag.

Samantha knew only one person could possibly live up there.

"Buffy," she said.

"I thought she spent most of her money," said Nipper.

"She did," Aunt Penny answered. "Poor thing. She's down to her last three hundred and twenty-seven million."

Samantha couldn't care less how much or little money her sister had. Horace Temple—Paul Spinner—might be nearby.

They came to a stop in front of the building. Samantha noticed a man in a brown leather coat by the entrance. At first, she thought he was going to approach the car and help them out, but he just stood there, watching them. His lips were pressed tightly together.

He looked irritated, or bored, or maybe both.

Aunt Penny hopped out of the car and opened the door for Samantha and Nipper.

"This is Nathaniel," she said. "He works for Buffy."

"I . . . I . . . am here to take you to your sister's place," he said, but he still didn't step forward.

They climbed out of the car and waited for him to come help with their bags, but he didn't budge from his spot by the door. He stood there and fiddled with a gold chain around his neck and continued staring at them.

"Oh, don't worry," Aunt Penny said with a laugh. "He doesn't bite."

She leaned over and hoisted their suitcases from the passenger seat. She carried them over to Nathaniel and waved for Samantha and Nipper to join them.

Nathaniel studied the bags carefully. Then he looked at Samantha again. He seemed suspicious.

"Arrrr . . . you sure that's your complete luggage?" he asked.

Samantha nodded.

He squinted and looked at Samantha, then at her bag again.

"I . . . I . . . cer . . . tainly don't want to miss anything."

Samantha studied Nathaniel as he picked up the suitcases. He was definitely searching for something that was missing.

"That guy sure talks funny," whispered Nipper.

Samantha nodded. Her sister's helper definitely had a very strange way of talking—and walking, too. He lurched from side to side as he carried the suitcases into the lobby.

"I'll see you two later," said Aunt Penny. "I have to do some more shopping for your sister."

She took out a small notebook and flipped to a page in the middle.

"Giraffe costumes, blue, with pink hooves," she said. "That shouldn't be too hard."

"Arrrrr . . . you coming?" Nathaniel called from the entrance.

"Go ahead," said Aunt Penny.

Samantha watched her aunt walk back to her car, climb inside, and start the engine.

"Goodbye, you two," she said cheerfully, and drove away.

Samantha and Nipper followed Nathaniel into a brightly lit lobby with marble floors and walls. Nathaniel paused, held out their suitcases, and let go. They dropped to the floor with a thud.

"Be a-carryin' these yourselves," he said. "It builds character."

He tucked his gold chain under his shirt, crossed his arms, and waited.

"Character?" Nipper blurted. "How about *you* be *a-pickin' up* our bags and start a-*buildin'* some a-*muscles* and—"

Nathaniel stepped extremely close to Nipper, bent down, and looked him in the eye. He pushed up his right sleeve, revealing a huge bicep.

"Wish to repeat that, laddie?" he snarled.

Samantha noticed a skull and crossbones tattooed on the man's arm. He continued to glare at her brother as he let out slow, raspy breaths that sounded like growls.

"Now that you mention it," said Nipper, reaching for his suitcase, "I always prefer to keep my luggage with me."

He faked a smile and picked up his bag quickly. Samantha picked up hers, too. Carrying her own luggage wasn't a big deal. She was excited that she'd be seeing Central Park and Cleopatra's Needle—and starting to look for Uncle Paul. Besides, if *she* had to work for Buffy, she'd be pretty grouchy and miserable, too.

Nathaniel led them through the gleaming white lobby. When they reached a set of elevator doors, Nipper tried to tap a button, but Nathaniel grabbed his finger and held it tight.

"It's the freight elevator for you," he said, and let go of Nipper's finger. "Special instructions from Ms. Hydrangea."

"Hydrangea?" Nipper asked, confused, and looked at Samantha.

She waited for him to remember.

"Who the heck is Ms. Hy— Oh, okay. I got it."

When Buffy first got her billions from Uncle Paul, she decided to become a big movie star. She moved to Hollywood, California, and had her high school shipped along with her—building, kids, and all. And she chose Scarlett Hydrangea as her "fabulous movie-star name."

Samantha didn't think the name was fabulous. She thought it was ridiculous and clownlike. Then she thought about Nelly McPepper, the one girl Buffy had refused to bring with the school.

"Poor Nelly," she said softly. "I wonder if we'll ever find out—"

Nathaniel tapped her on the shoulder.

"Don't dawdle," he said. "Ms. Hydrangea is expecting you."

He led them past the elevator and through a set of double doors. They entered a hallway that was much less fancy than the lobby. Years' worth of scuffmarks covered the cement floor, and the walls were streaked with grime.

Every ten feet, wooden pallets lined the hallway. Each one had a dozen burlap bags piled on it.

" 'Candy corn,' " said Nipper, reading one of the bags as they passed.

"You sister wants to be ready for . . . the unicorns," Nathaniel said dryly.

"I don't think he believes in unicorns," Nipper whispered to Samantha.

Nathaniel glared and led them down the long hall. At the end, they reached a cavernous space, cluttered with refrigerator-sized boxes and large wooden crates. Samantha counted a dozen black metal drums stacked three high.

"A vast . . . amount of material has arrived for your sister's show," said Nathaniel.

He pressed a button on the wall and machinery began to hum. He stood staring at the two kids as they waited.

Samantha looked at a nearby crate and read, " 'Bagpipes, fifteen count. Do not squeeze.' "

Nipper peered at the top of one of the metal drums. " 'Glycerol,' " he read carefully. " 'Fifty-five gallons.' "

Nathaniel tapped the barrel.

"That's fog-machine juice," he said. "Horace Temple ordered it for the performance."

"Horace?" said Samantha, getting excited. "Is he really gone?"

Nathaniel grunted but didn't answer.

Samantha waited for him to say anything else about Horace. He fiddled with his gold chain for a moment. Then looked away.

"Glycerol," Nipper repeated, looking at the barrel.

With a grinding squeal, the doors to the freight

elevator slid open and Samantha inhaled the scent of grease and rubber. The elevator was crammed with tires, gears, and shiny metal tubing. There was barely enough room for her and Nipper.

"This is the only place to store the monster-truck parts," said Nathaniel. "You'll fit."

Samantha and Nipper picked up their luggage. Samantha followed her brother into the elevator, squeezing between stacks of shiny hubcaps. She turned and looked back at Nathaniel.

"Why did Horace Temple order monster trucks, fog machines, and—"

"Apartment ahoy!" he shouted.

Nathaniel reached inside the elevator, pushed a button, and stepped back. The doors slammed closed, leaving the man on the other side, and the elevator lurched upward. Samantha looked at the long vertical panel with dozens of buttons. Nipper pointed to the glowing top button, labeled "PH."

"Penthouse?" he asked.

Samantha nodded. Then she remembered her sunglasses. She took them from her purse, put them on, and studied the buttons as the elevator traveled up. The elevator came to a stop and the doors slid open. Buffy stood waiting with open arms.

"Oh . . . my . . . gosh!" she screamed. "Look at those hideous purple glasses!"

CHAPTER EIGHT

BROTHER, CAN YOU SPARE A DIAMOND?

"I am passionate about the arts," declared Buffy as she led Samantha and Nipper through the first level of her apartment. Paintings, posters, and glittering objects covered every inch of every wall. Samantha counted at least ten portraits of her older sister. She also noticed Buffy's scarves, gloves, and shoes—size 9½—hanging as artwork.

To Samantha, it looked like a candy machine had exploded inside a jewelry store on a fashion runway.

"This is what the inside of Buffy's brain looks like, too," she whispered to Nipper.

He nodded.

Samantha was about to make another joke about her sister when she spotted a pair of boots leaning against a wall and stopped to examine them. They were huge, greenish-gray rubber waders. She waved to get Nipper's attention and pointed with excitement.

"Maybe Morgan Bogan was telling the truth," she said.

"What are you talking about?" asked Nipper.

Their neighbor Morgan Bogan Bogden-Loople was a boy who always said ridiculous things. Nobody ever believed him. When Uncle Paul first disappeared, Morgan Bogan said he saw her uncle Paul walking to a cello lesson wearing big rubber boots and carrying an inflatable raccoon on his shoulder. Samantha hadn't believed him at all. It seemed preposterous. Now she wasn't so sure.

"What are you two looking at?" asked Buffy, walking back to them.

She noticed Samantha staring at the boots.

"Oh, those hideous things," said Buffy. "You're surrounded by fabulous fashion, and all you care about are ugly rubber boots."

She shook her head.

"They were Horace's," she added. "Before he disappeared."

"That's what I thought," said Samantha. "What happened to Horace?"

"Enough with the boots!" Buffy shouted. "You're here because I need you. There is a whole world of shoes upstairs. Follow me."

Samantha growled softly and was about to argue, but her sister had already walked ahead down the long, accessory-lined hall.

They walked to the foot of an escalator. Beside it, a glass case was perched on a marble pedestal. The case was labeled "Hope Diamond." Inside, a photograph of a blue gem rested on a tiny easel.

"I tried to buy that, but apparently it's not for sale," Buffy told them. "Nate says he knows a company that can make an exact copy. That's probably a good idea because, well, I *am* almost out of money."

"I've seen that gem before," said Nipper, looking at Samantha.

Samantha nodded at him knowingly.

"Uh-huh," said Buffy, uninterested. "Now come on."

They rode the escalator up to the second level. It was a maze of hallways lined with gray metal doors. Samantha stopped following Buffy to read a sign on one of them.

JULY FOOTWEAR

The door looked very sturdy, like that of a bank vault. The painted metal had rivets that reminded Samantha of the Eiffel Tower. There was a keypad above the doorknob.

"My personal shoe rooms are here," said Buffy. "Nate and I are the only two people who know the combinations."

She banged on the door.

"Battleship-grade steel," she said. "You can't be too careful with fine footwear."

"A room for each month?" Nipper whispered to Samantha. "For shoes?"

Samantha opened her mouth to answer, but her sister interrupted.

"Less talking. More walking!" Buffy barked, and waved for them to follow.

They turned a corner, where a massive roll of blue cloth blocked their path. Samantha noticed the words *Seattle Fabric Center* embroidered on the edge.

"It's a flag," Buffy told her. "The Federated States of Micronesia."

"Micronesia?" asked Samantha. "Why?"

"Oh, I don't know," answered Buffy. "I asked Nate to find something that would make the building look fabulous. Light blue with white stars really makes the red of the bricks pop, you know."

"What's it doing in the hall?" asked Nipper.

Buffy sighed.

"When we hung it from the balcony, everyone from floor fifty-five down to floor ten started screaming," she explained. "They said it blocked their windows or something."

"Maybe they wanted to be able to see," said Nipper.

"Maybe some people aren't as interested in accessorizing as I am," said Buffy.

Samantha made a mental note to ask Uncle Paul about Micronesia . . . when he wasn't missing, of course.

Buffy and Nipper climbed over the giant rolled-up flag. Samantha waited, examining the fabric-store logo through her glasses as they climbed.

"Stop!" Buffy shouted. "Keep those hideous things away from my flag!"

Samantha frowned at her sister.

Buffy double-triple super-frowned back at her.

Samantha shuddered and put the sunglasses away

in her purse. Then she climbed over the big blue obstacle and followed her sister and brother up another escalator.

Buffy led them around the top floor of the apartment, through the main entrance, the formal dining area, and a dozen other rooms. Everywhere they went, she pointed out expensive and ridiculous details.

"It's a shame we have to keep all these $167,000 rugs on the floor," said Buffy.

Samantha looked down. Bright golden threads zigzagged through the fabric.

"But I suppose we don't want to cover the twenty-four-karat-gold-plated ceiling," Buffy added.

Samantha looked up. The ceiling was definitely shiny.

"If I have to walk all over someone—I mean, something—it might as well be expensive," said Buffy, and she marched ahead of them through a set of glittering double doors.

Samantha looked back and saw Nipper fidgeting with a picture frame. Then he tapped on a sculpture. He had definitely reached the limit of his attention span. On a good day, he could stay interested in something for about ten minutes without getting distracted. Looking at shoes and scarves and portraits of Buffy did not count as "a good day." The fidgeting, touching, and tampering had begun.

Samantha took out the purple glasses and was about to put them on again when Nathaniel entered the hallway, walking up behind Nipper.

"Loose fingertips sink ships," he growled.

Nipper jumped and turned around quickly.

Smiling nervously at Nathaniel, he inched backward toward Samantha and stopped beside her.

"Let's go see some more shoes, or art, or fashion thingamajigs," he said.

Together, they walked through the double doors.

CHAPTER NINE

UNEXPLAINED VANISHING PRODUCER

The living room . . . was actually amazing. Crystal vases perched on pedestals. Diamond chandeliers sparkled. A mahogany grand piano stood majestically. The ceiling was gold here, too. But none of this was what impressed Samantha. It was the view!

Tall windows stretched across three walls. Turning slowly, Samantha saw the towers of Wall Street all the way downtown, the entirety of Central Park, and completely up the West Side, north toward Harlem.

"Look," she told Nipper, and pointed at a glowing white rectangle on the far side of the park. "That's the Metropolitan Museum of Art."

Somewhere close to it would be Cleopatra's Needle.

"Eyes on me," said Buffy. "I flew you here to be part of something very important."

Samantha gritted her teeth. She didn't care why Buffy had brought her there. She was here to look for Uncle Paul.

Samantha turned away from the windows. Nipper was hovering over the grand piano. He tapped on a key twice. Then he lifted the mahogany lid and reached inside. He plucked a few of the strings closest to him.

Buffy heard the sound and looked over. She clapped her hands loudly and glared. He let go of the piano lid and it dropped with a heavy thud. A loud B-flat minor chord reverberated through the room.

Buffy waited for the musical notes to fade. She made a sad face and sighed loudly. Tears began to well up in her eyes.

Samantha was not impressed.

"You look like a chinchilla," she told her sister.

"I'm working so hard on my play," Buffy blurted. "I moved to New York City because the world-famous Broadway producer Horace Temple was going to make me famous."

Samantha nodded patiently and smiled. She waited for her sister to get to the point.

"He kept telling me over and over that I should be careful and stay away from sunlight, or something like that," said Buffy.

"She means 'Watch out for the SUN,' right?" Nipper asked Samantha.

"Just let her talk," Samantha replied.

"That's right. Let *me* talk," Buffy snapped.

She looked at Samantha.

"*Somebody* invited Charles von Bagelhouven, licensed theater critic, to come see a special performance of my play," she continued. "That was when I told Horace that he had to change out of those hideous rubber boots."

She started breathing heavily.

"And . . . ?" said Samantha, waiting to hear more.

"He said . . . 'I'll see you in June.' And then he was gone!"

"June?" Samantha asked.

"Yes," said Buffy. "I knew I had to go through with the exclusive one-night preview or . . . or—"

Nathaniel appeared.

"Did someone say . . . 'or'?" he asked.

"I was Horace-less," said Buffy, ignoring Nathaniel. "There was no Horace at all."

Samantha perked up, listening for any clue about the whereabouts of Uncle Paul.

"I almost gave up," said her sister, wiping away a tear. "But then I remembered—I'm a fabulous star!"

Samantha's heart sank. She was *not* going to get a clue about Uncle Paul.

"I had everything I needed to put on a Broadway show myself," said Buffy.

"Three hundred and twenty-seven million dollars?" Nipper asked.

"I mean talent!" she answered. "I designed extremely realistic costumes and historically accurate sets. I created tasteful advertisements and hired the best-looking actors. I even designed a cave for all the mermaids and unicorns!"

She raised both arms as she shouted.

"Von Bagelhouven came to see my preview . . . and he wrote . . . this!"

She snapped her fingers at Nathaniel. He held up a silver tray with a single piece of paper.

" 'Once in a lifetime, a show appears that makes you say *wow*,' " Buffy read.

Samantha saw Buffy's hands trembling.

" 'As in *Wow! That was the worst thing I have ever seen!* ' " she wailed.

Samantha watched as her sister dropped the letter and put a hand up to her forehead dramatically. Then she made eye contact, blinked three times, and collapsed onto a $167,000 rug. "I think I'm dying," Buffy sobbed into her hands. "Tell the unicorns I loved them."

Samantha reached for the letter, but Nipper hopped forward and grabbed it first.

"Let me read," Nipper said cheerfully and wiggled his eyebrows. "I love reading."

"Really? Since when?" Samantha asked.

She was never going to sleep until this performance was over.

Nipper cleared his throat.

" 'From the first sour note to the final, confusing spoken word . . . ,' " he began in a loud, dramatic voice. He held the page in one hand and waved the other. " 'What I saw left me shocked, shuddering, and speechless.' "

"He was shocked," Buffy moaned with her face buried in her arm.

"Oh well," said Samantha. "Maybe you don't need to go through with this play at all. You can save your—"

Buffy sat up quickly and pointed at her.

"Pay attention," she snapped. "This is why I need you."

" 'I am so certain that Ms. Hydrangea's play is going to flop,' " Nipper kept reading, " 'that I am willing to make a *generous offer*.' "

Buffy nodded at Samantha.

" 'If the show survives all the previews and makes it through opening night, I will climb to the top of the Empire State Building in my underwear,' " Nipper continued.

"Underwear?" Samantha asked. "That's *exceptionally—*"

"Wait for it," Buffy commanded.

" 'Then I, Charles von Bagelhouven III, will race to Hollywood, where I will raise the money for a spectacular big-budget movie of the play.' "

Buffy jumped up and put a hand on her sister's shoulder.

"Scarlett Hydrangea's *Secret of the Nile* has to survive!" she hollered. "So I'm making you the producer!"

"What?" Samantha asked, surprised.

"You're going to help make sure my show survives. We can't miss opening night!"

The surprise wore off quickly and Samantha yawned. This was interesting, but she was exhausted from their four flights. And hearing her big sister wailing and whining was double-triple super-exhausting. She wasn't in New York to become a producer. She had come to see Cleopatra's Needle. She had come to find Uncle Paul.

"Honest, Buffy, I'd love to hear more about your show, but I have to wake up very early tomorrow," she said.

"Are we staying in this castle?" Nipper asked, looking around the room.

"Oh, yes," Buffy replied, wiping her eyes. "I've got special guest rooms for you two."

She turned toward Nathaniel.

"Nate. Did you prepare the stables?" she asked.

"Yes," he replied, "but we're not any closer to finding the rainbow unicorns for you, Ms. Hydrangea."

"I know that," said Buffy. "But I asked you to put in mattresses for my kid sister and little baby brother."

"*Stables?*" asked Samantha.

"Little *baby* brother?" asked Nipper.

Buffy gestured for them to follow her. She led them back to the main entrance. Nathaniel followed. They passed a huge, round stone with a hole in the center. It was as tall as Nipper and stood on a base with a sign that read **STONE COIN OF YAP**.

"Yap?" asked Nipper.

"It's in the South Pacific, laddie," Nathaniel told him.

"Well . . . *Yap* reminds me of Dennis, our dog," Nipper said.

The giant stone circle reminded Samantha of a big waffle. And that reminded her of Uncle Paul. Where did he go? What did he mean about June?

"That coin reminds me," said Buffy. "Where's Penny?"

"She dropped us off out front," said Nipper. "She went shopping for giraffe costumes."

"Good," said Buffy. "That's for my rain forest tree-top tap dance number."

Samantha was extremely done hearing about her sister's play for the night, but she had to speak up.

"Giraffes don't live in the rain forest," she told her. "Or in trees."

"You're my producer, not a zookeeper," Buffy barked.

"Why didn't you just get animals from the zoo?" Nipper asked.

"Nobody uses real animals on Broadway anymore," she answered. "They can't learn their lines, and they're no good at standing still when an enormous wind machine starts blowing."

"Except for the Great Flingo," Buffy added. "He's a monkey, and a true professional."

Samantha and Nipper looked at each other, alarmed.

"A monkey?" Nipper asked. "There was a monkey in the RAIN! In Seattle!"

"Sure, whatever," said Buffy. "There's always rain in Seattle. But Nate helped me find this monkey for my show. The monkey's not much of a singer. He just screams 'breep' all the time. I have no idea what that's about. But he sure can dance and use a Hula-Hoop. And he does tricks with throwing stars and a ninja sword."

"Oh . . . my . . . gosh!" Samantha gasped, and looked at Nipper. "What else do you know about that monkey?"

"Well, he was in some kind of trouble with the law," Buffy explained. "He was supposed to go to jail in France, but the U.S. doesn't extradite animals to other countries."

"The beast has to do sixty-two thousand hours of community service," Nathaniel added. "The police agreed that being in a musical is an equal punishment."

They reached the elevators.

"Wait, Buffy," Samantha pleaded. "Where did Nathaniel find that monkey? How did he bring it here? Didn't you hear that I helped capture a bunch of ninjas at the art museum in Volunteer Park and—"

"Oh, there you go again," Buffy interrupted. "Rattling on about things you like to do in boring Seattle. Nate!"

Nathaniel walked over to them quickly. He pushed Samantha and Nipper away from the main elevator and tapped the freight elevator call button several times.

"But, Sis." Nipper raised a hand and waved to get her attention as the doors creaked open. "We traveled to France and Egypt and—"

"Not remotely interested," Buffy said.

Nathaniel shoved them both into the freight elevator and stepped inside.

The doors closed, leaving Buffy on the other side.

CHAPTER TEN

MANHATTAN HAYSTACK

Samantha woke early in the morning to the smell of bananas and coconut. It was a pleasant, fruity smell. It took her a moment to remember where she was. Then she looked around the room and saw bales of pink hay, a sack of candy corn, and a pair of rainbow saddles.

"Ridiculous," said Samantha as she shook her head. She didn't have time to spare on her sister's mythological-livestock problems, though. She got out of bed and woke her brother, and they left the stables.

She and Nipper headed to the dining room, where Nathaniel had prepared a thick, creamy breakfast. He served it in big bowls with rubber handles. Samantha suspected they were the type of bowl used for feeding horses . . . or unicorns.

"I don't want to eat a giant slimy brain!" Nipper shouted.

"It's fruit pudding, boy," said Nathaniel, looking irritated.

Samantha was starving—and in a hurry to explore Central Park before Buffy found them and they'd have to hear more about her big Broadway show. She ate quickly, and so did Nipper.

"Yum," said Nipper, scraping the bottom of the bowl with his spoon. "That tasted better than it looked."

"If you be a-complimentin' me, you're welcome," said Nathaniel.

After breakfast, they headed back down to the stables so Samantha could grab her purse. She checked to make sure her notes—and the purple sunglasses—were inside. Then she and Nipper rode the freight elevator down to the street and crossed into Central Park.

After only four minutes, it began.

"Are you sure you know what we're looking for?" Nipper asked. "When do I get to go see Yankee Stadium? Maybe you shouldn't have left the umbrella at home. Do you think you fixed it enough with the tape? Maybe we should have brought Dennis. When do we go see the Yankees?"

Samantha groaned. She'd thought she had at least ten minutes before her brother would get impatient.

He wore a New York Yankees T-shirt and a cap with

the team's emblem. A Babe Ruth bobblehead stuck out of his back pocket. It was a miracle that he was willing to accompany her to Cleopatra's Needle at all.

"Just keep walking," she said. "We're looking for a little plaza near the back of the Metropolitan Museum of Art. We're more than halfway there."

She took out a page and unfolded it.

"I printed this out from Dad's computer before we left," she said, and handed it to Nipper.

It was an aerial photograph of the east side of the park. A cluster of shapes combined to form a rectangular building that hugged the street. To the west of the building sat patches of trees, open green spaces, and something that looked like a red octagon with a pole in the center.

"We're headed here," she said, pointing to the page.

He nodded. She took the paper from him, folded it up, and returned it to her pocket. They walked on. A pair of early-morning joggers passed them. Samantha and Nipper were getting close now. Excited, Samantha started to walk a little faster. She and Nipper dodged a woman pushing a baby carriage, walking three dogs, sipping coffee, and talking on a phone. They went through a brick-lined tunnel and reached a flight of wide stone steps. A monument rose high into the sky.

"Cleopatra's Needle," she sighed.

As they climbed the steps, Samantha squinted at the

stone obelisk. Perched on a huge granite block, it towered over an octagonal red brick terrace. A black metal railing, about three feet high, surrounded the terrace. Closer in, another railing surrounded the obelisk itself.

When they reached the top of the stairs, she glanced around. It was still early on a Sunday morning. They were alone.

"Let's get to work," she said to Nipper.

Samantha reached into her purse for the sunglasses. She put them on, and the world turned purple.

"I'm going to look from a distance," she told Nipper. "You search the Needle up close, and don't miss *anything*."

"You got it, Sam," he said cheerfully, and sprang forward.

He climbed over the railing and began tapping and pressing everything. He shoved at corners and pushed in a dozen places. He poked at shapes and traced any carvings he could reach. Steadily, he worked his way around the monument.

Samantha smiled. It was satisfying to see her brother's fidgeting, touching, and tampering skills put to good use. She took two big steps back and stared.

Cleopatra's Needle is an ancient monument covered from top to bottom with carvings. Samantha had read that it had been moved to Central Park from Egypt more than a hundred years ago. Some of the carvings looked like birds and others like people. Most were Egyptian symbols that Samantha didn't recognize. A few of the images were crisp and clear. Most were faint, worn away by years of wind, rain, and pollution.

She saw nothing unusual on the first side.

"Side two," said Samantha as she walked to the next corner of the plaza.

She'd started to examine the Needle when she heard noises. She turned to see Nipper, hands flat against one corner of the huge granite base. He pushed at it, grunting as he shoved.

"What are you doing?" she asked.

He stopped shoving.

"I'm trying to turn it," he answered. "Maybe if I push hard enough the whole Needle will spin."

Samantha looked at the massive stone monument.

"Why do you think it would do that?" she asked.

"Just a hunch," he answered, and went back to shoving.

Samantha tuned out her noisy brother and went back to scanning the obelisk. She moved her head slowly, up and down, taking everything in. Nothing. She kept going, exploring all four sides. Still nothing.

"I give up," she said, and stopped squinting at the obelisk.

"I'll take a break, too," said Nipper, sitting down on the railing.

"But only for a minute," she added quickly.

"Sure, sure," he said. "But we're going to see the Yankees soon, right?"

He started kicking at a railing post with his heel.

"They need me," he added, sounding serious.

Samantha noticed a change in her brother's expression. He looked thoughtful for a moment. At least kid-brother thoughtful.

"They're my team," he said, still kicking at the post. "My mind is made up. I really, truly want them back."

Samantha looked at Nipper, and then to the railing as he kicked, and . . .

"Stop!" she yelled. "Don't move."

Nipper froze.

Through her glasses, Samantha saw the railing by her brother's foot blinking bright yellow.

"What do you see? Can I move?" Nipper asked.

"Yes, yes," she answered. "Get out of the way."

Samantha ran to the railing and crouched to inspect it. A section glowed exactly like the leg of the kitchen table at home. She reached out and pulled. It slid open—just like at home. Air rushed out.

"Whoa," said Nipper. "These things are everywhere."

"Maybe," said Samantha.

Her brother reached into the railing and took out a piece of paper.

"And everyone's writing to Uncle Paul," he said.

"What are you talking about?" Samantha said. She snatched the paper from him and read it aloud.

" 'Paul/Horace:
" 'Where are you?' "

"That's *my* note," she said, exasperated.

Samantha heard voices approaching. She turned and saw a cluster of people talking to one another as they walked up the steps. Seconds later, a pack of skateboarders rolled onto the terrace. Samantha sighed. Her and Nipper's time alone at the Needle had ended and still no Uncle Paul. She took off the glasses and put them in her purse along with the note.

"All right," she said. "I guess we can go back to Buffy's place."

Samantha turned to leave, but Nipper was standing still again.

"No way!" he replied, crossing his arms. "We're going to Yankee Stadium."

"Oh, yeah," Samantha said. "Let's go."

They crossed to the steps on the other side of the terrace. The path led past the museum and toward the east edge of the park. As they walked, Samantha wondered if there were any more clues in Buffy's apartment. It wasn't going to be easy to find out, with her sister whining and her weird helper Nathaniel watching.

She decided she'd help Buffy with her show. She could try to be a producer or something like that. It would keep her sister busy and give Nipper time to search for clues.

And who knows? Maybe she could even save the play and stop it from turning into a big, zany circus. Samantha had never cared about show business before. But maybe she had hidden talent.

She pictured her name in the program—beneath *Scarlett Hydrangea* in giant letters, of course. She might turn out to be a great producer. Maybe she could write her own play, or even start acting.

She heard Nipper shouting. While she had been thinking about the play, he had walked ahead to Fifth Avenue at the edge of the park.

"Come on, Sam," he called. "My Yankees need me."

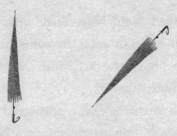

CHAPTER ELEVEN

LOCK ME OUT OF THE BALL GAME

Samantha and Nipper rode the number 4 subway north to Yankee Stadium. She watched the map to make sure they got off at the right station.

"Not like the magtrain at all, is it?" she asked Nipper.

He shook his head. He couldn't hear her over the noise of the subway.

They were the only two passengers to exit at Yankee Stadium. They marched up from the subway onto a quiet, empty plaza. They saw a dark stadium. The ticket booths were shuttered and the gates were closed.

A poster on a ticket booth displayed the team's schedule for the month of May. The Yankees were currently playing a three-game series against the Nationals in Washington, D.C.

"Don't trust a *Nat*," Nipper said quietly.

"Oh, come on," said Samantha, exasperated. "Couldn't you have checked the schedule before you dragged me all the way up here?"

She looked up at the empty stadium.

"The ride was a big waste," she grumbled. "And we don't have much time left in New York."

Nipper had already turned and bounded up the stairs. He poked his head through a closed entrance gate. He gripped a metal bar with each hand and peered around the grounds, standing up on his toes to get a better view.

A vendor pushing a squeaky cart stacked with T-shirts and hats made his way along the sidewalk. He flashed a hopeful smile. Then he saw that Nipper already had a bobblehead and the complete Yankees wardrobe. The man lost some of his enthusiasm.

"That's my team and my stadium," Nipper told the vendor.

"Your team?" the man said, chuckling a little. "I hope you didn't pay a lot for it."

Nipper noticed a sign on the vendor's cart.

LOSING STREAK SPECIAL
90% OFF

Nipper was about to say something to the vendor

about his Yankees, how they were going to turn it around, and the magical World Series ring he would wear someday. But the man was already walking away.

"I wouldn't pay three hundred bucks for those bums," the vendor said as he rolled his creaking cart away down the sidewalk.

Samantha let her brother pace around the outside of the empty stadium for a few more minutes. Then she led him back to the subway and they headed to Buffy's castle in the sky.

CHAPTER TWELVE

"NO" BUSINESS

Samantha sat across from her sister at the ornate dining room table. Together, they reviewed scripts and set designs.

"Nate's in the kitchen," said Buffy. "He says he wants us to get ready for a 'Polynesian Surprise.'"

Samantha wasn't exactly sure what that meant, but her sister's grouchy assistant sure was a good cook. The food would probably be delicious.

After a frustrating day, she was starting to feel better. While Samantha helped Buffy with the play, Nipper borrowed the purple sunglasses from her and snooped for clues about Uncle Paul. Samantha had to admit, she was actually looking forward to becoming a producer.

Maybe she could help her sister turn the play around. And then, who knew where it could lead?

"What's up with the monster trucks and the fog machines?" she asked Buffy.

A blueprint on the table showed a big propeller inside a cage.

"And what's that?" she added. "A big fan?"

"Horace Temple told me it was very important to have all these things," said Buffy.

Samantha nodded, rubbing her chin thoughtfully. Were these clues? Did they have something to do with watching out for the SUN? Or was Uncle Paul just pretending to think like a Broadway producer, so Buffy would keep him around?

"The bagpipes and the giraffes were my idea," Buffy said proudly. "And the fireworks."

"Stop," said Samantha, gesturing with both hands. "Never cause an explosion in a theater. That violates a dozen safety codes and regulations."

Buffy frowned.

"I have some ideas for the opening number," Samantha said. "But first we have to talk about the unicorns."

"What about them?" Buffy asked quickly.

"Face it," said Samantha. "There aren't any unicorns. So I don't think we should plan the whole production around them."

"What?" Buffy asked, much louder.

Nipper tapped Samantha on the shoulder.

"Hey, Sam," he whispered. "I think I found some clues."

"Hold on one minute," she told Buffy, and turned to her brother.

Nipper handed her four Word Whammy! cards.

"A, L, I, and M," he said. "They were on the floor in a hallway."

Samantha looked at the cards.

"Did you find them in this order?" she asked.

"Mmmm—maybe," he replied.

He shrugged his shoulders and looked like he had no idea.

"Samantha . . . I'm waiting," said Buffy.

Nipper handed the glasses back to Samantha and shrugged again.

"Are these the only letters?" she asked quickly. "Were there any other cards around?"

"I dunno. Probably." He shrugged. "I was in a hurry and I didn't really—"

"You didn't really pay attention, did you," Samantha snapped.

"Sammy!" Buffy called.

Samantha hated it when people called her "Sammy." She turned back to the table to see Buffy scowling at her.

"Okay, okay," said Samantha. "Let's talk about these mermaids."

She pointed to the drawing of a big cave. Huge letters above the entrance spelled out *Hydrangea*!

"I don't think ancient Egyptians had anything that looked like—"

"You're fired!" said Buffy.

"What?" Samantha asked.

"Go home. *Now*."

CHAPTER THIRTEEN

PLANE SAMANTHA

Samantha sat quietly in her double-triple super-economy class seat. The plane hit a bump and the seat flushed, but she ignored the sound of rushing air and water. The whole weekend had been a disappointment.

"We never got that Polynesian Surprise, Sam!" Nipper shouted from his cabin. "Missing dessert violates a dozen of my personal codes and regulations!"

Samantha didn't answer him. She looked down at the four cards in her hands and flipped through them twice.

"A-L-I-M," she said quietly. "M-A-I-L."

Maybe it was meant to spell *mail.*
They could certainly go back and
check the magtrain mailbox again.

But what if her brother had missed some letters? She couldn't be sure.

In fact, there was only one thing she could be sure of: *It wasn't fair!*

She didn't find Horace or Uncle Paul.

She didn't find the SUN.

She didn't get to be a producer, a writer, or a Broadway actor.

It really wasn't fair.

In her heart, Samantha knew that if anyone ever wrote a series about her life, every book would have a chapter titled "It Wasn't Fair."

Cleopatra's Needle

A sixty-nine-foot solid-granite obelisk stands on a small terrace in New York City's Central Park, just west of the Metropolitan Museum of Art.

It is popularly known as "Cleopatra's Needle," even though it was built around 1450 BCE, more than a thousand years before the Egyptian queen was born. It's the oldest outdoor monument in New York City.

It was transported to New York in 1880 as a gift to the people of the United States from the government of Egypt. Tourists have been marveling at its design and mysterious inscriptions ever since.

* * *

The monument rests on a heavy-duty roller bearing. Push hard to rotate the obelisk on its giant stone base. It is very heavy, however, so it may take more than one person to get it going.

Once it starts to move, turn the Needle three complete rotations in both directions. A section of the base on the north side will unlock. Push inward and you will find an opening. There is a ladder on the far wall. It is seventy-nine feet down to the start of a narrow railway tunnel.

A slingshot trolley waits to launch you under Manhattan. Depending on how the secret switch under the Hess triangle has been set, you will zoom to the west, east, or south.

CHAPTER FOURTEEN

THE TROUBLE WITH KIBBLES

Dennis sat under the kitchen table.
    Where was the man with orange shoes?
    He looked there and here.
    He looked here and there.
    Fuzzy things were everywhere.

They chewed on his toys.
    They made squeaky noise.
    It hurt his ears.

Dennis looked in his bowl.
His bowl was empty.
Fuzzy things stole his food!

Attack! Attack!
Attack! ATTACK!

CHAPTER FIFTEEN

WHOA, NELLY!

It was a short, four-day school week, but it seemed to drag on forever. Samantha started out exhausted, having arrived home late Monday night, after midnight. And she hadn't slept well. She couldn't stop puzzling over the letters A, L, I, and M.

During lunchtime, she had used a computer in her school's media center. She learned that *alim* means "All-Knowing" in Arabic and "scientist" in Azerbaijani. *Ilma* means "air" in Finnish. There's a butterfly species with the Latin name *Tetrarhanis ilma*. None of those seemed like useful clues, however. She shuffled the Word Whammy! cards over and over again.

Mali and *Lima* spelled names of places. *Mila* and *Liam* spelled personal names. *Mail* could refer to the mailbox.

And of course, there was the very real possibility that Nipper missed some cards on the floor in their sister's apartment.

After school on Friday, she went to her room and made a list of countries with names that included A, L, I, and M.

COLOMBIA

DEMOCRATIC REPUBLIC OF THE CONGO

DOMINICAN REPUBLIC

MALAWI

MALAYSIA

MALDIVES

MALI

MARSHALL ISLANDS

MONGOLIA

SOMALIA

Then she wrote down all the magtrain stations listed on the wall of her station.

DYNAMITE (United States)

PARIS (France)

BARABOO (United States)

DUCK (United States)

ZZYZX (United States)
EDFU (Egypt)
WAGGA WAGGA (Australia)
WAHOO (United States)
SEATTLE (United States)

The two lists had no countries in common.

"Dead end," she muttered, and put down her pen.

She closed her notebook, covered her ears to mute the sound of squeaking chinchillas, and tried to think.

Nipper tapped her on the shoulder. She jumped.

"Didn't mean to scare you, Sam," he said cheerfully. "But I've been thinking carefully about Uncle Paul."

"Thinking carefully?" Samantha asked. "That's refreshing."

She didn't really believe him, but it was nice to hear that he was trying to solve this mystery, too.

"He always talked about the Great Wall of China, and the *Titanic*, and Machu Picchu," Nipper said, pacing around her bedroom. "That's a WALL, a SHIP, and a CITY."

"Go on," said Samantha.

"I added SUN," he continued. "You know, 'Watch out for the SUN.'"

She nodded.

"I put everything in alphabetical order," he said.

He took out a piece of paper.

" 'ACHIILLNPSSTUWY,' " he read.

Samantha couldn't tell where this was going.

"Now, we all know that Uncle Paul loves waffles," he continued. "And Cornelius Swartwout patented the waffle iron in 1869."

"Cornelius Swartwout?" she asked. "How come you remember that, but you can't keep track of—"

"Stay with me," said Nipper. "We've got ACHI-ILLNPSSTUWY, CORNELIUS, and SWARTWOUT."

"Nipper," said Samantha, louder than before, but her brother couldn't be stopped.

"Did you ever wonder what's in a GRANOLA bar?" he continued. "Well, I checked. They're mostly OATS, HONEY, and NUTS. I'm leaving out raisins because they're too sticky. I added HOPE DIAMOND instead. Now take a look!"

He turned over his paper and held it out for her to read.

Samantha stared at the page.

```
  D O R P              C H E W
S W I N T Y          S N U L A D
G O R L O N          S T O T S I
S N Y T O T          C H I N S U
M A W E A L          P E N H O O
  U L I A              A R U A
```

"Dorp? Swinty?" she asked. "Gorlon?"

"Don't you see?" he said excitedly.

Samantha stared at him.

"They're all letters!" he continued. "And . . . letters come from . . ."

"Let me guess," she said. "A mailbox."

"Yes!" he shouted. "M-A-I-L! Let's go there again."

Samantha let out a heavy sigh.

"You could have just said that in the first place."

"And let you do all the puzzling?" he replied. "No way!"

He turned and headed to the hall.

"Meet me at the corner in five minutes," he said.

There was no point in arguing. She closed her notebook and left the room.

The Waffle Iron

On August 24, 1869, an American inventor named Cornelius Swartwout filed a patent for a waffle iron.

Up until then, most people cooked waffles by pouring batter into hinged plates with long wooden handles.

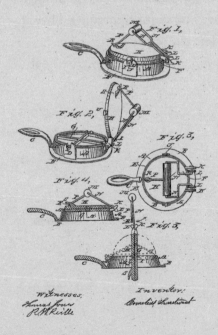

C. SWARTWOUT.

Waffle Iron.

No. 94,043.

Patented Aug. 24, 1869.

Swartwout's invention had a special design that allowed breakfast makers to open, close, and turn the waffle iron, spreading the batter evenly.

To commemorate this great moment in breakfast history, August 24 is celebrated in the United States as National Waffle Day.

* * *

If the waffle iron in your kitchen has been modified to include *miniaturized infrared diodes*, it can help you find super-secret clues. Once you get used to taking a closer look at things, you'll find that there are messages hidden in all kinds of places—even in words that seem like gibberish!

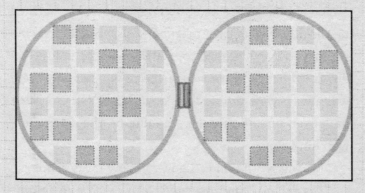

Compare the shaded squares in these waffles with any crazy, mixed-up letters that your annoying kid brother shows you. He might not even realize it, but there's a secret message waiting for you. Whoa, Nelly!

CHAPTER SIXTEEN

NEIGHBORHOOD WATCH

Nipper walked far ahead of Samantha. He had a special errand to run before they visited the mailbox. He marched up the driveway of their neighbor, Missy Snoddgrass. As he hopped over smashed toys, a Hula-Hoop, and several discarded balls of yarn, he started to wonder why there was always yarn around the side of Missy's house. Then he looked up and saw her standing on the side porch, watching him.

"Hi, Missy," he said. "Did you know I was coming?"

"Yes and no," she answered. "I'm keeping an eye out for all kinds of suspicious characters."

"Um, okay," he said, stopping at the bottom of the stairs beneath the porch.

She was double-triple super-evil, so he didn't want to get too close.

"I'm the new captain of our neighborhood watch," she told him.

"Watch?" he asked nervously. "Captain?"

"We've been getting reports of strange activity around here," she said.

Her eyes narrowed. She looked him up and down.

"I see you're wearing some of my team's official licensed merchandise," she said.

Nipper looked down at his sweatshirt. It had a big New York Yankees logo on it.

"Oh, yeah," he said, looking back up at her. "That's the reason I'm here."

He reached into his front pocket.

"I want my Yankees back," he said. "I have a new trade for you."

"I already told you," she snapped. "*No backsies.* Besides, the team isn't doing very well these days. It would be bad luck to change ownership midseason."

Nipper pulled out a shiny golden sculpture. It was shaped like an egg, and crisscrossed by rows of red and white gems. It glistened in the sun.

Missy's eyes widened. She looked excited, maybe even pleased.

"See?" Nipper said. "I knew you'd be interested in this."

Her expression returned to its natural scowl. Then, slowly, it slid into an evil sneer. She leaned forward over the edge of the porch. Nipper noticed that she was still wearing the scorpion ring he had given her. Its emerald eyes flashed briefly.

"Interesting egg," she said, scratching her chin. "From whom was it stolen?"

"Whom? What? Stolen?" said Nipper. "It's not stolen."

"Then how did you get it?" Missy asked. "Do you have any documentation or paperwork?"

"Paperwork?" he asked, getting nervous. "It was from my uncle."

"Oh. Pajama Paul," she said slowly. "And how do you suppose *he* got it?"

"Well, um, gee," said Nipper. "I'm not sure. It was a present and—"

"Okay," she said, cutting him off. "I'm willing to pretend this whole encounter didn't happen."

"Didn't happen?" said Nipper, frustrated. "What do you mean? I'm here to talk about my baseball team."

Missy reached into the pocket of her yellow polka-dot blouse and took out a small notebook. She jerked it open with one hand, raised a red pen with the other, and stared into his eyes.

"You don't want me to write your name on this list, Jeremy Bernard Spinner," she said without blinking.

"Once somebody gets on it, they never get off."

Missy was one of the few people who knew Nipper's real name, and the only person who used it.

Nipper gulped.

"No. No, Missy," he said quickly. "I don't want that."

He held up both hands.

Missy snatched the egg from him and placed it on a chair, far out of reach.

"Hey!" Nipper shouted. "That's mine and—"

"Jeremy ... Bern ... ," she said slowly, starting to write in her notebook.

"Okay, okay," he said. "I don't like eggs anyways."

"Good," she grunted.

Missy put down the notebook and raised a hand to shade her eyes.

"The SUN is really bothering me today," she muttered.

"What did you just say?" asked Nipper.

"Nothing," she said quickly, dropping her hand and pointing a thumb sideways. "Your sister's waiting for you."

Nipper turned and saw Samantha on the sidewalk. She waved at him and pointed toward the mailbox.

"I give up," Nipper said. "For now."

He stomped back down the driveway to join his sister.

"Sam!" he called. "I lost my egg!"

CHAPTER SEVENTEEN

UNDER

"What was that about?" Samantha asked her brother.

"Forget it," he answered. "Put on those specs and spot some clues."

Samantha pulled the sunglasses from her purse, put them on, and stared. A few feet ahead, the now-familiar word glowed on the side of the magtrain mailbox in bright yellow letters.

"*PSST?*" Nipper asked.

Samantha nodded.

"Yep," she answered. "But that's all. There doesn't seem to be anything else to it."

She took the glasses off and wiped the purple lenses on her sleeve. She handed the glasses to Nipper. He put them on, leaned forward, and squinted.

"*PSST,*" he repeated, reaching for the handle of the mailbox.

Samantha caught his arm and stopped him.

"Don't bother," she said. "I've checked the station at least twenty times. This is the only message."

Nipper ignored her. He opened and closed the metal door three times. It clicked and hummed. Then the mailbox began to rise, revealing the chamber beneath it.

"I just told you, I already checked under there," Samantha called over the sound of grinding gears.

"Under where?" asked Nipper, watching the mailbox rise

"Under there," she repeated.

"Under where?" he asked again.

The rectangular structure stopped in place.

"Under— Nipper," she said, getting annoyed. "Are you trying to be funny?"

He looked at her with a serious face.

"I never *try* to be funny . . . I just am," he told her.

Samantha sighed.

"Wait! Under there!" he said quickly, and pointed up to the mailbox, now perched atop the entrance chamber. He handed the glasses back to Samantha and pointed again, shaking his finger at the gap between the bottom of the box and the top of the chamber.

"Take a closer look," he said.

She put the glasses on again and squinted upward. The mailbox stood on short legs, creating a space about a foot high. On the underside of the box, a yellow arrow glowed. It pointed into Volunteer Park.

Nipper grinned at her and gave her a thumbs-up.

"Let's explore the park," he said.

He started to cross the street, but Samantha stepped in front of him.

"It's almost time for dinner," she said. "And besides, I want my umbrella before we do any more exploring."

"Got it, Sam," said Nipper. "You had me at 'dinner.' "

He handed her the sunglasses and they waited. A minute later, the mailbox clicked and whirred and sank back into place. Then they headed back down the block.

As they passed the Snoddgrass house, Nipper slowed and gazed up the driveway. Samantha kept going, then turned and walked back to him.

"It's okay," she said, putting a hand on his shoulder. "We're both explorers, and we're not coming home empty-handed."

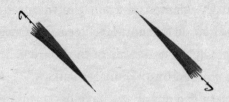

CHAPTER EIGHTEEN

HYDRANT-GO-SEEK

Samantha rose early Saturday morning. She chased a pair of chinchillas out of her room, then took a quick shower and got dressed. She grabbed her umbrella and put the sunglasses in her purse. On the way down to the kitchen, she passed Dennis, who was chasing a chinchilla headed up to the second floor. She was only half awake, so the sound of rodents squeaking and plastic cone clattering was extra-irritating. She and Nipper had a new clue, though, a good one, and they were about to check it out. That improved her mood.

She made breakfast while she waited for her brother. She filled a bowl with cereal and went to the refrigerator for milk. Before she could sit down, a chinchilla dashed across the table and scampered away with her spoon in its mouth.

Samantha watched the rodent retreat to a far corner of the kitchen. It looked up at her and opened its tiny mouth, letting the spoon drop on the floor. It began to squeak at her repeatedly.

Samantha thought it sounded like the chinchilla was laughing at her.

"You know what animals I *really* love?" she said to the chinchilla. "Owls, skunks, and foxes."

"Really? Since when?" Nipper said cheerfully, walking into the room.

Before she could respond, he grabbed a bowl and two spoons. He handed one of the spoons to his sister and they both dug in, eating quickly.

"I've got my hand lens," said Nipper, waving his magnifying glass at Samantha.

She nodded, then grabbed her purse and umbrella, and they headed out the front door.

"Sam, did you know that owls, skunks, and foxes are natural predators of chinchillas?" Nipper asked as they headed north on Thirteenth Avenue.

"Yes," she replied. "An eight-year-old boy told me that several times this week."

Nipper tilted his head sideways and stared off into space. She could tell he was replaying events of the week in his mind.

"That was me, Sam, wasn't it?" he finally said.

Samantha noticed Missy Snoddgrass watching

them through the bay window of her house. She wore the same yellow polka-dot blouse as always and pounded one fist rhythmically onto her open palm as she watched them walk by.

Samantha quickly took the purple sunglasses and put them on Nipper's face.

"Huh?" he asked. "What are you—"

"You should try these first today," she said.

Samantha was determined to get to the park before her brother paid another punishing visit to their neighbor's house. He always came back in a bad mood.

"Keep a watch out for any lights or clues," she said.

"I'm on it," said Nipper.

He began to stare straight ahead toward the end of the block.

"Distraction prevented," Samantha said quietly to herself.

They passed the Snoddgrass lair and reached the mailbox. She pictured the arrow beneath it pointing across the street into Volunteer Park.

"Follow me and keep looking," she said, and led Nipper across the street.

They walked around the water tower and crossed to the front of the art museum.

"Take your time," she told him. "Make sure you don't miss anything."

Nipper stood with his hands at his sides and began to turn around slowly.

"Beep . . . beep . . . beep," he said, imitating radar or some kind of warning device.

"How is it possible," she asked, "that you can be annoying in any situation?"

"Beep . . . beep . . . oh, I don't know, Sam," he replied. "It just comes natural to me. Beep."

"Stop it," she said. "Right now. No more noises."

He stared at her. His lips moved, but he stopped making beeping sounds out loud.

Samantha waited as Nipper went back to staring and turning. Slowly and silently, he spun all the way around. He looked at the art museum, south toward their house, west over Downtown and to the Olympic Mountains beyond. He finished his 360-degrees rotation, then stared at her.

"Anything?" she asked.

He pointed to his mouth. His lips were closed tight.

"Speak," she said.

"Bee-eep . . . prepared to keep walking," he said. "There's nothing secret here."

Samantha groaned.

"You are *exceptionally* annoying," she said. "Let's move on."

They walked past the museum and farther north into the park. The sidewalk curved around a field dotted with picnic tables. It continued to the Volunteer Park Conservatory, a two-story, glass-and-iron greenhouse.

"Beep," said Nipper.

"Again?" Samantha asked, irritated. "When you make those sounds you are super-annoy—"

"Listen, Sam," he insisted. "Bee-beep-beep. I see—beep. Something yellow—beep. In front of the—beep. Conservatory and—"

She snatched the glasses from her brother's face and followed his gaze. To the right of the walkway, a few feet from the glass doors to the greenhouse, a red fire hydrant stood in the grass.

She put the glasses on. The hydrant glowed yellow. Toward the top, extra-bright yellow letters flashed:

PSST

She stared at the hydrant. It was waist high and had a domed cap. A large round outlet on its front faced her. Two smaller outlets stuck out on either side like stubby arms. Short chains connected the pentagon-shaped bolts to the body of the hydrant.

While Samantha put the glasses in her purse, Nipper pushed past her.

"I've got this," he said as he reached the hydrant.

First, he put his hands on the domed cap and tried to twist it. Then he tugged at the chains. Finally, he pulled on the two arms and tried to get the whole hydrant to turn.

"I can do it, Sam," he grunted, putting his full weight into it. "I'm sure there's . . . a way . . . to make it . . ."

Nipper lost his grip and his footing, falling onto the grass behind the hydrant.

"Ouch!" he said, looking up at Samantha. "I just fell on my hand lens."

"Get up and pass it to me," she replied. "I want to check the Plans."

Samantha unslung the umbrella from her shoulder, raised it above her head, and popped it open. Then she extended a hand to Nipper, who was still lying on the ground. As she waited for the magnifier, she looked past her fingertips at the hydrant. The large bolt on top of the cap caught her attention. She quickly turned and looked at the open umbrella. Then she looked down at the bolt again. Each had eight sides. They were both octagons! It couldn't be a coincidence.

Samantha stepped off the path toward the hydrant. Meanwhile, Nipper was running his fingers through the grass.

"Hey, this is fake," he said. "It's artificial turf."

Samantha focused on the octagonal bolt. She reached out, grabbed it, and gave it a quick turn. Immediately, she heard a soft click and a loud hiss. The ground shook. She reached out again to steady herself. The lawn surrounding the hydrant, about three feet in all directions, began to drop slowly. They were sinking into the park on a green, ring-shaped platform.

"Interesting," said Nipper, standing up quickly.

Samantha watched the fire hydrant rise above them in the center of the ring as they descended. They dropped below street level and continued downward until, with a gentle bump, they came to a stop. Looking up, she saw the fire hydrant thirty feet above, framed by the sky. Some light trickled down, but not much. Machinery droned softly, and she heard what sounded like sheets of sandpaper rubbing together.

Something clicked and lights came on.

They stood in the center of a small room It was about ten feet to the wall all around. The floor beyond the edge of the platform was rotating clockwise.

The white tile walls surrounding them had four wide rectangular openings, spaced evenly around the chamber. Samantha read a large sign above each one.

NORWAY
4,500 MILES

PERU
5,000 MILES

MALI
6,500 MILES

INDONESIA
8,300 MILES

In the past few months, Samantha and Nipper had done so much traveling on mysterious, barely labeled trains, tubes, and ladders, it felt strange to be in a place with such clear signage.

Painted on the walls between the openings, Samantha saw:

SLIDEWALK
KEEP RIGHT

"Ever hear of a 'slidewalk'?" she asked.

Nipper shook his head.

They stepped onto the rotating floor.

"'Slidewalk . . . slidewalk . . . slidewalk,'" she read, watching the walls go by. "I have a feeling we're about to find out."

As they began their second orbit around the room, they peeked through the entrances and saw that each had two conveyor belts. The one on the right led away. The one on the left led back to the chamber.

"Okay, Sam," said Nipper. "Where to?"

Samantha started to reach for the umbrella on her shoulder, but then stopped. She scanned the signs above each opening again. Then she smiled.

"A-L-I-M," she replied. "Unscrambled, that's . . ."

She waited for her brother to answer.

He stared at her blankly.

"I-L-A-M backward *is* . . . ," she tried again.

"Mali," he said.

"It's in Africa," she told him.

"Oh, yeah. Of course," he said. "It's one of the sixteen landlocked African countries."

As they stepped through the entrance, Samantha marveled at her brother's capacity for useless facts.

Fire Hydrants

There are an estimated 8.9 million fire hydrants in the United States. Each one allows firefighters to tap into the local water system. Users attach hoses to the hydrant, then open a valve to unleash a powerful water flow.

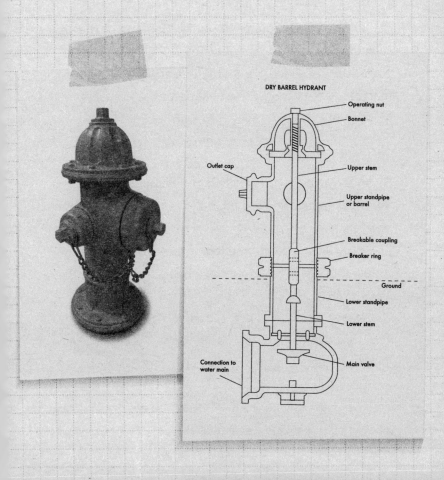

DRY BARREL HYDRANT

- Operating nut
- Bonnet
- Outlet cap
- Upper stem
- Upper standpipe or barrel
- Breakable coupling
- Breaker ring
- Ground
- Lower standpipe
- Lower stem
- Connection to water main
- Main valve

the most common designs is the "dry barrel" ...nt. Turning the bolt on the top opens a valve located ...ur below ground to prevent freezing.

Most hydrants have pentagon-shaped bolts to keep unauthorized persons from using them. The bolts require special tools, usually a large wrench with a pentagon-shaped socket.

* * *

Twenty hydrants in the United States do not connect to water. Instead, they are part of the international slide-walk system.

If you look closely at the top of these hydrants, you will notice that the bolts do not have five sides. Instead, they have eight.

No special tools are required to activate these hydrants. Simply twist the bolt left or right. The areas around these hydrants are ring-shaped elevators, disguised with artificial turf.

The green elevator ring will lower you gently to a lobby about thirty feet below street level.

CHAPTER NINETEEN

SLIP, SLIDE, AND AWAY!

As they rode the conveyor belt through the Mali entrance, it reminded Samantha of the moving sidewalk they'd ridden in Newark airport about a week earlier. The slidewalk quickly moved, however, into a space unlike anything she had ever seen before.

A huge room, the size of two football fields laid end to end, stretched out in front of them. The ceiling arched high above, with glowing panels that bathed everything in bright white light. Humming, swishing sounds filled the air. The floor was covered with conveyor belts.

"Slidewalks?" said Nipper.

Samantha nodded.

She quickly counted twenty conveyor belts, all moving at different speeds. The ten belts on the right—including the one they were on—moved away from the entrance. To the left, ten belts moved back toward the ringed platform. Ahead, on the other side of the hangar, the belt on the far right disappeared into a tunnel.

Samantha looked down at the belt immediately to her right. It was moving faster than the one they were on. She couldn't be sure how much faster. Then she looked at the far wall. They definitely had to reach the tunnel before they got to the end of the room.

"Grab my hand and wait until I tell you to go," she said.

Samantha knew that, normally, Nipper was not the kind of boy who would want to hold any hands belonging to any of his sisters. But after their climbing, sliding, and tumbling around the world together, she figured he'd join her for a quick synchronized leap onto a moving walkway.

"One, two, three . . . go!" she shouted, and they hopped to the right.

Nipper let go quickly. He looked around. He frowned.

"See that?" he said, pointing at the surface of the belt.

There were yellow stripes every few feet, stenciled with black numbers and letters.

10 MPH

Samantha could tell Nipper was a little bit disappointed. He clearly thought it was going to be a more exciting ride. She nodded and pointed to her right. She didn't try to hold his hand a second time.

"Ready, set . . . walk," she said, more calmly this time, and stepped sideways onto the next belt.

Nipper followed and stepped beside her. They looked down again.

15 MPH

The end of the hangar was still far away.

"Ready, set, walk," she said quickly, and they stepped again.

20 MPH

"Ready, set, walk."

25 MPH

It didn't feel like they were accelerating quickly. Each new conveyor belt added five miles per hour to their speed. She stopped directing Nipper as they continued walking from belt to belt.

30 MPH
35 MPH
40 MPH
45 MPH

Samantha felt a steady breeze through her hair as the slidewalk carried them along. It was a smooth ride.

They had almost reached the other end of the vast hangar. Ahead, nine of the ten conveyor belts ended at the wall. The tenth slidewalk, to the far right, disappeared into a tunnel. Samantha checked to make sure Nipper was beside her. Together, they stepped to their right, onto the last belt. A minute later, they coasted out of the hangar.

Samantha's ears popped as she and Nipper entered the tunnel. The ceiling was just a few feet above their heads, and the brilliant light of the hangar panels had been replaced by rows of green and white lightbulbs that whizzed by. It was still easy to see, but everything had taken on a greenish tint.

Samantha glanced down, looking for stenciled speed stripes. She didn't find any. Instead, she noticed that the surface of this belt was different from the others. It was completely covered with small plastic bumps. She figured they were meant to help riders' feet grip the surface on the fastest belt.

"Okay, Sam," Nipper called to her. "We're on our way."

She looked up. He pointed at a sign flashing the words **TO MALI.** She started to think about the letters A, L, I, and M again. She closed her eyes and tried to think. Were they going to the right place?

When she opened her eyes, Nipper had his arms out at his sides pretending to surf.

"Whee!" he shouted. "I'm going to do this all the way to Africa!"

Samantha began counting to herself. *One, two, three . . .*

Nipper put his arms down. He was bored, of course.

"So," he said. "How fast do you think we're going now?"

"Well, each belt sped us up five miles per hour," she replied. "I think we're moving at about fifty miles per hour."

He nodded and started watching the white and green lights flash past them. After a minute, he turned back to her.

"How long do you think it will take to get to Mali?" he asked.

Samantha did some math in her head. It was 6,500 miles to Mali. Divided by 50, that was . . . 130 hours. Divided by 24 hours in a day, that made . . .

Nipper, waiting, watched her.

"Five and a half days," she said, and bit her lip, concerned.

Nipper stared. He looked around the tunnel and rubbed his chin thoughtfully.

"We really should have brought lunch," he said. "And dinner . . . and breakfast . . . and lunch . . . and . . ."

It was going to be a very long ride.

CHAPTER TWENTY

SPEED BUMPS

Fish must swim.

Mosquitos must bite.

People must pop bubble wrap.

As Samantha stood on the slidewalk and pondered how long it would take to reach Mali, Nipper noticed the plastic bumps along the belt. He bent down and touched one of the bumps with his finger. It jiggled.

"Wait!" shouted Samantha. "Don't touch that. You don't know what will—"

Bubble wrap waits for no one.

He pressed harder on the bubble. It popped.

With a blast of air and a loud crackle, two giant circles burst from the hole in the belt. They inflated in a fraction of a second and whipped around Nipper, sealing him tightly in an upright position. Instantly, all the green lightbulbs changed to yellow. An alarm began to sound.

"Nipper!" shouted Samantha.

He was locked tight between layers of bubble wrap, unable to move. His right hand was pinned a few inches from his head. He wiggled his fingers at her. He had a smile on his face.

"I'm okay," he said, his voice muffled by thick layers of bumpy plastic.

The alarm honked again and again. Samantha thought it sounded like a car alarm, or maybe a dive warning on a submarine.

She rushed over to Nipper and started tapping on his inflated enclosure.

"No, Sam," he shouted. "Pop your own bubble."

It was difficult to hear him, and harder still to think over the sound of the alarm.

The yellow lights turned red.

Samantha felt the slidewalk starting to accelerate.

Quickly, she looked down at the belt, chose a nearby bubble, and stomped. It popped, and two clear disks exploded upward. The sheets of industrial-strength packing material closed around her.

All sound became muffled. Facing forward and locked in place, Samantha looked ahead. She couldn't turn to see the umbrella or her purse, but she could feel them bubble-wrapped tightly against her. Ahead, Nipper smiled back at her from within his own shell. The green and white stripes moved faster and faster. The walls of the tunnel became a blur.

As she raced along, Samantha decided that her weird plastic enclosure was kind of comfortable. The bubble wrap formed an exact mold around her, with practically no pressure anywhere. It was like floating in space. Outside the container, however, the tunnel walls were zooming by at an amazing speed. She had no idea how fast. Were they traveling at a thousand miles per hour? Maybe more?

Unable to move, Samantha started to think about Uncle Paul again.

Were they on their way to meet him? Had she been too quick to decide which slidewalk to take? In all the stories he had shared, night after night, she was sure he never said anything about Mali. She racked her brain to remember facts or places he might have mentioned. Nothing. She couldn't recall anything about Mali's people or culture. What was the most common language of Mali anyway? Even her brother knew more about the landlocked African nation than she did.

Samantha felt pressure against her face. The slidewalk was slowing. Ahead of her, Nipper was sinking. Their bubble wrap shells had started to deflate.

The walls of the tunnel were no longer a blur. The lights passed by more slowly.

"Ta-da!" Nipper called, and hopped free as his bubble wrap fell to the floor. Samantha's plastic enclosure dropped away, too. She felt a blast of fresh air as the slidewalk tunnel widened. There were nine conveyor belts to her left.

Samantha and Nipper began to step from belt to belt, slowing down with each new slidewalk. They had reached the belt labeled *25 MPH* when they coasted into a new chamber. Just like before, twenty belts filled the room, but it was much smaller than the vast hangar they'd left behind them in Seattle. The ceiling here was lower, and the far wall wasn't quite as far. They continued to step and to slow down. When they reached the last belt, Nipper began to skip ahead of Samantha.

There wasn't a rotating floor in this slidewalk station. Instead, Samantha spotted a wide circle painted on the floor where the conveyor belts ended. A silver pipe rose from the center.

Samantha watched Nipper hop to the edge of the conveyor belt. At the same time, she noticed the round elevator platform dropping from the surface above them.

"Look out!" she yelled at Nipper, afraid that he was about to be flattened, but the green ring touched down well before he reached the landing zone. He turned back and gave her a thumbs-up.

Samantha stepped off the slidewalk and felt for her umbrella and her purse. Then she and Nipper walked onto the elevator ring. It began to rise.

"Good golly, it's Mali!" Nipper announced.

Samantha thought about Uncle Paul again. She had a nagging feeling about this. Were they in the wrong place?

"A-L-I-M," she said softly, and shrugged as they rose toward a circle of blue sky.

The Accelerated Moving Walkway (AMW) Concept

The 1893 World's Columbian Exposition in Chicago, Illinois, showcased the first moving sidewalk. In 1900, the Paris Exposition Universelle demonstrated a motorized walkway with multiple lanes moving at different speeds.

Writers, inventors, and urban planners have dreamed of high-speed conveyor belt systems ever since.

Using names such as slidewalk, glidepath, and speed-away, people have described and even tested many systems. The dream is to transport passengers at speeds of several hundred miles per hour.

Today, many airports have slow-moving automated walkways. However, there has never been an accelerated moving walkway made available to the public.

* * *

The Seattle slidewalk station is located under the conservatory at Volunteer Park. From there, you can access four slidewalks running to and from Norway, Peru, Mali, and Indonesia.

Walk onto a slidewalk and you'll reach a speed of fifty miles per hour simply by stepping from belt to belt.

To reach supersonic speed, activate the inflatable restraint cushions. Suspended inside a bubble-wrap shell, you can safely travel to the farthest reaches of the slidewalk system in less than an hour.

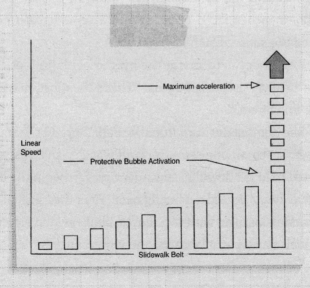

CHAPTER TWENTY-ONE

ON YOUR MARKET, SET, GO

Samantha and Nipper rode the elevator ring up to the surface. When it stopped, they found themselves standing beside a fire hydrant in the center of a small park. Stone benches faced outward and a cement path outlined the square patch of green grass.

Nipper began to kick at the hydrant with his foot.

"Really?" asked Samantha. "That's the most interesting thing here?"

She pointed outward from the park. Beyond the small green space on one side, the land was dry and dusty. A paved road led downhill toward a city. Farther in the distance, boats dotted a winding river. The other side faced a parking lot filled with cars, buses, donkeys, and bicycles as well as people, pushcarts, and wheelbarrows.

She noticed that the lot and all the roads leading from it were red dirt. Actually, vehicles, buildings, and just about everything else was covered in a thin layer of red dust.

Except for the people.

Men and women milled about, dressed in a swirl of colors. Some wore brightly colored shirts. Others wore long, patterned tunics. Women walked by wrapped in gowns of dazzling purples, yellows, and blues, with matching headscarves. The fabrics flowed with fruit, flowers, and geometric shapes. Men sported colorful turbans and hats small and large.

Samantha also saw people wearing T-shirts and blue jeans, but the swirl of amazing colors caught her eye.

People passed under a pink stucco arch with large wooden letters.

MARCHÉ DE MOPTI

Samantha guessed that the words were in French. If so, then *marché* meant "market." Uncle Paul had taught her a few things in French, and she had added a hundred words or so since then.

"I'm guessing Mopti is the name of this city," she told Nipper.

"Yes, Americans," said a smiling woman. With one hand she balanced a basket loaded with fruit on top of her head. With the other hand, she waved toward the city and the river.

"Welcome to Mopti," she said.

Samantha tried to think of a question to ask that might help them search for Uncle Paul. Before she could say "Where's your tallest building?" the woman disappeared into the busy market.

"Try the glasses," said Nipper. "Do your look-for-clues thing."

Samantha nodded and put them on. She gazed all around, hoping for a *PSST* or an arrow, or even "This way to Uncle Paul," written on a wall.

Nothing.

She put them back in her purse and waved for Nipper to follow her under the arch and into the market.

Buyers and sellers filled the red dirt street. Kids tugged at parents, workers pushed wheelbarrows, and vendors displayed everything from tools to clothes to fresh fish from the river.

All around, Samantha heard people talking, arguing, and even singing. But she didn't hear any more words that sounded like English or French.

She approached a table covered with brightly colored sheets and towels. She saw circles and squares and a dozen different patterns. One green towel had lines and stripes.

"Does this look a little like plaid to you, Nipper?" she asked, pointing at the towel.

Her brother didn't answer. She lifted the fabric for him to see.

"What do you think?" she asked.

Samantha looked over her shoulder. Nipper was gone.

"Happens all the time," she said to herself.

She dropped the cloth on the table, sighed heavily, and headed deeper into the market to find her brother.

Samantha passed carts with sizzling rice dishes and tables of jewelry made from animal teeth and beads. As she scanned the crowd, however, she couldn't shake the feeling that this trip was a big mistake. Maybe Uncle Paul was waiting for her on the other side of the planet.

"Pancakes! Hotcakes! Get your silver-dollar flap-jacks!"

The sound of English pulled Samantha's attention to a small crowd gathered around two men. They stood beside a tripod supporting a cast-iron pan and waved spatulas in the air.

Both wore one-piece outfits with what looked like little pictures of bananas all over them. What made them stand out the most, though, was that each had a bright red ball covering his nose and wore shoes that were enormous—at least a foot longer than Buffy's size 9½.

These were not local food vendors in colorful African clothes. They were circus clowns and, judging by their accents, they were American.

Without warning, they both scooped disks up from the pan with their spatulas and began flinging them at the crowd. Samantha froze, watching as the man closest to the clowns got slapped in the mouth. A woman next to him was hit on the side of her head. The object bounced off her ear.

In a panic, several people started to run. Samantha stayed in the street, watching the strange scene unfold. Pancakes ricocheted around the market like rubber balls. They knocked bowls off tables and ripped through plastic shopping bags, scattering seeds and nuts into the street.

"*We're* making pancakes, but *they're* getting battered," said one of the clowns.

The other clown laughed as if this was the funniest joke in the history of the world. Samantha noticed that no one else was laughing.

The clowns flung their pancakes, picking up speed, flinging them faster and faster.

One pancake zoomed at Samantha's head. In a flash, she swung her umbrella and batted it away. It bounced into the crowd.

"Rubber pancakes?" she asked out loud.

"Aiee!" an elderly woman screamed, covering her head with her hands.

A little girl stood in the street nibbling a peeled mango. One of the fake pancakes whacked the back of her hand. The mango fell into the dirt and the girl started to wail loudly.

"Bull's-eye," said the clown.

"Watch this," said the other clown as he stacked three rubber disks on his spatula. He raised his arm to fling them. Then he noticed Samantha, standing in the street, still holding her umbrella upright.

The clown froze. He stared at the umbrella, and then at Samantha. Not taking his eyes off her, he dumped the pancakes back into the pan and tapped his partner on the shoulder.

Samantha didn't wait to see what would happen next. She turned and walked away quickly. When she got far enough to feel like she could, she looked back, only to see the two clowns following her. Immediately, she turned into a side street and sped up. She could hear the clowns' big, flat shoes slapping the dirt street at her back. Where was Nipper?

"Come back, girl!" one of them shouted. "We've got some hilarious hotcakes for you."

The street curved left and Samantha reached a dead end. Her heart was racing now. She stopped and turned. There were market tables to her left and her right. Straight ahead, the pancake clowns marched toward her.

Keeping an eye on the clowns, she stepped backward and bumped against a table. A spice merchant stood there, displaying his wares. Small baskets and wooden bowls covered the table, and each one overflowed with a brightly colored powder. Open bags of seeds and spices were laid out around the table. A dozen powerful smells swirled her way.

As the clowns drew close, one suddenly stopped. He sniffed, taking in the spice smells. He started coughing and pounding his chest with his fist. He didn't come any closer. The other clown kept walking toward Samantha. He reached out to grab the umbrella.

"Give me that," he snarled. "Then I won't have to waste any more time in Dynamite, or stupid Zzyzx, where there's nothing except for—"

The clown's nose began to twitch, and he stopped talking. He looked past Samantha at the spices and then back to the umbrella. She could see his eyes getting red and tears beginning to form.

The clown took a step backward.

"Achoo!" he sneezed, and bent forward with his face in his hands.

Samantha bolted. She sprang past the sneezing clown, around the coughing clown, and back to the center of the market.

She still didn't see any sign of Nipper. Vendors, workers, and shoppers swirled around her. Samantha started to get more worried than usual about losing her brother. With so many people, it would be nearly impossible to find him. She decided to make it easy for *him* to find her. She raised the umbrella over her head and popped it open, hoping that Nipper would spot her— before those awful clowns found her first.

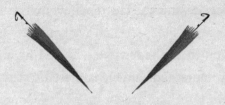

CHAPTER TWENTY-TWO

DUCK SEASON

Nipper walked through the crowded street, inspecting tables and carts. Vendors stood beside buckets of rice and bags filled with dried chili peppers and herbs.

Up ahead, a tall woman sat in a chair, watching the shoppers pass by. Nipper could tell that the woman was more than just tall, she was very tall. Seated, she was at eye level with the people walking past.

She wore baggy blue coveralls with big yellow polka dots and had a red ball on the end of her nose. On her bright red mop of hair, she wore a small gold crown. Her shoes were huge yellow triangles. They looked like big, webbed duck feet.

Nipper was pretty sure that this was not a typical out-fit for someone from Mali. She looked like a circus clown.

Without warning, the strange woman stuck out one of her webbed shoes. A man walking past tripped and tumbled onto the ground. He looked up and his eyes widened. He stood, brushed off red dirt, and walked away quickly.

A moment later, the clown did it again. This time, she tripped an old woman carrying a basket of mangoes. The woman started to pick up her fruit, but when she noticed the clown, she hurried away, leaving several mangoes behind.

Nipper stood watching the bizarre spectacle as another man passed by. He carried a stack of baskets, balanced one on top of the other. Each basket was full of eggs. He was heading right by the duck-foot clown.

"Watch out!" Nipper shouted to the man. "She's gonna trip you!"

The man peeked cautiously around his egg baskets. He spotted the clown, turned, and walked the other way.

The tall clown rose from her chair. She was huge— almost seven feet tall! She turned very slowly and gave Nipper an evil look. He watched as she reached into a pocket of her coveralls and pulled out a slingshot. She raised it, pulled back, and let go.

Smack!

Something hard and yellow hit Nipper in the face.

"Yow!" he cried.

Nipper bent down and picked up the projectile. It was a rubber duck.

He threw the object on the ground. Angrily, he marched toward the giant woman. Fists clenched, he was ready for war.

Halfway there, he stopped.

Two men had appeared, standing beside her. They were looking up at her, waving spatulas, and shouting over each other. Nipper noticed that they were dressed as clowns, too. Their shoes were big and ridiculously wide, and they had red plastic balls on their noses.

All three turned toward Nipper at the same time. One clown pointed a spatula at him. They all looked really angry.

Nipper didn't want to find out why. He started walking, weaving between pedestrians and carts, and turned onto a new street. It was just as crowded. He picked up his pace and turned another corner. He was sure he'd lost the clowns, but he kept going. He might run into them again, or there might be other weirdos in the market. He sped down aisles packed with people and didn't slow down until . . . he smelled something delicious.

Nipper stopped and sniffed the air. He decided then it was safe to explore again. Or at least safe enough— because he hadn't eaten for hours.

"Clowns can hurt you, but hunger can kill," he said out loud, and started looking around the market.

A man stood in front of a tent, stirring onions and some kind of marinated chicken in a large pan above a burner. Bags of spices cluttered the table.

Nipper approached, smiling.

"Hi there," he said in his best I'm-so-charming voice. "Do you speak English?"

The man looked up from his cooking and smiled.

"*Yassa*," he said.

"Good," said Nipper, rubbing his hands together. "What's in the pan, man?"

"*Yassa*," he said again.

A woman with a black headscarf rushed out of the tent. She looked at Nipper and shook her head while she pointed at the man stirring the food.

"Husband," she said to Nipper. "No English."

She pointed at the chicken and onions.

"Food is *yassa*," she explained.

Nipper looked down at the sizzling food. Then he heard the faint sound of ducks quacking. He looked around but didn't see any clowns. Nervously, he pointed to the woman's tent.

"Can I come in?" he asked.

The woman wrinkled her brow, confused. She picked up a bag of greenish-brown powder and handed it to him.

"Cumin," she said.

Nipper looked at the bag, then back at the woman.

"No," said Nipper, talking faster. "I need to hide from

some goons. They look like clowns, but they're not silly."

"Not silly?" asked the woman. She studied the spices on the table.

The quacking sound grew louder.

"Here," said the woman, pressing a plastic bag into Nipper's other hand. This one was filled with bright red powder.

"Hot chili," she said, smiling.

"Hold on," said Nipper. "I meant that I want you to—"

A big shadow drifted over Nipper. He turned.

The giant duck-foot clown faced him. Two clowns holding spatulas stood at her sides.

He looked over his shoulder. The man and woman slipped inside their tent. They looked from him to the clowns and quickly closed the flap.

Nipper felt something tap his chest. He turned back to see a clown jabbing him with a spatula.

"Stick 'em up, boy," said the clown.

Terrified, Nipper held out his hands, filled with bags of colorful powder.

"I mean way up," the clown said, and poked Nipper's chest again.

"Okay, okay," said Nipper, lifting both hands high above his head.

"Where's the girl with the umbrella?" the clown asked, and twisted his spatula into Nipper's breast-bone, hard.

Nipper flinched and, shutting his mouth and eyes, let go of the open plastic bags he'd been given by the woman who was now back in her tent. They dropped to the ground and exploded at his feet. A cloud of brown and red dust enveloped them.

The clown who'd jabbed him with the spatula gasped. His eyes turned redder than his fake nose. He took a step back and began to cough violently.

"What did you . . . ? I can't . . . ," he wheezed, and crumpled to the ground.

The spices swirled around the other clowns and they began to sneeze, too.

"Achoo!" one of them shouted, sneezing so violently his red nose flew off. He dropped to his hands and knees immediately and began searching for it.

A dozen shoppers stopped shopping and gathered around, watching the weird people in strange outfits coughing, crawling, and shouting and screaming in English.

Nipper pushed his way through the crowd and ran. He sprinted through the market. In the distance, he saw the pink stucco arch where he and Samantha had first entered the market. Halfway there, a bright red umbrella hovered above the crowd.

Behind him, the sound of quacking ducks started up again.

"I see you, Sam!" he shouted. "Get ready to run!"

CHAPTER TWENTY-THREE

FLEE CIRCUS

Samantha heard her brother shouting and saw him racing toward her. Behind him, three clowns stomped through the market. She recognized two of them as the men with the rubber pancakes. The third clown was an incredibly tall woman with a tiny gold crown on her head. Samantha heard ducks quacking.

"Run, Sam!" Nipper called. "This isn't a joke!"

She snapped her umbrella shut and waited for him to reach her.

"Stay with me this time," she said, and grabbed his arm as he bolted past.

With the umbrella in one hand, she followed him around the corner and onto another crowded street. As they threaded between shoppers and stalls, babies and bicycles, Samantha sniffed the air and looked at her brother. He was smeared with red, brown, and green powder. He smelled like one of the rice dishes in the market.

"What happened to you?" she asked.

"Clown seasoning," he answered.

She had no time to ask what that meant as they zigzagged down the dirt road. When she spotted a gap between two mud-brick buildings, she stepped sideways and yanked her brother behind her into the space.

They both leaned back against the wall, panting. The sound of quacking rose as the tall clown in the duck shoes marched past, followed by the pancake clowns, still huffing and wheezing. The sound of giant shoes slapping began to fade.

"Sca-ree," said Nipper.

"Strange, too," added Samantha, stepping away from the wall.

She checked for the glasses in her purse and adjusted her umbrella.

"When the coast is clear, let's get back to that hydrant."

She peeked around the corner after the clowns. Far down the street, she saw the gold crown bobbing above the crowd.

"Come on," she said, stepping back into the crowded market and heading in the opposite direction.

They retraced their path. Every few steps, Samantha looked back to make sure that Nipper was still following—and that clowns weren't.

"Sca-ree," he said again.

When they reached the parking lot near the hydrant, Samantha stopped. She pointed to a stone bench, ran over, and crouched behind it, motioning for Nipper to follow.

"What's going on now?" Nipper whispered as he slid next to her.

She peeked around the corner of the bench and pointed into the park.

A new clown was sitting on top of their fire hydrant. He wore a bushy rainbow wig and the same red nose as the clowns from the market. A strange device, the size of a suitcase, rested on the ground beside him. It looked like a metal vacuum cleaner.

"How many clowns are there in this town?" Nipper asked.

"I have no idea," said Samantha. "This is really odd."

She started to count all the clowns they had seen; then she stopped and squinted at the one in the park.

"What's he juggling?" she asked.

As he perched on the hydrant, the clown tossed small orange objects into the air.

Nipper was an expert on all types of candy. He could tell a chocolate-covered raisin from a black jellybean at one hundred yards. He could name at least 783 varieties of candy without breaking a sweat. This included a dozen types of Halloween candy. The clown could only be juggling one thing.

"Marshmallow circus peanuts," he said confidently. "The saddest candy of all."

Samantha looked at her brother. Streaks of brown powder covered his face. A bright red spot, about the size of a quarter, poked through the powder on his cheek. She reached a thumb out to rub the spot.

"Don't touch," he said, pulling back from her. "The big lady with the duck feet did it to me."

Samantha stared at his injury. Then she looked over to the juggling clown and his strange machine.

She opened the umbrella, turned it over, and placed it gently on the grass.

"It's time to find another way out of here," she said.

"Hand lens, ready for action!" said Nipper loudly.

"Shhh," said Samantha. "That weirdo will hear you."

She peeked over the top of the bench. The peanut clown had stopped juggling. He sat up straight, looking around.

"Hand lens," Nipper repeated, whispering this time.

Samantha watched the clown. He looked left and right a few more times. Then he shook his head and went back to juggling. Samantha crouched down again.

Nipper passed her the magnifying glass and leaned

in to watch as she examined the Super-Secret Plans. She stared at the picture of a hydrant near Seattle and began to trace the four lines from it.

One line extended across the umbrella to what looked like mountain peaks. That definitely was not this place in Mali. Another line ended at a cluster of dots that looked like islands. Nope.

The next line ended at a picture of a building. It looked like some of the mud-brick buildings around them. Samantha took an even closer look.

The tiny image could definitely have been one of the buildings they'd passed in the market. An oval sat next to it, connected by a wavy line to the cluster of islands.

Samantha looked up, past the clown, and out toward the river.

"I have a theory," she told her brother. "If we can find the right building, there's a way to travel . . . here."

She moved her finger from the oval to the islands.

"Then, from this place," she continued, "we can catch a slidewalk home."

Nipper nodded in agreement. Then they both crouched low and snuck around the edge of the park, making sure the peanut clown couldn't see them. When they reached the other side, they stood up and ran.

Samantha looked back several times and didn't see anyone following them. After a few blocks, she gestured to her brother and they slowed to a walk. They walked on paved streets in this part of town and, unlike the market, it wasn't bustling with people. Occasionally, they saw a man or a woman wearing colorful fabrics—but they weren't clowns. No one paid much attention to Samantha or Nipper.

"Keep your eyes out for a little oval," she said. "Or maybe a big one."

As she walked, Samantha examined each of the buildings lining the street. Most seemed like simple one- or two-story structures, like the ones in the market. A few blocks ahead, however, a giant mud-colored rectangle rose high above them.

Three triangular towers, connected by shorter walls, made up the face of the structure. The walls took up the entire city block and had small square windows running along the top. Dark wooden posts jutted outward from the towers and the corners of the building. Samantha thought it looked like a combination sandcastle and giant wooden porcupine.

In the months since Uncle Paul had gone missing, she and her brother had seen many huge towers, cathedrals, and skyscrapers made of glass, stone, and steel. This giant building looked like it was made out of mud. It also looked a lot like the illustration on the umbrella.

Samantha squinted at the towers, trying to decide if they matched the ones on the umbrella. She started to reach for it on her shoulder when Nipper tugged the back of her shirt.

"What now?" she asked, stopping and turning toward him. "We've almost reached that building. I don't see a big oval, but it might be inside somewhere."

"Is that oval big enough for you?" Nipper replied. He pointed to their left.

A large sign with the word *STADE* rose over a set of open metal gates. Beyond it, bleachers surrounded a huge, green, oval soccer field. Samantha had been so focused on the building ahead that she had missed it entirely.

"Good eye," she said. "It's a stadium."

They passed through the gates and headed down a cement path to the edge of the field. She took out the purple sunglasses and stared all around.

Nothing.

She walked with Nipper toward the center of the field. They marched up and down, testing for hidden trap doors or secret panels. Twice she stopped and checked her umbrella for more clues.

Nothing.

Nipper got down and tugged at the grass.

"What are you doing?" she asked.

"I'm checking to see if it's fake," he answered. "Like the turf around the fire hydrant."

Nipper held out a fistful of grass. It was real. He shrugged and let it fall.

"Maybe there's a clue in the seats," she said.

Samantha took off the glasses, put them away, and pointed toward a section of bleachers.

Crack!

Something flew past her face. She felt it brush an eyelash as it barely missed her. She turned quickly.

The pancake clowns stood in the center of the field. Between them, the peanut clown from the park crouched over his strange machine.

Crack! Crack!

"It's a marshmallow-circus-peanut gun!" Nipper shouted.

"Let's head over there," Samantha said, pointing to the seats.

As they ran, an orange peanut whizzed past Samantha's head, missing her ear by an inch. She reached the metal staircase first. She pointed up the steps and waved for Nipper to follow. Then she stopped. Someone had appeared at the top of the stairs. Another clown!

This one wore a bright blue dress and an apron. Four yellow pom-poms decorated the front of her dress. Two more pom-poms flopped on the tips of her giant shoes. She had a huge head of frizzy blue hair and the same red plastic nose as the other clowns. She grinned and held up a silver pan dripping with foamy gray goo. Samantha could see green shapes wriggling on top of the disgusting mess.

"Who wants pie?" the clown croaked.

Samantha and Nipper looked at each other.

"Yuck," he said quickly.

"Move," said Samantha, pointing left to the end of the bleachers.

They turned and bolted along the row of metal seats. *Crack! Crack! Crack! Crack!*

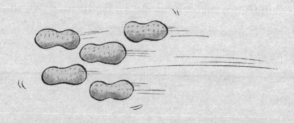

As they ran, orange circus peanuts zinged past, bouncing everywhere. One ricocheted off a railing and smacked Samantha on her right shoulder. It stung. She stopped and looked back. The pie clown bounded down the stadium stairs toward them. Her oversized shoes clanged on the metal steps and the pom-poms bobbed wildly with each stride.

"There's always room for *pie-eee*," the clown sang, raising her foul pan high above her head.

Samantha turned and raced to catch up with Nipper. As she ran along the seats, she saw the pancake clowns on her left, marching in from the field.

Quack-quack!

She and Nipper both stopped. Ahead, the duck-foot clown stood at the end of the row. She reached into her pockets.

"We're surrounded by idiots!" Nipper yelled.

A sudden roar reverberated through the stadium. Everyone froze—kids and clowns.

A bright red motorcycle raced across the field. It had a sidecar—a round pod with a seat and one wheel—attached to the right side. The bike sped past the pancake clowns and skidded to a stop along the bleachers beside Samantha and Nipper.

The driver pulled off his helmet and flashed a big smile.

"Come with me, guys," he said.

Samantha stared. She guessed the driver was four-teen years old. Maybe fifteen. He had curly hair, cut very short, and was wearing a white sleeveless T-shirt and blue jeans. Still smiling, he gestured for her and Nipper to come forward.

"Hurry," he said.

Samantha watched Nipper hop off the metal bench and try to climb on the back of the motorcycle, but the boy sniffed and made a face. He held up one hand and covered his nose with the other. Then he reached into the sidecar, picked up a helmet, and held it out while gesturing for Nipper to get inside.

Swack! Swack!

Two pancakes sailed over their heads and slapped against stadium seats. Nipper grabbed the helmet and hopped into the sidecar. The boy looked back at Samantha and nodded, then gestured toward a helmet hooked to the seat behind him. She picked up the helmet and put it on.

Samantha had never ridden on a motorcycle before. She carefully climbed onto the seat, keeping both hands at her sides.

"Hang on," the boy said.

He revved the engine and kicked it into gear. The bike lurched forward. Reflexively, Samantha grabbed onto him.

"Order up!" screeched the pie clown, and hurled her pan at them.

"Watch out!" shouted Samantha.

The boy ducked as the gooey gray pie sailed over his head. He sat back up, leaned forward, and steered the bike straight at the clowns in the center of the field.

Samantha took a deep breath and held on tight.

The pancake clowns tossed their spatulas in the air, screamed, and dove out of the way. The sidecar smacked into the peanut clown, knocking him down. Samantha heard a loud crunch and looked over at Nipper.

"Wahoo! We crushed the circus-peanut gun," he called, his voice muffled by the helmet.

"Three clowns down," said the boy.

Samantha tried to hold on a little less tightly as they zoomed out of the stadium.

CHAPTER TWENTY-FOUR

SAY, DO YOU?

The boy steered left and they sped to the end of the block. He made another left and put three more blocks between them and the stadium before he rolled to a stop and cut the engine.

Samantha let go and dropped her hands awkwardly to her sides.

"Who are you?" she asked.

He took off his helmet and flashed another big smile.

"My name's Seydou," he said.

"As in 'Say, do you hate clowns as much as I do?'" asked Nipper, rubbing the bruise on his cheek.

"No, some clowns are funny," Seydou said. "But those guys were bad news."

Samantha hopped off the back of the motorcycle.

"I'm Samantha Spinner, and this is my brother, Nipper," she said. "Thanks for the lift."

She hung her helmet on the hook at the back of the motorcycle and brushed some dirt off her pants.

"Of course, we were about to get the situation under control," she added.

Seydou raised his eyebrows.

"What my sister means to say," Nipper called from his seat, "is thanks for saving our butts!"

"That's all right," said Seydou. "The clowns were following you. I figured it was my chance to knock a few of them down."

He leaned over and wiped a red-and-white smudge of clown makeup from the front of the sidecar.

"What are you guys doing here anyway?" he asked.

"We're looking for our uncle—I mean, oval," said Nipper. "There's an oval, and it's a secret, and—"

"What my *brother* means to say," Samantha interrupted, "is that we're trying to get home and— Hey. How come you speak English so well?"

"I've been to the U.S. a bunch of times," Seydou answered. "I was in Spokane, Washington, last year."

He stepped off his motorcycle and pulled a flattened baseball cap from his back pocket. He unfolded it, put it on his head, and smiled. Samantha saw the words *Pacific Pandemonium* stitched across the front.

"Wait," said Samantha. "You've been to Washington State recently? Why were you—"

"Holy cowabunga!" Nipper interrupted. "I rode the roller coaster at Pacific Pandemonium amusement park thirteen times, until I barfed."

Seydou laughed and rubbed his chin. "Now, tell me about this oval you're looking for."

"I'm pretty sure it's near that big structure," Samantha answered. "Is that the tallest building in the city?"

She pointed to the structure in the distance with her umbrella. She was about to pop it open but changed her mind. Instead, she found a patch of dirt next to the street and began to sketch the building, using the umbrella's metal tip.

Seydou looked at her sketch and shook his head.

"Right country, wrong building," he said.

He took off his baseball cap and scratched his head. Then he crouched beside Samantha's drawing and waved for her to look closely.

"That big structure is a mosque, where many people here go to worship. Some of the mosques in West Africa are more than five hundred years old," he said. "Look at these towers."

He pointed to Samantha's sketch in the dirt.

"Rectangles, right?" he asked.

Samantha nodded.

He stood up and stretched an arm toward the large building in the distance.

"What shape towers do you see?" he asked.

"Triangles," Nipper chimed in. "I was just telling Samantha that she should try to take a closer look at things."

"Fine," said Samantha. "What building *are* we looking for?"

"The Great Mosque of Djenné," Seydou answered.

"Djenné? Where's that?"

"Don't worry," said Seydou, smiling. "I'm happy to drive you there."

He popped a snap on each side of his baseball cap. He gripped the visor and pulled it out two feet, unrolling it like a window shade.

Samantha gasped slightly. The visor held a map.

"Cool hat-map," said Nipper.

Seydou held it out for them to see.

"Here's the Niger River, and this is the main highway," Seydou said as he moved a finger along the fabric. "It takes about two hours to get from Mopti, here, to Djenné, there."

Samantha watched as he tugged on the visor and the map snapped back into his cap.

"Ready to go?" Seydou asked.

"Yes, please," said Samantha, putting on her helmet and climbing back onto the motorcycle.

Seydou stood looking at her.

"And . . . thank you," she added.

"That's *i ni che* in Bambara," he said, and winked.

Then he climbed onto the bike.

CHAPTER TWENTY-FIVE

ROAD WORRIERS

The main highway was a two-lane dirt road.

As Seydou drove them south to Djenné, Samantha watched the country of Mali roll by.

They passed an airport and a few modern office buildings. Occasionally, they passed neighborhoods that reminded Samantha of Spokane, Washington. Most of the time, however, it was like looking through a window to another century.

They drove by clusters of mud-brick buildings. Farmers rode donkey carts overflowing with piles of hay. At one point, they swerved to avoid a goat. Men and women walked along the road balancing baskets and boxes on their heads. A barefoot man urged a herd of cattle onward with a stick. Fishing villages hugged bends in rivers, and dusty red fields stretched far into the distance.

"Major mosque at twelve o'clock!" Nipper called.

From his seat in the motorcycle's sidecar, he pointed at a huge tan structure rising ahead.

"Now, *that* is the Great Mosque of Djenné," Seydou told Samantha.

The mosque resembled the one in Mopti but was much bigger. Three rectangular towers rose above a main entrance. High walls connected many other towers and entrances. A curved wall surrounded the building, separating it from a busy market outside. Wooden posts stuck out from all sides. Just like the building in Mopti, it reminded Samantha of a porcupine.

"The towers are over fifty feet high," Seydou told them as they approached. "It's the tallest building in the city, and the tallest mud-brick building in the world."

As they drove closer, he pointed up.

"Look carefully," he said. "Each tower has a real ostrich egg on top."

Samantha squinted at the tiny white dots on the tips of the towers.

"Wonderful," she said. And it was. The shapes of the towers and along the top of the mosque walls made her think of sandcastles.

"I never thought you could make something so beautiful out of mud," she added.

"Well, it's kind of in the middle of nowhere," said Nipper.

"No place is in the middle of nowhere," said Seydou.

Samantha nodded in agreement. Then she stopped and stared at Seydou.

"Wait," she said. "Did you just make that up, or did you hear somebody else say—"

Honk! Honk! Honk!

Behind them, a very loud horn blared. It sounded like that of a huge truck. Samantha turned to see a tiny car speeding toward them. The horn kept honking as the car gained on them. There were balloons and angry clown faces pressed against the windows inside the car. A huge shoe, caught in the passenger-side door, flapped in the wind.

Samantha had no idea how many clowns were inside the little car. She guessed at least five. They screamed and pointed at her and Nipper, but she couldn't hear their words over the roar of the motorcycle engine and the honking horn. Seydou looked at the car, then at her. She looked at him.

"Clown car," they both said at the same time.

Seydou nodded, faced forward, and revved the engine. Samantha held on tight.

The motorcycle blasted ahead, leaving the tiny car behind. They sped along the highway, weaving past cars, buses, and goats, and pulled off, coasting into a crowded neighborhood. They continued on, coming to a market swarmed with merchants and shoppers. It was as big as the one in Mopti. Seydou steered the bike around food carts and pedestrians. They skidded into a space between two parked buses and came to a stop.

"Hop off here," said Seydou. "I'll lure those goons out of town."

Samantha nodded and climbed off the bike. She put the helmet back on its hook and smiled at him.

"Thanks for all your help," she said. "I really mean it."

"That goes double for me," said Nipper.

He hopped out of the sidecar, gave Seydou a thumbs-up, and joined his sister.

"I hope you find your uncle—I mean, oval," Seydou said.

Then he revved the engine and took off around a corner.

Seconds later, Samantha heard the tiny car's loud horn again. Then the sound of shouting clowns and a rumbling motorcycle faded into the distance.

CHAPTER TWENTY-SIX

BOTTLE ROCKET

Samantha and her brother stood between two buses. She opened her umbrella. Then she turned it over and lowered it gently to the ground. Nipper passed her the magnifying glass, and she knelt down to search.

"The line next to the oval looks like waves," she said, squinting through the lens. "I'm going to guess that means it has something to do with water."

She thought about the water slide in Florence, Italy. That started at a big fountain. Little by little, she was figuring out how to decipher the Plans.

She closed the umbrella and used it to help her stand up. She stepped out from between the buses and looked around.

"Let's go . . . there," she said, and pointed to a narrow side street.

A block away, it sloped down and ended at a river.

Walking side by side, they headed toward the water. As the river grew closer, she could tell that Nipper was on the lookout for clowns.

A woman carrying an empty woven basket in each hand passed them, heading in the opposite direction. A boy—who looked about Nipper's age—walked beside her, dragging a stick along the dirt road.

The woman stopped and barked at the boy. Samantha couldn't tell what language she spoke, but she clearly told him to stop fidgeting and poking things with sticks. "Some things are truly universal," said Samantha.

"Did you say something, Sam?"

She shook her head and pointed down the road. The smooth dirt street ended, becoming a rocky slope. She hopped down a few feet and landed on the sandy shore of the river. Nipper skidded behind her.

"Hold on," she said, and took in the scene.

A man was using a long pole to push his boat through shallow brown water. A dog and two goats rode in the boat with him. He smiled and waved as he passed. To their left, a dozen yards away, a paved street extended all the way to the water's edge. Cars and pedestrians boarded a bright blue river barge. To their right, a sandy strip separated the water from the slope up to the town.

Samantha took the sunglasses from her purse, put them on, and looked around. The world grew purple, but nothing else changed. She squinted at the man in the boat, now coasting away. He smiled and waved again. One of the goats bleated.

"Nothing there," she said.

"Great, Sam," Nipper replied.

"Didn't you hear me?" she asked, putting the glasses back in her purse. "There's nothing. I'm not even sure we're supposed to be in Mali. *You* didn't pay attention when you picked up the letter cards, so we—"

Nipper tapped her on the shoulder.

"One more time," he said, pointing to the embankment a few yards to their right. "*Grate,* Sam."

A metal grate was set into a steep section of the embankment. It was shaped like an oval.

"Great," said Samantha.

"I told you," said Nipper.

She walked up to the grate. A screen of crisscrossed metal bars was about her height. She pulled on one bar and the grate swung open like an oval screen door.

"That was easy," she said to Nipper.

"Not if you count getting attacked by clowns and chased through a crowded market," he replied. "Did I mention that I got hit in the face with a rubber duck?"

Samantha nodded and examined the grate more closely.

"Oh, yeah," Nipper continued. "There was a two-hour motorcycle ride. Tiny car, angry clowns. You know. That kind of *easy*."

She ignored him and leaned forward to peek inside the oval doorway. A narrow staircase curved down to the left.

"Come on," she said, and held the grate open for her brother to climb through the entrance.

Then she followed him. She heard the grate clang shut behind her as she went down the steps.

Light filtered in through the grate, so the way was easy to see as she marched downward. As she descended, she realized that the staircase hugged a curved wall of thick brown glass. She paused and examined the wall. No. It was clear glass, filled with brown water, probably from the river outside.

"Nipper," she called. "We're walking around the outside of a giant glass water bottle."

He was already around the bend ahead of her and didn't answer.

As she continued down the steps, she could hear the huge tank creaking. She stopped and listened. The whole big thing seemed to be under tremendous pressure. This didn't feel especially safe. She walked faster down the steps.

The longer she walked, the farther she got from the grate above, and the darker it became, making it more and more difficult to see. She pressed forward and discovered only more curve. In near-total darkness, she stepped down onto a flat surface. A light came on.

Nipper stood beside a panel of light switches. He was grinning from ear to ear.

Samantha gazed up. They had walked down and around a glass tank of brown river water. The tank, about four stories high, narrowed at the bottom and connected to a pipe that ran past them into a chamber beyond. She had been right. They were standing at the base of a giant *upside-down* bottle.

The huge glass tank creaked once more. Samantha guessed it held a million gallons of water. She looked around nervously—and saw Nipper.

He stood there, watching her with a half-crazy smile. Samantha could tell he was waiting for her to ask him something.

"Okay. I'll bite," she said. "What did you find?"

"Nothing much, Sam," he answered calmly. "Just . . . *this!*"

He flipped another light switch with one hand while waving dramatically with the other.

He stood beside a shiny silver vehicle. It looked like a jet fighter without wings—or maybe a rocket lying on its side. A hole on top revealed an open cockpit. Inside, two seats faced forward. There was no canopy or cover. A thick metal pipe connected the back of the vehicle to the bottom of the giant bottle.

With the lights on in the chamber, Samantha could see that the strange rocket pointed at the entrance to a tunnel. A sign dangled over the entrance.

JAVA

Nipper scampered into the cockpit.

"This is going to be great," he said.

Samantha definitely didn't like the sound of that.

A little over a year ago, their dad had given Nipper a Hydro Howitzer for his birthday. It turned out to be one of George Washington Spinner's worst decisions ever. He warned Nipper not to turn the power up past level five. Nipper insisted that because he was seven years old, he should be able to fire the water gun at level seven. Then, when no one was looking, he turned it all the way up to ten. When he fired it, the water blasted a hole in their back fence. Kids ran for their lives. The cake disintegrated. The birthday party ended early that day. And half of their lawn furniture was gone.

"Hurry up!" Nipper shouted.

He was already strapped into the left seat, adjusting a headrest behind him.

Samantha climbed over the side of the rocket and settled into the cockpit on the right. The spongy padded chair fit snugly around her body. She checked for her purse, wedged the umbrella between the two seats, and tugged to make sure that it was secure. Then she reached for the safety belt. It snapped together across her chest, holding her tight under a big orange X.

"Pilot to copilot," said Nipper.

Nipper stared at a glowing red button on the dashboard. It had one word: *Push.* He couldn't take his eyes off it. His finger moved toward it.

"Wait a second," said Samantha.

She glanced around the cockpit, looking for anything that said *Roof* or *Close hatch.* She peeked out over the top.

The connection between the bottom of the giant bottle and the metal pipe was vibrating, and a fine stream of mist hissed from the joint. There was a lot of water pressure between the bottle and the rocket. She scanned the chamber quickly.

Along the wall, behind where Nipper had stood, Samantha noticed a row of hooks with orange jumpsuits, helmets, and boots. A sign above them said:

SURVIVAL SUITS
HIGHLY RECOMMENDED

"Ten. Nine. Eight," said Nipper in a robotic voice.

"Wait," said Samantha.

She unsnapped her X restraint and stood up. With both hands, she started to pull herself out of the cockpit.

"Three-two-one . . . blast-off!" Nipper shouted quickly, and pressed the button.

Boom!

In Samantha's history class, they'd learned about atomic bombs the United States tested over islands in Micronesia in the 1950s. Those tests probably sounded half as loud as this did.

Wham!

A shock wave knocked Samantha backward into the cockpit. She landed on her back as the rocket shot forward. She was pinned to the padded seat, with her feet where her head should have been! As she looked up through the cockpit opening, the top of the tunnel became a blur.

The rocket blasted into the mouth of the tunnel and everything went black. Water gushed into the cabin.

"Hydropower is so awesome, Sam," Nipper called.

Samantha tried to move her arms, but the force of acceleration was too strong. She grasped a strap of her purse and held on tight. The rocket rumbled as they continued to speed up. She shut her eyes tight and gritted her teeth, as wave after wave of swirling spray whipped at her face and hair.

Her left shoe flew off. Her sock was instantly soaked, and water began to pour down her leg.

"Hey, Sam!" Nipper shouted. "Did you notice the sign over the tunnel before we took off? It said 'Java.'"

The rocket roared again. Water soaked Samantha from every direction.

"Maybe that was a clue we're headed to Seattle," Nipper continued. "You know . . . *java* is another name for coffee."

Samantha had already told him they were going to Java, Indonesia. There didn't seem to be much point to repeating it.

The rumble grew louder, drowning out the sound of her brother's voice.

It was probably a good thing, thought Samantha. If she heard him say "great," "cool," or "awesome" one more time, she would have to summon superhuman strength, overcome the force of the acceleration, and strangle him.

The vehicle rattled as they zoomed onward in the dark.

Lying on her back with no way to move, Samantha thought about how she wound up there. She was absolutely sure that going to Mali was a mistake. There was no sign of Uncle Paul, and nothing showed up through the purple glasses. Either her brother had missed some cards or A, L, I, and M spelled something different.

The rocket's acceleration pinned her hands to her sides.

Now they shot through a tunnel on their way to Java. Samantha knew that it was an island in Indonesia with a slidewalk to Seattle. She'd go home and start over.

Of course, there were those awful clowns. What were they doing? What was all that coughing and sneezing about? And why did they mention *Dynamite* and *Zzyzx*?

"Holy cowabunga!" Nipper shouted. The rumbling of the rocket had begun to fade. "This is great, cool, and really awesome!"

The rocket slowed down.

Now that she could move freely again, it took all of Samantha's self-control not to grab her little brother by the neck.

The Great Mosque of Djenné

The Great Mosque of Djenné, in Mali, is the world's largest mud-brick building.

It was originally constructed in the thirteenth or four-teenth century and rebuilt as recently as 1907. It is one of the most famous landmarks in Africa.

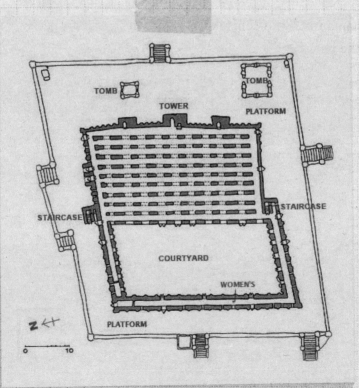

It is considered by many to be the finest example of adobe architecture. Because it is constructed entirely of local mud, clay, and straw dried in the sun, many modern builders praise it as a model of sustainable design.

The mosque's three largest towers have spires topped with ostrich eggs. These eggs are symbols of good fortune. The distinctive wooden poles projecting from the building are used for decoration and also as scaffolding for repairs.

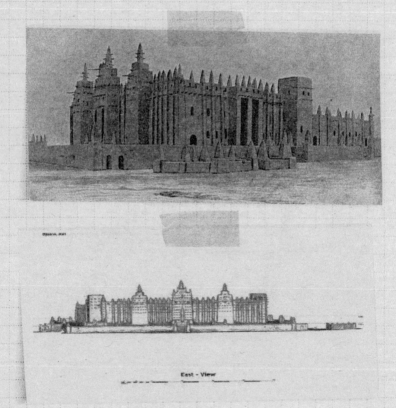

Djenné, Mali

East - View

* * *

A few blocks from the Great Mosque is an underground, high-power water rocket that can transport one or two passengers to Java, Indonesia, in less than an hour.

Search the embankment between the south side of Djenné and the Bani River for an oval grate. It opens freely, leading to a secret staircase. The stairs wrap around a huge tank, filled with water from the nearby river.

Be sure to take advantage of the survival suits stationed conveniently beside the rocket. Otherwise, the ride to Indonesia will be wet and extremely uncomfortable.

CHAPTER TWENTY-SEVEN

JAGALAH KEBERSIHAN

"Watch out for the SUN!" Nipper shouted.

Light poured in as the rocket screeched to a stop.

Looking up through the cockpit opening, Samantha saw a metal grate above them. Sunlight shined through. She shielded her eyes from the glare and watched the bottoms of shoes going by overhead. Whatever was up there, it was crowded.

Groaning, she lowered her legs, rolled over, and sat upright in the seat. She looked straight ahead. She was wet and extremely uncomfortable. Water dripped down her face as she gathered her thoughts. She heard squishing sounds as Nipper climbed up and out of the rocket.

Samantha looked over at the space between the two padded seats. Her heart started pounding. The umbrella was gone!

She searched all around the cockpit, under both seats, and in all the spaces where an umbrella might fall. She didn't see it. She scurried over her side of the rocket. She checked the ground, and in all the gaps where the metal floor met the sides of the silver vehicle.

It wasn't anywhere.

She staggered around the front of the rocket, her left sock squishing on the floor.

Nipper stood smiling. Patches of brown paste clung to his face and neck. He held the umbrella out for her.

"Here you go, Sis."

Samantha adjusted her purse on her shoulder and snatched the umbrella. She bent down. With her free hand, she removed her remaining shoe. As she stood back up, she whacked Nipper on the side of the head with it.

"Hey!" he shouted, rubbing his temple. "What was that for?"

Spice globs sprinkled the floor as he rubbed.

"*That* was to get your attention," she growled.

Samantha put the shoe back on her right foot. Then she popped open the umbrella. When Nipper held out the magnifier, she snatched that, too. The handle was sticky.

"Let's get back to work," she said impatiently.

She examined the drawing of Indonesia on the Super-Secret Plans. She saw a circle inside a circle inside a circle. She looked closer and saw that each circle was made up of tiny dots. One dot in the center circle wasn't filled in like all the rest. From there, a line stretched across the umbrella, all the way back to Seattle.

She closed the umbrella. When she started to hand the magnifier to Nipper, he flinched.

"Don't worry," she said. "I'm not going to hit you. We need it to get home."

"So, where are we?" he asked.

"Somewhere in Java, Indonesia," she answered.

She tried to run her fingers through her hair to flatten it, but it was so twisted and knotted that she gave up. The splashing, spraying, upside-down rocket ride had left her with crazy hair. And only one shoe. Samantha pointed at narrow steps along the wall.

"Let's go find something with circles and dots," she said. "It's our slidewalk home."

Nipper hurried up the stone staircase in front of Samantha. At the top, he pushed aside a metal grate and climbed out onto the street. As he disappeared into the sunlight, Samantha caught a whiff of his cumin-and-chili coating. She thought of the strange clowns again, and how they'd backed away when she stood near the table of spices.

She adjusted her umbrella, followed Nipper up the stairs, and climbed out. She used her left foot—the one with a shoe—to shove the grate back into place.

Immediately, Samantha was hit by a warm, humid breeze. It was much hotter here than in the clammy rocket tunnel. She looked around and realized she stood in a crowded plaza. Two children raced by, playing tag. Backpackers in heavy boots trekked in the other direction. A vendor pushed a cart with sizzling sticks of meat. A dozen people with cameras and phones snapped pictures of themselves, one another, and their surroundings.

A stone mountain towered overhead. At first, she thought it might be a pyramid. Then she noticed that it was covered with sculptures. She saw lions, elephants, monkeys, birds, and trees. There were human figures, too: men and women, kids and babies, warriors, workers, dancers, and kings. Samantha guessed that the ones shown floating in clouds represented gods. Every few feet, stone figures sat nestled in arches along the side of the monument. Columns and intricate carvings covered every surface.

The structure had even more images on it than the Super-Secret Plans.

Samantha shielded her eyes and gazed up. She counted nine levels. Each one swarmed with tourists. Way up at the top level, she saw a huge pointed dome.

More people milled about.

Teenagers in matching shirts took pictures of one another in front of carvings. Parents grabbed at toddlers standing too close to ledges. Couples in shorts and hiking boots sat on steps, thumbing through guidebooks. She scanned the crowd. There was no sign of an annoying spice-covered boy with a bruised face.

"Over here, Sam!"

She turned again. Nipper stepped out from around a corner, smiling and waving.

"I found a sign," he told her. "We're in a place called Jagalah Kebersihan."

"Not you're not," said a bearded man with a backpack. "*Jagalah kebersihan* means 'Keep clean.'"

He sniffed Nipper and frowned.

"Or at least 'Don't litter,'" he added.

Based on his accent, Samantha thought the man might be a tourist from Sweden or some other Scandinavian country.

The man adjusted his bulky backpack and turned to face the wide stone steps leading to the top.

"I don't know how anyone could get here without knowing this is Borobudur Temple," he muttered, and walked away.

Samantha looked at her brother. He smiled and shrugged. He was about to say something else, but she held up a hand to stop him.

"*Gedung tertinggi*," she said, and pointed to the temple. "That's 'the tallest building' . . . in Indonesian. It's definitely the tallest building around here."

Samantha and Nipper joined the throng of tourists marching up a central staircase. They climbed past a second level, then a third.

As they continued up the temple stairs, Samantha noticed people staring at them. It wasn't hard to figure out why. When they'd gone to Paris, Florence, and Edfu, they'd blended in with the other tourists. And in any case, everyone was busy looking at the Eiffel Tower or the other attractions, so no one really looked at them. At this moment, blending in was not possible. A boy smeared with spicy brown sludge, and a girl with crazy hair and one shoe, did not blend in.

When they reached the sixth level, Samantha stopped and looked around. The view could not have been more different from the cities in Mali. In every direction, the world was lush and green. Crystal blue lakes dotted the landscape. Tropical trees covered rolling hills. Some looked familiar. Samantha recognized palm trees. Others seemed more like giant flowers than trees. Over the tops of the statues and domes, she could see more forests and, far in the distance, jagged mountains. Steam rose from one of the larger peaks—perhaps an active volcano.

Samantha took out the purple glasses and put them

on. Slowly, she panned left and right, examining walls and steps and sculptures.

Nothing turned yellow. Nothing said *PSST*.

That didn't surprise her. They weren't here because of any clues from Uncle Paul. She was using the Super-Secret Plans on her own now, and she was confident that the circles and dots on the umbrella held the path home.

The top three levels of the temple were circular and ringed by large, bell-shaped domes. Each dome stood at least six feet tall.

"Here we go," said Nipper, peeking through diamond-shaped openings. "I bet we're looking for something inside one of these bells."

"Stupa," said a girl holding a brochure in one hand.

She seemed about the same age as Samantha. She was wearing jeans and a yellow T-shirt. Stenciled on the front of her shirt were the words *Tour du Jour*.

Nipper frowned at her.

"What did you call me?" he asked.

"You said 'bells,'" she replied. "It's not a bell. It is called a *stupa*."

The girl smiled at Nipper. She unfolded her brochure and held it up for him and Samantha to see. It showed a view of the temple from above. Three rings of dots surrounded the central dome. The words on the page were in French, but an arrow pointing to one of the dots said "stupa."

The girl lowered the brochure and turned to Samantha. She looked at her, up and down. She studied the red umbrella, then looked over her shoulder.

"*Excusez-moi,*" she said quickly. "I must go."

Samantha watched the girl skip off to join a crowd of teenagers, all wearing matching yellow T-shirts. The girl pointed back at her and Nipper, and everyone in the group turned quickly to see. When they noticed that Samantha was watching them, they all looked away in different directions. They began to point at sculptures around the temple, pretending to study them. Several pointed with loaves of French bread. It all seemed very odd.

"Did you see that?" she asked Nipper. "Really strange."

"I'm getting used to it," he replied. "We've been to a lot of strange places full of strange people."

Samantha shook her head.

"That's not true at all, Nipper," she said. "Some places just seem strange because we haven't been there yet."

She noticed the Tour du Jour teenagers again. They were still pointing loaves of bread in all directions. Every now and then, one of them snuck a glance at her and Nipper. What did they want? She didn't have time to find out.

"Never mind," said Samantha. "Let's move on . . . and go home."

She pulled up her right sock and used the umbrella to wave her brother onward to the top of the temple.

CHAPTER TWENTY-EIGHT

I'M WITH STUPA

Nipper skipped ahead of Samantha to the top of Boro-budur Temple. She only had one shoe, so she limped up the steps more slowly. She leaned on the umbrella as she climbed. When she reached the ninth level, she saw Nipper, at the far side of the platform, leaning against the base of a stupa. As she walked toward him, she saw he was wearing an I've-got-a-secret smile on his face.

"Check out this dome," he said, pointing a thumb over his shoulder. "Notice anything unusual?"

"Hmm . . . let's see," she said, looking to the top of the stupa and back down to him. "There's a boy soaked with smelly brown sludge leaning on it."

"Ha ha, Sam," Nipper replied. "But really, take a look up close."

She studied the side of the dome and noticed it was dark gray, darker than any other stupa on the temple. It was also a little shiny. It didn't look like stone.

"Good eye . . . for once," said Samantha.

"Just wait a minute," said Nipper. "Here's the fun part."

Nipper punched the side of the dome with his fist. It made a hollow, ringing sound, like a basketball bouncing. The stupa moved a few inches and then drifted back to the center.

"It's a big balloon!" he said, and punched it again.

As the fake dome moved, Samantha peeked under it. Several ropes connected the balloon to the bottom of what looked to be a shallow pit.

"Very good," she said, nodding slowly. "Maybe you're starting to pay attention to things."

Nipper frowned.

"Just keep that shoe where it is," he said, pointing at her foot and rubbing his head.

Samantha glanced around the platform. When no one was watching, she leaned against the dome with both hands, shoving it as far to one side as she could.

"Go for it," she said.

Nipper climbed over the side and dropped into the pit beneath the statue.

The fake stupa shook slightly.

"Your turn," he called up.

Samantha pushed the stupa balloon aside and lowered herself over the edge. Her shoe and sock touched the bottom, about five feet below the balloon. The floor creaked as she landed, and it seemed to give a bit.

"Odd," she said, and began to gaze around the pit warily.

Light trickled in from around the stupa balloon overhead. The top two feet of the rounded walls were made of stone. The floor and the lower part of the walls, however, were made of wood. She didn't see any doors or exits.

Samantha sniffed the air. Her brother still reeked. A lot.

As she looked up at the bottom of the balloon, there was a splattering, trumpeting noise. It was long and loud, and it sounded very close by.

Anyone with a brother or a sister knows that sound.

Anyone who eats a lot of beans knows it, too.

"Oh . . . my . . . gosh, Nipper," said Samantha. "Do you have to do that while I'm trapped in an enclosed space with you?"

"That wasn't me," said Nipper. "You smelt it, you dealt it."

The sound started up again. It was a long, drawn-out, gurgling squeal.

"And may I say," he added, "really impressive."

The squealing noise kept going. It became louder, and a scraping sound joined in. Alarmed, Samantha looked around to find the noise. The walls of the pit seemed to be moving. No, they were sinking!

"It's the pit!" cried Samantha.

She grabbed on to a rope in the center with one hand and held her umbrella tight with the other.

"Hah! I told you it wasn't me," said Nipper.

"I'm not talking about your smelly noises!" she shouted.

The squealing, scraping noise grew even louder. As they sank farther, the ropes pulled the dome balloon into the pit, blotting out the light.

"At least not this time," Samantha added.

POP!

The noise was like that of a huge cork pulling free from a giant bottle. The bottom half of the pit was a big wooden bucket! It had disconnected from the stone walls and was pulling the balloon down. They dropped through the opening, faster than before.

As Samantha looked up, a new noise rang out. A replacement dome inflated above them. It expanded quickly and filled the hole, blotting out the sky.

"Balloon-o-matic!" said Nipper.

Everything took on an orange glow. The light came from beneath the bucket.

Ragged rock walls rose around them. As they dropped, several razor-sharp stones passed within inches of the balloon.

"Hold on tight," said Samantha.

"That was my plan, Sam," Nipper answered.

The deeper they drifted downward, the brighter the orange lights below glowed.

CHAPTER TWENTY-NINE

DOWN, DOWN, AND AWAY!

A gust of hot wind blew against Samantha's matted hair. They stopped descending and started moving sideways through the cavern as a new stream of air caught them. The balloon lurched, and the bucket shook.

They moved faster now. Samantha guessed they were sailing at least twenty miles per hour.

Her ears popped. The cavern walls parted, and they entered a vast open space. It made the slidewalk hangar in Seattle seem tiny.

And the space was hot. So hot that Samantha started to sweat.

A deep, low rumble filled the air, and everything around them lit up in the bright orange light.

It was getting even hotter!

Her weight shifted and the bucket wobbled. She straightened up quickly.

"Careful, Sam," said Nipper. "I don't want to get dumped out here."

He tilted his head to gesture at the cavern floor below.

She looked down.

Sharp limestone spikes pointed up. She and her brother drifted above a field of stalagmites. The light came from glowing orange rivers of lava, splashing and rumbling across the rocky floor. Plumes of sulfurous steam rose from bubbling craters filled with molten rock.

Samantha wiped sweat from her forehead and looked up.

The balloon coasted below a field of sharp stalactites. Slivers of light came through cracks in the stone above, joining reflected orange light from the lava below.

It finally dawned on Samantha: they were inside a volcano!

Samantha wanted to try on her glasses and look around, just in case there was a *PSST* or a clue, but it seemed wiser to stay still.

"Watch out!" Nipper shouted.

A black shape moved toward them from the side. It swerved and zoomed, squeaking and fluttering away.

"Don't worry," Samantha said. "It's just a bat. It won't bother us."

"No, Sam," Nipper said, waving urgently. "Look where we're going."

Ahead of them, the cavern ended. A wall of sharp rock pointed at them like needles. Samantha squinted and saw an oddly shaped opening in the wall. It was wide and round at the top, then narrow at the bottom. The shape reminded her of a soft-serve ice cream cone. They were coming up on it, fast!

"Hands inside the bucket," she said to Nipper, and prepared for impact.

They fit through the hole—just barely. The balloon carried them into a new room and landed gently on a flat surface. They waited, staying still in the center of the bucket.

"Sca-ree," said Samantha.

Nipper nodded. After another minute, he hopped out of the bucket and onto the floor.

Samantha felt the bucket rising again and she got out, too. As soon as her feet were on the floor, the balloon and bucket floated up and away.

Bang!

The sound made Samantha jump. Somewhere overhead, a stalactite had popped the balloon.

The wooden bucket crashed to the floor a few yards from them.

It was colder in this new area, and quieter. Samantha heard the familiar swishing-sandpaper noise.

"Slidewalks," she said.

They stood in the center of a smooth concrete slab. It was about the size of a tennis court, but square and without a net. A set of twenty slidewalks moved to and from each side of the square. The belts disappeared into tunnels labeled with glowing signs similar to the ones under Volunteer Park.

AUSTRALIA
2,100 MILES

CHINA
3,700 MILES

INDIA
4,000 MILES

UNITED STATES
8,300 MILES

"Where to?" Nipper asked.

Samantha glanced down at her left foot. There was a hole in her sock. She looked at her brother. Brown sludge caked his body from head to toe. Her shoulder stung from the circus peanut. She was exhausted, and they had zero clues.

"Home," she said. "We'll start again tomorrow."

Samantha was about to step onto the slowest U.S.-bound slidewalk when she noticed something in the distance.

"Wait," she said, and walked over to investigate. "Come see this."

Just past the edge of the concrete slab, a slender stalagmite, about two feet high, stuck out between some rocks. A plastic crate rested beside it. Samantha bent down and lifted something from the crate. It was a deflated inflatable animal. She stretched it out on the floor. It had a black-and-white-striped tail and a black mask across its eyes.

"That's kind of neat," said Nipper, studying the stalagmite. "Do you think it does something super-secret?"

"Not that," said Samantha. She pointed at the deflated animal. "This."

"A raccoon," said Nipper.

"It figures," said Samantha. "Morgan Bogan was telling the truth . . . and Uncle Paul was here."

Nipper looked confused.

"It was all in that note from opening day," Samantha said. "I think this raccoon is meant to let us know that Uncle Paul was here."

Nipper shook his head.

"Beats me," he said. "But I'll take your word for it."

Samantha frowned. How could anyone remember 783 varieties of candy, the name of the waffle iron inventor, and that Mali is one of sixteen landlocked countries in Africa, but not recall important details that could help them find their missing uncle?

"*You* are a master of useless facts," she said, irritated.

"Thank you," Nipper replied.

Samantha hadn't meant it as a compliment, but she gave up on the conversation.

She took another look inside the crate and saw three sheets of scratch-and-sniff stickers—the ones she had given Uncle Paul months ago. She ran her hand along the top page, being careful not to scratch. Near the bottom, the strawberry sticker was missing, of course. Uncle Paul had placed it on the letter he left for her in Edfu, Egypt. She felt the empty outline of the berry and looked next to it at the sticker of a tomato.

"I know what you're thinking," said Nipper.

"What?" she asked.

"You're wondering if a tomato is a fruit or a vegetable," he replied. "Fruit."

He flashed a smile.

Samantha scowled.

"So's a chili pepper," he added. "Did you know that the Scoville scale is how scientists measure—"

"A pepper is most definitely not a fruit," said Samantha.

She flipped through the three pages of stickers. On the third sheet, between a banana and a cranberry, she saw a chili pepper.

Nipper crossed his arms and flashed her another big smile.

"I've had it with you!" she shouted, and stood up.

She felt her right toe poke through the hole in her sock.

"You know every kind of stupid fruit there is, but you're too stupid to NOT press the stupid button on a stupid rocket before I'm strapped in!"

Nipper stopped smiling.

"I'm going home," she said, rolling up the sticker sheets and stuffing them into her pocket.

She stepped onto the slowest-moving conveyor belt.

"I'll see you in Seattle," she said. "If you can manage to get there without doing something incredibly dumb."

Samantha stepped quickly to the farthest, fastest Seattle slidewalk. She caught her balance and watched Nipper recede into the distance.

Then she stomped on a bubble and zoomed away.

CHAPTER THIRTY

OFF TO SEE THE LIZARD

Nipper watched his sister slide out of sight.

He didn't feel great. Not after she'd said "stupid" four times.

He hopped onto the first conveyor belt leading to Seattle.

"Ten, fifteen, twenty, twenty-five," he counted as he moved from slow to fast and even faster.

When he reached forty-five miles per hour, he wasn't sure what to do. Samantha had already popped a bubble and triggered the fastest belt, so it whizzed by at supersonic speed. Nipper figured it would be an hour before the belt slowed down. He wasn't good at waiting.

He hopped onto the speeding belt.

Pow! Pow! Pow!

He landed, breaking three bubbles. Immediately, three inflatable shells burst upward, slammed into each other, and launched Nipper into the air. He landed ten feet back and set off more bubbles.

Pow! Pow! Poppity-poppity! Pow!

He bounced from bubble to bubble as the conveyor belt raced toward the tunnel.

Poppity-pow!

Another patch of bubbles exploded under Nipper, flinging him off the slidewalk completely. He tumbled onto the floor of a hallway beside the slidewalk. He stood up, ready to try again; then a ladder caught his eye. There was one word stenciled on the wall beside it:

KOMODO

He was already off the belt, so he decided he might as well have a look around.

Nipper climbed the ladder and reached a metal panel at the top. Holding the ladder with one hand, he pushed upward with the other. The panel flipped open and light streamed in.

Nipper pulled himself up . . . onto a pink, sandy beach.

He stood up and brushed sand the color of bubble gum off his legs. He was alone on a beach, not a street or sidewalk in sight. In front of him was a dense jungle. Beyond the trees, jagged peaks rose into the sky.

"A mountainous island," Nipper said to himself thoughtfully.

Waves gently lapped against the shore, and he heard a seagull cry. He took in a whiff of warm, salty air and gazed out over the water, but he didn't see any birds. A thick veil of fog rose from the water. He couldn't see more than a few feet past the shoreline.

"In a mist-covered ocean," said Nipper.

He closed his eyes and thought about the poster he'd seen in his mother's office.

Twigs snapped behind him and he opened his eyes. He heard rustling leaves. Something moved through the dense vegetation along the jungle's edge.

"Hello?" he called out. "Samantha?"

Of course, his sister wasn't there. He'd seen her stomp on a bubble and go home. But what was it? No one—and nothing—answered.

"'Mantha?" he called. "Is that you?"

Something burst from the bushes. Before Nipper could react, it raced up to him, hissed, and stared.

It looked like a small alligator, about three feet long, with a short, flat head, kind of like a snake's. It had wrinkly, greenish-gray skin and a thick tail as long as its body. A forked tongue flicked in and out of its mouth.

Nipper stared into beady black eyes.

"In a mist-covered ocean far, far from home," he said breathlessly, "there's a mountainous island where . . ."

His voice trailed off.

He gazed at the animal in wonder.

A baby dinosaur!

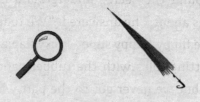

CHAPTER THIRTY-ONE

HAVE A BALL

"SUN-rise!" shouted Chuckles J. Morningstar. He adjusted his top hat and tried to concentrate. Five soldiers stood before him. Their faces were pale. Their hair was wild. Their uniforms were wrinkled. Of course, they *were* clowns.

He sniffed three times. Two short snorts, then a long one. Even through his odor-minimizing nose filter, he could tell that several of the soldiers reeked of cumin and chili pepper.

"It was a routine seek-and-annoy mission, boss," said a pancake soldier standing near the left corner of his desk.

"Routine?" asked Chuckles. "What was the routine, Sergeant Hotcakes?"

"We found the secret underground conveyor belt you told us about," he answered. "We rode to Mali and started the flippy-floppy super-sticky flapjack prank. We started hitting folks with the rubber pancakes. It was hilarious, but we never got to the part with the super-glue syrup."

Chuckles tapped one of his enormous shoes on the floor impatiently.

"Yeah," said the other pancake soldier, raising his spatula. "We looked out in the crowd and saw a girl with a red umbrella. *The* red umbrella."

He waved his spatula and accidently bumped his partner's shoulder, releasing a puff of brown dust.

"We tried to follow her," he continued. "Then a super-annoying . . . ahh-annoying boy— Ahhhh-choo! Ahhhh-choo!"

The soldier's odor-minimizing nose filter came loose on the second sneeze and fell off. He quickly bent down and picked it up. Wheezing loudly, he reattached the bright red ball to his nose.

Chuckles waited for him to stop wheezing. Then he waited a little longer, just to make the soldiers extra nervous.

"I can't believe I'm hearing this," he said finally. "This is a total disaster, Private Griddles."

"Um, sir"—the extra-nervous soldier raised his spatula—"I'm *Captain* Griddles."

"Not anymore!" barked Chuckles. "That umbrella holds the Super-Secret Plans to the whole world. You had a chance to grab the complete map of hidden tunnels and secret transportation everywhere . . . and you blew it!"

He pounded his fist on the metal desk. The sound of a dozen mousetraps snapping rang out from inside one of the drawers.

Four out of five soldiers flinched. The giant woman with duck feet stood at attention.

"This is what you are all going to do now," Chuckles said, leaning forward.

He took off his hat and pointed its flat top at them.

"Get on your unicycles and pedal to the map department, pronto."

Sergeant Hotcakes and Private Griddles stared at the top hat. They both nodded.

"*You* will tell them everything you saw in Mali," Chuckles continued. "*They* will tell you where to go next."

The pie soldier raised a goo-covered hand.

"But, boss," she protested. "The map guys are fools. They're worthless. It's like their brains are made out of cotton candy. They wouldn't know a secret staircase from a porta-potty."

"Not. Remotely. Interested," Chuckles said forcefully. "Now leave, before I send you to practice the barefoot-booby-trap routine . . . in Antarctica."

The soldiers looked at one another helplessly and slunk out of the room.

"You stay here," he said, pointing at the tall woman with the duck shoes.

Chuckles listened for the sound of squeaking wheels. He opened the top drawer of his desk and rummaged through a dozen shiny, red plastic balls. He picked one up and studied it. Still fresh. He removed his odor-minimizing nose filter, tossed it on the floor, and replaced it with the new one. Then he fished around in the drawer, found his phone, and dialed.

A high-pitched noise squeaked from the phone.

"Major Helium!" he barked. "Those worthless fools in the map department actually got something right, for once. Dressing up like police officers and spying on that Spinner family paid off."

The phone squealed.

"Yes," he answered. "The magtrain isn't the only way to get around. The kids led us to a system of conveyor belts."

He listened to more squeaks on the phone.

"No, Major Helium," he replied. "Nobody found the guy in the green plaid pajamas. But they saw the umbrella."

Chuckles stood up and walked around to the front of his desk.

"I'm sending you someone who can identify the kids who have it," Chuckles said, looking up to make sure the tall woman was listening.

His phone squeaked and squealed.

"Yes, yes, Major. The kids got away," he answered. "But I'm glad they did. We'll keep following them, until they find their uncle for us."

With a soft crunch, he stepped on the used nose ball and ground it into the concrete floor with one of his massive shoes.

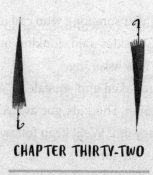

CHAPTER THIRTY-TWO

COUNTING CHEEPS

Samantha rose from under the fire hydrant by the Volunteer Park Conservatory.

She walked home slowly, as she only had one shoe and didn't want to step on anything sharp. Even more than that, she was exhausted.

It was going to take Nipper a while to catch up, so she headed to her bedroom for a nap. She hung her purse on the back of the door and stowed the umbrella under her mattress. She spent ten minutes struggling with her hairbrush before giving up.

"*PSST*," she said, dropping the brush on her dresser. "Puzzled, sore, shoeless, and tired."

Samantha looked at her clock. It was only two p.m., and she had already been around the world. Literally.

All the way around the world. Super-secret travel was tiring, especially when you were also running from clowns.

She flopped down on her bed and tried to take a nap.

Her mind was full.

She thought about Buffy's crazy play and Cleopatra's Needle.

She thought about slidewalks and tables piled high with spices.

She took a deep breath and closed her eyes.

Her muscles relaxed.

She drifted. . . .

Screee! Screee! Zicky zicky zicky scree-dleeee!

She sat up quickly. Out in the hall, a chinchilla had let loose a piercing squeal. It made Samantha's teeth hurt, but she was too exhausted to get up. She lay back down and closed her eyes again.

She thought about Seydou, with his big smile and his cool hat with the secret-map visor. She pictured him on his motorcycle, leading away the tiny car full of clowns.

Horrible clowns. Were they the SUN that Uncle Paul warned her about?

How did they know about the umbrella? And how come they all sneezed and fell down when they smelled spices in the market?

Did they follow her there? Or had they been in Mali before?

Samantha sighed. Too many questions. She stretched her shoulders.

Zicky zicky zicky scree-dleeee!

She tensed up again. A chinchilla had found a brand-new way to irritate her. She turned sideways and tried to ignore the sound of the shrieking rodent. She clenched both fists.

Zicky. Zicky. Zick—

The noise stopped suddenly. Samantha waited for the chinchilla to start shrieking again. But it didn't. Everything stayed quiet. Dead quiet.

"Whatever," she whispered.

Samantha started thinking about Uncle Paul and the stickers.

She pictured glowing yellow letters A, L, I, and M, spinning around and around.

Her hands relaxed. She breathed deeply and drifted off to sleep.

CHAPTER THIRTY-THREE

LUCKY DAY

Samantha awoke to thumping and banging across the hall. She sat up and looked at her clock. It was eight a.m. She'd slept all afternoon and night!

She'd had no intention of sleeping so long ... but she felt great. She stood up and stretched. She took a quick shower, got dressed, and then headed across the hall to make sure her brother had made it home safely.

Samantha walked through Nipper's open bedroom door and into his room. He was crouching in front of his dresser, pressing hard on the bottom drawer with both hands.

"Oh. Hi, Sam," he said, looking up at her. "Mom and Dad came by last night, but you were snoring so loud, they let you sleep."

Samantha frowned.

"I don't snore," she said. "Well, maybe I was so tired that I— Wait. When did you get home?"

"Uh . . . a while ago," he said, standing up.

She sniffed. He still smelled like spices. Dried powder streaked his shirt. She glanced down. He had spices on his pants, too.

She looked farther down to see he was pressing one foot against the drawer.

"And what's in the dresser?" she asked.

"Nothing," he answered quickly.

Nipper glanced down at the bottom drawer, then back to her.

"I think I . . . need some socks," he said, looking around the room. "Oh, right here."

While keeping his foot pressed against the bottom drawer, he opened the top drawer of the dresser.

Everything about this seemed very strange to Samantha. Stranger than regular kid-brother strange, and *that* was already strange. She sniffed again.

"Did you really sleep in your spices?" she asked.

One at a time, Nipper pulled socks from the drawer and used them to wipe away powdered spices from his body.

"I'm kind of like a chinchilla, Sam, if you think about it," he said. "I'm taking a dust bath."

"Or . . . you could just take a real bath and put on clean clothes," she replied.

"Don't worry," he said. "I'll get to it tonight."

Samantha looked at him, then at the sock drawer. It was almost empty. Socks were scattered all over the room now.

Still holding the bottom drawer of the dresser closed with a foot, he reached into the back of the sock drawer and pulled out a rolled pair of tube socks.

"Gotcha," he said. "I always keep a special emergency pair in the back."

"Really?" asked Samantha. "Since when?"

Nipper whipped the socks in the air to unroll them. Something flew out and clattered to the floor. He bent down and picked up a shiny silver object. It was a coin from 1913 engraved with a woman's head surrounded by stars. He turned it over. There was a big letter V on the back.

"My lucky nickel!" he shouted.

Uncle Paul had given Nipper the coin a year ago.

Samantha remembered her uncle telling Nipper, "She's one of a kind. Look after her," and then giving Samantha a wink. Her brother lost track of the coin a few hours later.

"It's a sign," said Nipper, waving the coin at her. "Today is a lucky day."

"Maybe," said Samantha.

She thought about the last time Nipper invoked the *Lucky Day*.

A little over two years ago, Samantha's parents

threw her a deluxe birthday party with a magician, a pirate, and a clown. Their dad did lightbulb tricks and put on a super-bubble science show. Uncle Paul dressed up in his "formal" tuxedo T-shirt and made snow cones for all the kids in the neighborhood.

Right before the magic show started, Nipper picked a clover. He told everyone it had four leaves and that this meant it was his lucky day.

Uncle Paul offered him a sour-cherry snow cone, but Nipper insisted he make it extra-super sour. Uncle Paul doubled the syrup. When no one was looking, Nipper poured the rest of the bottle on his snow cone.

Then Nipper tasted the extra-extra super-sour snow cone. He screamed and flung it across the yard.

It splatter-painted half the kids bright red and knocked the hat off the magician's head. The magician had been hiding a pet rabbit in the hat, and Dennis chased the terrified animal around the backyard for an hour, knocking over kids and Samantha's cake. The party ended early that day. After all the guests left, Samantha took the clover from Nipper and counted five leaves.

Samantha ignored the silver coin her brother was waving in her face.

"Lucky, huh?" she asked him. "Should I move everything out of the way?"

"No, this really is a lucky day and things are going to

go my way," he insisted. "You keep using your big brain to figure out what 'Watch out for the SUN' means and where we should have gone instead of Africa. While you do that, *I'm* going to go and get my Yankees back."

Nipper tucked the coin into his pocket, put on the tube socks, and forced on his dusty shoes without untying them.

"Lucky day," he said one more time, and headed downstairs.

CHAPTER THIRTY-FOUR

BIRD BRAIN

The sun blazed high in the sky. The view of mighty Mount Rainier, fifty-nine miles to the south, was crystal clear. That's usually another sign that it's a lucky day in Seattle.

Nipper strolled down the driveway to his neighbor's side porch.

"Lucky, lucky day," he said softly.

Missy Snoddgrass stood just inside the screen door, waiting. She folded her arms across her yellow polka-dot blouse as she watched him climb the steps. The moment he reached the porch, she pushed the door open with one hand and leaned forward.

"Hello, Jeremy Bernard Spinner," she said. "I don't remember inviting you."

Nipper ignored her. This was his lucky day. He patted his front pocket and felt his lucky nickel.

"Hi, Missy," he said cheerfully. "I'm here to talk about my Yankees."

"Those losers?" she snapped, twisting her face into a weird half-grin.

Nipper did his best to keep smiling.

"At first, I worried that nobody would take them at all," said Missy, rubbing her chin. "It's been so long since they won a game."

"Take them?" said Nipper. He forgot to keep smiling.

"I had to keep lowering the price," she said. "Eventually, I found a buyer."

Nipper heard a loud fluttering noise. A large red-and-blue parrot flapped through the open side door and landed on Missy's shoulder.

"I used the three hundred bucks to buy Sammy here."

"Three hundred bucks, three hundred bucks," the bird squawked.

"Sammy?" Nipper asked. He watched the parrot as it picked at Missy's blouse with one dirty gray claw. It reached out with its beak and tapped twice at the scorpion ring on the end of Missy's finger. Then it stopped tapping and picking and stared at him.

Slowly, Nipper began to realize what happened. His eyes went wide and his heart raced.

"You sold my Yankees for three hundred dollars and bought a *dumb bird*?" he screamed.

"Sammy's not a dumb bird," said Missy calmly. "I like to think of her as my discomfort pet."

"*Discomfort pet?* What does that mean? Whose 'discomfort' is it?"

She glanced at the parrot on her shoulder and turned slowly back to Nipper.

"Yours," she said in a low voice. She grinned and stared directly into his eyes without blinking. "And I wouldn't make her mad if I were you."

Nipper scowled back at her.

"I'm not scared of a—"

"Not scared. *Boo!* Not scared. *Boo!*" the parrot shrieked, and it leaped forward.

"*Boo! Boo! Boo!*" it squawked, flapping its wings in Nipper's face.

Nipper tried to bat it away, but all he could see was a blur of blue and red feathers.

"Who's the bird brain now?" asked Missy.

The parrot found a small hole in Nipper's collar and worked its beak into it.

"Bird brain!" it squawked. "*Boo! Boo! Boo!*"

It scratched at Nipper's neck through the hole. He shoved at the awful creature with his elbow until it let go of his collar. Then he stepped backward down the stairs, shielding his face and neck with both arms.

When his feet touched the pavement, he turned and uncovered his face.

He didn't look back.

Nipper walked down the Snoddgrass driveway, silently picking feathers from his hair as he went.

He stopped and reached into his pocket. His lucky nickel was gone.

"*Boo!* Bird brain! *Boo!*" the parrot screamed in the distance.

The walk to his house seemed like fifty-nine miles.

CHAPTER THIRTY-FIVE

WATCH OUT FOR THE SUN

Samantha felt energized. She sat at her desk, tapping the yellow notepad with a pencil. The closed umbrella leaned against the wall near her. She had a hardcover book—the *Encyclopedia Missilium*—open on the desk. This huge book about weapons and projectiles came from her uncle's apartment.

Nipper staggered in through her bedroom door.

"I clearly heard one of the clowns say 'Dynamite' and 'Zzyzx,'" she said, not looking up from her notes. "Do those sound familiar to you?"

Nipper didn't answer.

"Well, they're both stops on the magtrain line, remember?" she asked.

"Three hundred dollars," Nipper muttered.

"Whatever," said Samantha without looking at him.

She had written a list of all the magtrain destinations from the station under their mailbox. She drew a circle around the word *Baraboo*.

"I tried to use the computer in Dad's office, but chinchillas had chewed through the power cord," she continued. "So I used Mom's laptop, and I researched all the places on the magtrain line. And guess what? Baraboo! That's what."

"Boo," said Nipper softly.

"There used to be a clown school in Baraboo where all the big circuses practiced."

"Boo," Nipper said again.

Samantha looked at her brother. His hair was a mess. His shirt collar was twisted. Small blue and red feathers stuck to his face.

"You are double-triple kid-brother-strange today," she said. "Work with me here. Uncle Paul is counting on us."

She put down the notepad and held out the encyclopedia.

"I still don't know what A-L-I-M means," Samantha said. "But look at this."

She pointed to a spot on the page for Nipper to read.

RUBBER PANCAKES

Ranging from thin and bendy flapjacks to steel-rimmed, armor-piercing johnnycakes, rubber pancakes are the projectiles of choice for slapstick pranksters and comic vandals.

Breakfast historians believe airborne faux consumables date back to the nineteenth century, beginning with the cultivation of rubber trees for commercial use.

In modern times, antisocial clowns often employ rubber pancakes, most notably the organization known as the Society of Universal Nonsense.

See also: LEAD BALLOONS, CANDY PEANUTS

"'The Society of Universal Nonsense,'" Nipper repeated. He had snapped out of his stupor and nodded enthusiastically. "Watch out for the—"

Samantha raised one hand and cut him off. She glanced left and right. The squeaky, chittering noises had stopped.

"Weren't there a bunch of chinchillas up here?" she asked.

Samantha got up and started looking around. The room seemed remarkably quiet. She bent down to peek under her bed, and then stood up again. She spotted a thin blue strip of tape lying in a corner and picked it up.

" '*Chinchilla lanigera.* La Paz, Bolivia,' " she read.

The tape had big teeth marks through it.

She studied the bite. Then she glared at Nipper.

"Show me what you've been hiding," she said. "Show me now!"

Baraboo, Wisconsin

Founded in 1838, the city of Baraboo, Wisconsin, takes its name from the nearby Baraboo River.

Conveniently located only a few miles from Interstate 90 and the train station at Wisconsin Dells, Baraboo features many fine restaurants, a dozen outdoor recreation attractions, and the Circus World Museum.

From 1884 to 1917, Baraboo was the headquarters of the Ringling Brothers circus as well as several other circuses. This earned the town the nickname Circus City.

Officially, the population of Baraboo is about twelve thousand.

* * *

The official population count does not include one hundred clowns who live in secret buildings beneath the streets of Baraboo.

The Society of Universal Nonsense (aka the SUN) is an army of failed circus performers. Every member of the SUN has *hyperosmia*, meaning that their sense of smell is super-powerful. They are so sensitive to smells that they cannot spend much time close to people or animals. Thus, they can never join the circus.

They wear special red ball nose filters to protect themselves from odors. They wear enormous shoes to keep people at least twenty inches away from their faces.

Since they are unable to entertain, these clowns have banded together to annoy. They interrupt music festivals and sabotage parades. They ruin parties and vandalize art fairs. They play mean-spirited pranks on unsuspecting people around the globe.

Until very recently, the SUN has been crepuscular, choosing to stage most of its pranks around dawn and twilight. Now that the foul-smelling ninjas of the RAIN have been caught, the SUN has stepped up its attacks during all hours of the day and night.

Governments worldwide are trying to put a stop to the SUN and their cruel tricks. The New York City Police Department has assigned twenty-two officers to hunt them down.

CHAPTER THIRTY-SIX

FEROCIOUS BEASTS AND WHERE TO HIDE THEM

"What have you been hiding?" Samantha repeated.

Nipper led her across the hall. He stopped just outside his bedroom door and held a finger to his lips.

"Shhh," he whispered excitedly. "We don't want to wake her if she's sleeping." He gently pushed open the door.

"*She?* Who's *she*?" asked Samantha.

Her eyes went wide.

A giant, greenish-gray lizard moved around the room. Its feet thumped against the wood floor as it darted back and forth. A chinchilla scampered under Nipper's bed.

The lizard knocked over a chair and stopped at the

foot of the bed. It hissed loudly and tried to jam its head between the bed and the floor, but it didn't fit.

"It's a baby dinosaur," said Nipper giddily. "I found her on a mountainous island, in a mist-covered ocean far, far from home."

Samantha looked at the animal. It was at least three feet long.

"See, Sam? I remembered what you told me yesterday," he said.

"Remembered what?" she asked.

"You said that we're both explorers," he answered. "And you said we shouldn't come home empty-handed. Didn't you?"

Samantha slapped her forehead and let out an exasperated sigh.

"I think she's a lythronax," he said happily.

"A lythro-*what*?" asked Samantha.

"A lythronax," he answered. "That means 'king of gore.' Lythronaxes are the largest carnivorous dinosaurs ever discovered."

Samantha glanced across the room. The creature had stopped trying to get under Nipper's bed. It moved slowly toward them, sniffing the air as it crawled.

"She'll be house-trained, soon," Nipper continued. "*Then* I'll teach her how to hunt for birds."

"Birds?" Samantha asked.

"Oh yes," he answered, rubbing his hands together and grinning fiendishly. "Sammy the parrot is in big trouble."

Samantha looked down. The giant lizard was slinking close to Nipper's feet. Its forked tongue flicked in and out of its mouth quickly. The creature tilted its head up and stared at Samantha with jet-black eyes. It hissed.

Samantha groaned. She took another look at the lizard. Then at her brother. She stepped backward into the hallway.

"Wait right here," she said, and shut the door.

CHAPTER THIRTY-SEVEN

BOOK CLUB

Samantha quickly walked down the stairs and into the living room. She saw her parents in the kitchen and turned the other way. They were talking loudly to hear each other over the sound of chinchillas. She left through the front door instead. She sped around the house, down the driveway, and up the steps to Uncle Paul's apartment.

The door was still unlocked. She turned the knob and entered. No one had been inside for several months now, except for her and Nipper. Samantha had been there earlier that day, when she borrowed the *Encyclopedia Missilium*. She headed back to the tall bookcase.

Among the atlases and dictionaries, a set of thick, leather-bound books stood where she remembered.

Each one featured the words *THE WORLD'S DEAD-LIEST ANIMALS* on the spine in red-and-gold lettering. She reached for the third book in the set.

VOLUME III
HIPPOPOTAMUS TO POISON DART FROG

" 'King cobra . . . Kodiak bear,' " she read out loud as she flipped through the pages.

She stopped at a photo of a giant, greenish-gray lizard.

" 'Komodo dragon.' " Samantha sighed, shaking her head. She snapped the book shut and raced back to the house.

A minute later, she pushed open the door to her brother's room.

Nipper held one end of a pillow. The lizard's mouth was clamped tightly onto the other end. They were engaged in a tug of war.

"Nipper," she said, holding up the book. "You've done a lot of incredibly dumb, dangerous things, but this is the worst!"

The lizard let go of the pillow and turned to look at Samantha.

Samantha started thinking about some of the incredibly dumb things her brother had done. A little over two months ago, he'd tried to loot a secret tomb and it almost got them drowned in ancient Egyptian sewage. A little over ten months ago, he'd tried to build a roller coaster in the backyard and—no. No. *This* was much worse.

She raised the leather-bound book, opened it, and read loudly.

" 'Komodo dragons are giant lizards native to several islands of Indonesia. They can grow to be ten feet long and weigh up to one hundred and fifty pounds. They are venomous, and they dominate their ecosystem, feeding on bugs, birds, mammals, and each other!' "

She lowered the book and glared at her brother.

"That is not a baby dinosaur," she said. "It's a teenage Komodo dragon. And it's venomous!"

Nipper mouthed the word *venomous*. He looked down at the very large lizard, then back at his sister.

"That means their bite is poisonous!" she added angrily.

The lizard hissed loudly and bared a set of gleaming white teeth. It stuck out its long, forked tongue and wiggled it at Samantha. She noticed a glistening drop of clear goo dangling from one tooth. Slowly, the creature began to slink toward her. She took a step back. It continued moving in her direction. She stepped sideways around the room and kept reading.

" 'Komodo dragons have a powerful sense of smell,' " she continued. " 'They can detect their prey up to six miles—' "

The lizard lunged at Samantha. She closed the heavy book quickly and swung it, smacking the beast hard across its snout. It jumped back and retreated behind her brother.

"Watch out," said Nipper. "You could hurt her."

The Komodo dragon poked its head through Nipper's legs and looked up at Samantha again. It hissed fiercely. A thin strip of blue tape fell from its mouth and fluttered to the floor. Nipper picked it up and read.

"'*Chinchilla lanigera*. Lima, Peru.'"

He tilted his head thoughtfully.

"Lima . . . Lima . . . Lima. That sounds familiar."

His eyes widened.

"Oh. Yeah. Now I remember," he said. "Those cards in the hallway read L-I-M-A."

Samantha scowled at him.

"As in Lima, Peru," he repeated, and handed her the scrap of tape. "I guess we were really close. Weren't we, Sam?"

A hiss rang out. It wasn't a lizard. It came from an angry, angry sister whose brother didn't pay attention to things.

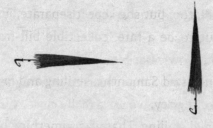

CHAPTER THIRTY-EIGHT

OPERATION FLAPJACK

They had another full week of school before they could head out on their next super-secret journey. Samantha made the most of the afternoons to get ready. She planned to be prepared for Peru.

She already knew a little bit of Spanish. On Monday, she started practicing phrases that might come in handy. She wanted to say a lot more than "Please," "Thank you," and "Where's the tallest building?" She also found a pocket guidebook to Peru—for any not-super-secret places they needed to find.

After school on Tuesday, they biked downtown to an international currency exchange. Samantha traded in sixty dollars of birthday money for one hundred and ninety-five Peruvian nuevos soles. Nipper contributed a ten-dollar bill, too, but she kept it separate, just in case it turned out to be a rare, collectible bill from Uncle Paul.

"Beautiful," said Samantha, smiling and fanning out the colorful currency.

She stopped smiling. That was something her big sister would say. At least Samantha didn't have the urge to go buy a thousand pairs of shoes or invent a goofy, movie-star name.

On Wednesday, Samantha sat at her desk, carefully stitching the umbrella, repairing the hole that the chinchilla had made, when she heard a loud ripping sound in Nipper's room. She stood up quickly and walked across the hall.

Nipper sat on the edge of his bed, cradling a huge hardcover book in his lap. It was over two feet tall and more than a foot wide. The words *Birds of North America* were engraved on the cover.

"Where did that book come from?" she asked him.

The Komodo dragon hunched on the floor, watching Nipper carefully.

"Uncle Paul gave it to me to learn about birds," her brother answered. "That's exactly what we're going to do."

Suddenly, Nipper tore a page from the book and held up an illustration of a speckled bird.

"Starling!" he announced.

The lizard reached up and snatched the page with its mouth. It chewed furiously and swallowed.

"What on earth are you doing?" asked Samantha.

"I already told you," said Nipper. "Kym is going to be an awesome bird hunter."

"Kym?"

"Yeah," he said, grinning. "And, Sammy, the three-hundred-dollar parrot, is in big trouble now."

He tore another page from the book and held up an illustration of a bright red bird.

"Cardinal!"

The Komodo dragon snatched it from him and chewed ferociously.

Samantha had absolutely no idea what this was all about. She left the boy, his lizard, and his giant bird book and went back to repairing her umbrella.

On Thursday, they met in the kitchen.

"Granola bars," she said, holding up a box.

Nipper snatched it from her, took out a bar, and ate it in four bites.

"Stop it," she said. "You're as bad as the lizard."

She grabbed the box back.

"The other five bars are for our trip," she told him.

Nipper had already moved on to the spice rack.

He grabbed jars of pepper, nutmeg, chili powder, cloves, and hot Hungarian paprika. He took a box of powdered dishwasher detergent from under the sink.

"What is that for?" asked Samantha, watching him mix it all in a bowl.

"Clown seasoning," he answered, and poured the mixture into two plastic bags. "*That* will get their attention."

He stuffed one in his back pocket and handed the other to Samantha.

"Wruf," barked Dennis, scampering up to investigate.

He sniffed twice at Nipper's pants and backed away slowly. His cone clattered as he backed all the way out of the room.

On Friday, Samantha laid out her clothes for the trip. Just like the tourists she saw in Borobudur, she'd wear hiking boots, shorts, a T-shirt, and a backpack. She'd bring a sweater in case it got chilly.

She tried to get Nipper to organize his clothes, too.

"It couldn't hurt to plan your outfit for the trip," she suggested.

"Outfit? What's wrong with you, Sam?" he snapped. "Are you turning into Buffy?"

She shut up immediately.

Later, he tossed her his New York Yankees sweatshirt for the backpack.

Saturday, at seven a.m., they sat together in the kitchen. The magnifying glass, Peru guidebook, granola bars, clothes, and currency covered the table.

"Umbrella," said Nipper.

"Check," said Samantha.

She lowered one hand and touched the red umbrella resting across her lap.

"Purple specs," said Nipper.

"Check," Samantha answered, tapping her purse.

"Hand lens?" asked Samantha.

"Check. And can I bring the dinosaur—I mean, the Komodo dragon?" he asked.

"Are you kidding me?" said Samantha. "Keep that monster in your room until we figure out what to do with it."

"How about Dennis?" Nipper asked.

"Not this time," she answered.

Her brother looked disappointed.

Samantha noticed the pug creeping around the edges of the kitchen. His plastic cone rattled on the tile floor. He was stalking a chinchilla, no doubt. She pictured the giant lizard stalking Dennis.

"I changed my mind. Bring the dog," she said. "When 'Kym' is done eating all the chinchillas, pugs are probably next on the menu."

"Dennis. Check," said Nipper.

"Now listen up," she said, tapping the table. "Last night, I told Mom and Dad we were getting up early to work on a science project next door with Morgan Bogan. I'm starting to believe him, but most people still think everything he says is preposterous."

Nipper looked at her, trying to understand.

"You see," she continued, "if he tells Mom and Dad we're not there, they won't be sure if that's true or not."

"Okay." Nipper shrugged. "That seems like a good plan."

Samantha didn't like sneaking around and misleading her parents. But maybe, if they didn't know about the SUN, the clowns would leave them out of it. Besides, they might not understand this was a mission to save Uncle Paul, and possibly the whole world.

She looked out the kitchen window. She saw the sun—the good kind of sun—shining, and a clear sky.

"It's a fine day to save the whole world," she said. "Let's go."

Nipper took the magnifying glass. Samantha stowed everything else in the backpack. Carefully, she slid the umbrella into a loop on one side of the pack. She stood up and put the pack on.

They headed down Thirteenth Avenue, past the mailbox, and into the park. Samantha didn't bother with the purple sunglasses this time. She knew where to go. They passed the water tower and the art museum to reach the special fire hydrant.

Samantha reached for the octagonal bolt, but Nipper held out his hand and blocked her.

"Wait," he said. "Can I have one of those granola bars?"

"Already?" Samantha asked.

"Yep," he answered. "I hate slidewalking on an empty stomach."

Samantha shrugged and reached into a side pocket of her backpack. She held a snack bar out for her brother.

Dennis started growling.

"This isn't for you," she told him.

Swack!

Something whizzed near Samantha's hand. It sliced the granola bar neatly in two. She stood there, stunned.

Clank! Clank!

Two pancakes sailed by. Sparks flew as they ricocheted off the fire hydrant.

CHAPTER THIRTY-NINE

HOW NOW, BROWN CLOUD?

Samantha thought she had packed everything they would need for a trip to Peru. Unfortunately, she forgot to include a defense against steel-rimmed, armor-piercing johnnycakes. She stared at two deep marks on the hydrant. Smoke rose from the dome, where the deadly pancakes had gouged the metal.

She turned toward the art museum. Four clowns in overalls marched toward her, waving spatulas. Samantha thought she recognized two of them from Mali, but she couldn't be sure—and she wasn't going to stick around to find out.

She made eye contact with Nipper. Together, they sprinted across the conservatory's front lawn. Dennis scampered at their heels.

Suddenly, the dog turned and sped back to the hydrant. He scooped up both halves of the granola bar. Then he caught up with Samantha and Nipper. All three of them made a sharp right turn at the corner of the building and slipped behind a tall bush.

"Should we head to the fabric store?" Nipper asked. "Maybe they'll pass out the way those ninjas did."

"I don't think that will work," said Samantha. "Did you see their outfits? They clearly have a textile immunity."

Samantha suddenly felt a twinge of fear, and it wasn't because of clowns. She'd just said *another* thing Buffy would say! At this rate, Samantha was going to wind up in a sky castle, shopping for flags to accentuate bricks.

"Wait," said Nipper. "I've got this one."

He took out his bag of clown seasoning. He walked around the bush and dropped the bag on the grass.

"Get ready," he said. "When I say 'Go for it,' run."

He pointed to the back of the conservatory. Then he stepped farther out and waved in the direction of the clowns.

"Hey, Bozos!" Nipper shouted. "Come and get us!"

He slapped at the bag with his foot, leaning as far back as possible. The bag popped, sending a brown cloud into the air.

"Run, Sam!" he shouted, and headed toward the back of the building.

Dennis took off after him. Nipper forgot to say "Go for it," but Samantha knew what he meant. She followed him around the corner, too.

They sped along the back of the brick-and-glass building. They made another sharp turn, hugged the side of the conservatory, and listened.

Everything was quiet for a moment. Then they heard an explosion of woe.

"Ah! Eek!" wailed a clown. "It's pepper."

"You mixed it up!" a second clown shouted. "It's pepper. Eek! Ah!"

"Help!" a different clown screamed. "This is NOT SILLY!"

"Aaaaah!" another clown shrieked, drowning out all the others. "The CUMIN-ity!"

Samantha and Nipper stayed put, listening to howls and coughs. After a while, the sounds faded to moans and wheezes.

"Four clowns down," said Nipper.

He stepped away from the wall and looked back along the building.

"Coast is clear," he said. "Let's go."

They reached the fire hydrant and journeyed down beneath the conservatory.

CHAPTER FORTY

DOG RUN

They hopped off the lift ring and onto the rotating floor. Samantha read the country names above the openings as they rotated past.

"This is it," she said, pointing at the entrance to the Peru slidewalk.

Before she could step through, Nipper tapped her on the shoulder.

"Can I have a granola bar?" he asked. "I told you I hate to slidewalk on an empty stomach."

Samantha reached into the backpack and held one out for her brother.

"Wruf!" Dennis barked.

He jumped and snatched the granola bar. His white plastic cone smacked Nipper on the hand.

"Hey!" Nipper cried. "That's mine! You're a bad—"

The dog sprinted into the left side of the entrance to Norway.

Nipper gasped. He looked at Samantha and pointed to the sign.

She waited.

The exit belt dumped Dennis back into the room. His cone clattered as he rolled across the floor. He righted himself and sat down, munching happily on his snack.

Samantha let him finish. Then she picked him up.

"Okay," she said. "*Now*, let's go to Lima."

With Dennis tucked under her arm, she stepped through the *right* side of the Peru opening, onto the five-miles-per-hour slidewalk.

Nipper followed her across the conveyor belts. When they reached the fastest one, he hopped in front of her and held out his hand.

"Slidewalking," he said. "I hate doing it on an empty stomach."

Samantha sighed, reached into her backpack once again, and fished out another granola bar.

"Here," she said, and tossed it.

When Nipper moved to catch the bar, he popped a bubble with his heel. A plastic enclosure shot upward, sealing him tight. The bar bounced off the bubble wrap and disappeared.

Lights turned yellow and the alarm sounded.

Samantha held Dennis tight and stepped on a bubble. The protective padding closed around them.

As they zoomed toward Peru, Samantha noticed her brother looking at her. His lips moved. *Five minus three.*

Samantha nodded and mouthed back at him. *Yes. I know.*

There were only two granola bars left.

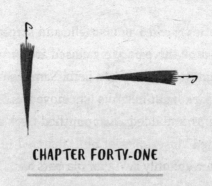

CHAPTER FORTY-ONE

PEP(PER) TALK

In a concrete bunker, twenty feet beneath Baraboo, Wisconsin, Chuckles J. Morningstar paced back and forth, shouting at the SUN.

"Giving you orders is like screaming into an empty garbage can!" he bellowed.

In three long rows, ninety-nine soldiers stood at attention. Chuckles walked slowly in front of them. He stopped at an extra-nervous soldier. He removed his top hat, held it by the brim, and took aim.

Bonk!

A red leather boxing glove shot from the top of the hat and whacked the soldier in the face.

"Ouchie!" wailed Private Griddles. "What did I do?"

Chuckles grunted and moved on to Sergeant Hotcakes. He stared at the pancake soldier's uniform. There were fresh, reddish-brown streaks on his overalls.

Chuckles sniffed. Two short snorts, then a long one. It was hot Hungarian paprika. He held his breath and leaned closer. Bits of blue sparkled in the powder. Was it detergent? Chuckles stepped back, exhaled, and began to shout.

"You used steel-rimmed, armor-piercing johnny-cakes," he said angrily. "You could have killed that girl."

"So?" asked Sergeant Hotcakes. "We'd get the map."

Chuckles moved forward again, within an inch of the soldier's red nose ball.

"It could have been a *fake* umbrella," he growled. "That girl's tricky. She might try to pull a stunt like that. Your job was to let them go and *follow them*."

"Oh, we know where they went, boss," said Private Griddles. "Peru. We found a trail of granola crumbs. First, we went all the way to Norway, but—"

"Enough," said Chuckles, turning away.

He started pacing again. The rest of the SUN remained silent.

"We need to find the uncle," he said, finally. "He knows *everything*."

"What about the other kid?" asked a pie soldier in the second row.

"That annoying boy doesn't know *anything*!" Chuckles shouted.

"What about that doohickey he was carrying?" asked a peanut soldier.

"Doohickey?" asked Chuckles. "You mean his magnifying glass? That's nothing special."

"No, sir," said Sergeant Shellshock. "When I was in the park in Mopti, I heard the kids talking about a *hand*-something-or-other. I think they used it to escape."

Chuckles thought about this for a moment and stared at his hand. He looked up at the soldiers again.

"A *hand*-something-or-other," he said thoughtfully. "With our luck, it's some kind of . . . *super weapon*."

"Super weapon?" asked a pie clown in the back row.

"He said 'super weapon'!" another peanut clown hollered.

Murmurs filled the bunker. The SUN began talking to one another about a super weapon.

Chuckles sneered at his soldiers.

"SUN-down!" he shouted.

Instant silence. Everyone stood at attention.

"I need a volunteer," he announced.

Quack-quack!

The giant woman's shoes echoed as she pushed her way to the front.

"Not you this time," said Chuckles, looking up at her. "This job calls for someone . . . stealthier."

She quacked back to her place in the formation.

"Meeeeee!" a high-pitched, squeaky voice rang out. "Pick meeeeee!"

A balloon shaped like a hand wiggled high above the second row.

"Good," said Chuckles. "Come with me, Major Helium."

A soldier in a checkered bodysuit pushed his way through the ranks. He wore a leather cap and goggles. Rainbow suspenders held a silver canister to his back.

Chuckles walked with the balloon soldier to the exit tunnel. He paused and looked back at the rest of the SUN.

"Listen up," he told them. "With those smelly ninjas gone, I thought it was safe to ride the magtrain to Seattle. But that's not the case. Nobody goes there again without my permission."

He looked at all the faces in the crowd. Heads nodded in unison.

"Wait for Major Helium to find out where the uncle is. Then we'll go and get him . . . together!"

The SUN cheered. And sneezed. And cheered some more.

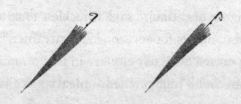

CHAPTER FORTY-TWO

PLAN, PUG, PARASOL

Samantha hopped off the conveyor belt and landed beside Nipper. Slidewalking was getting easier. The pug started squirming, so she let him go.

"Wruf," Dennis yapped as he plopped onto a cement floor.

The bark, already amplified by his plastic cone, echoed loudly in the chamber. Samantha followed the sound as it bounced around them and slowly faded. They stood at the bottom of a concrete silo. Metal scaffolding rose from the center of the chamber, filling most of the cylindrical space. Flights of stairs zigzagged up to the top of the metal structure.

"One, two, three, Peru," said Nipper, counting flights.

At the top of the third flight of stairs, a metal bridge extended to an open doorway. Light streamed in, along with the noises of a busy city.

"Ready, Sam?" Nipper asked, pointing at the steps.

"Almost," she answered. "Hand lens, please."

Samantha held out her hand. While Nipper passed her the magnifying glass, she used her other hand to pull the umbrella off her shoulder. She raised it high above her head and popped it open with her thumb. Holding the magnifier at arm's length, she closed one eye and peered through the lens with the other.

"Just what I thought," she said, and snapped the umbrella shut.

She was getting much better at figuring out the lines and shapes on the Plans. This, plus taking the time to prepare for their journey, made her feel confident. She was becoming an explorer. A true explorer.

"You're becoming a show-off, Sam," said Nipper. "A true show-off."

"Just wait," she replied. "It gets better."

Together, they climbed the stairs.

"I've had a lot of time to think about this," said Samantha as they marched up the metal steps. "All those nights we spent listening to Uncle Paul, what did he tell stories about the most?"

"The Great Wall of China," said Nipper.

"Okay, that's correct," she said. "But the slidewalk doesn't go to China. What's the *other* amazing place he talked about all the time?"

"A mountain city called Machu Picchu," Nipper answered, waving his hands and imitating their uncle's voice.

He stopped imitating Uncle Paul and wrinkled his forehead.

"Is that in Lima?" he asked.

"No," she said. "But we're close. It's in Peru, and we're on our way."

When they cleared the second set of stairs, they stopped at a landing.

Across from the stairs was a wide, round hole, ten feet in diameter, in the concrete wall. A thick steel cable came out of the hole and connected to the scaffolding. Samantha leaned over the edge of the landing, tugged on the cable, and peered into darkness.

"What's this for?" asked Nipper.

Samantha shrugged and shook her head.

"I haven't the foggiest idea," she said. "But let's keep going."

She pulled out the Peru guidebook. "I spent a lot of time studying the Plans and matching things up with this guide. I think I've found out a way to get to Machu Picchu in style."

They continued up the stairs.

"Are you sure we're headed in the right direction?" Nipper asked, looking back at the huge, dark hole.

Samantha stopped and took out the purple sunglasses. She put them on and looked around the silo.

Big yellow letters, each twelve inches high, pulsed on the concrete. They formed a message from the top of the chamber to the floor below:

Y
E
S
!

K
E
E
P

G
O
I
N
G
!

Samantha took off the glasses and put them back in her purse.

"Yep," she answered.

At the top of the scaffolding, they walked across the metal bridge, through the doorway, and into a small, square nook. They stood in a drainage pit with a metal screen overhead. A short ladder was bolted to one of the cement walls. Nipper went first, pushing the screen open when he reached the top. Samantha hooked the Plans over her shoulder, picked up the pug, and climbed. At the top of the ladder, she passed the pug to Nipper, joined them on the surface, and closed the screen behind her.

The scene couldn't have been more different from the market in Mali or the temple in Indonesia. They stood in a square plaza. Green patches of grass, dotted with palm trees and benches, surrounded a bubbling fountain.

Ornate buildings faced the plaza on all sides. Many were painted yellow, with white trim. Others were made of white stone. They were decorated with bell towers, flags, sculptures, and elaborate balconies.

"This is the Plaza Mayor," said Samantha. "The historical center of Lima."

From where they were standing in the plaza, they could tell that Lima was a bustling, modern city. Office buildings and apartment towers stretched in every direction. Taxis and buses clogged the streets. Horse-drawn carriages shuttled tourists about.

People walked through the plaza wearing everything from T-shirts and business attire to military uniforms and jogging suits.

A couple walked by wearing knit caps and ponchos crisscrossed with red and blue patterns. It reminded Samantha of the traditional Peruvian clothing shown in the guidebook.

She opened the book to a map of Lima and studied it. Then she looked across the plaza.

"The Government Palace," she said, pointing to one of the white stone buildings. "The train station is just a few blocks that way."

"I can't help but notice the fountain over there," said Nipper, gesturing toward the center of the plaza. "Do you need me to go poke something in the nose?"

"Not this time," she said. "Just pick up the dog and come with me. I have a plan."

Nipper grabbed Dennis and followed.

She waved to the driver of a horse-drawn carriage.

"A la estación, por favor," she said.

The driver smiled, hopped off the carriage, and helped Samantha inside. He nodded at Nipper and waved for him to climb in, too.

"Impressive," said Nipper, sliding beside her with Dennis on his lap.

"Not really," she said. "I did my homework this time."

Nipper shuddered. Then his eyelids started to droop. His head tilted forward. His breathing slowed. He let out a soft, croaking groan, like an old wooden door swinging slowly on its hinges.

"Not *school* homework, silly," she said. "I meant that I took time to learn about Lima and to practice some Spanish phrases. I just told the driver 'To the train station, please.'"

"Oh . . . okay," said Nipper, shaking off his homework-triggered sleepiness.

"You see, I have a plan," she added, and smiled.

The carriage pulled away from the plaza and the horse trotted forward along with the cars and buses. As they traveled through the city, hotels, museums, and palaces passed by.

According to the map in the guidebook, the station was only eight blocks away. They had been in traffic for at least ten minutes and they had only gone four blocks.

"Should we have walked?" asked Nipper.

"Just enjoy the ride," said Samantha. "I have a plan."

They arrived at the train station and headed up the stone steps. A woman in a uniform stood at attention. She smiled as she watched them climb the stairs. As they were about to enter the station, however, she held out a hand and pointed to a sign beside the open door.

NO SE PERMITEN PERROS

Nipper looked at Samantha.

"What's that about?" he whispered.

"It says 'No dogs allowed,'" she answered. "But don't worry. I've got a plan."

She picked up Dennis and cradled him like a baby. Then she looked at the guard with wide, soulful eyes.

"Are you trying to look like a chinchilla?" whispered Nipper.

"Shush," she said quickly, and turned back to the woman in the uniform.

The guard, looking pleased, smiled at her.

"*Por favor?*" Samantha asked, as sweetly as possible. "*Él es mi precioso bebé.*"

The guard smiled again.

"Your Spanish is *so* good, young lady," she said warmly. "I don't know why you're having trouble un-derstanding . . . *NO DOGS ALLOWED!*"

The woman shouted the last words and slammed the door.

Nipper waited for Samantha to speak.

She blushed.

"Do you still have a plan?" he asked.

"No," she said slowly. "But I have an *umbrella.*"

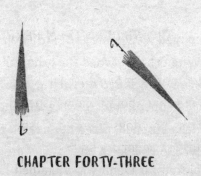

CHAPTER FORTY-THREE

PLAN B

Nipper handed Samantha the magnifying glass. To-gether, they studied the Super-Secret Plans. Between Peru's slidewalk line and the drawing of Machu Picchu, they saw a rectangle. It had a row of tiny squares inside and geometric patterns in each corner.

Samantha smiled, handed the magnifier back to Nip-per, and closed the umbrella.

"It's time for *plan B*," she said. "Walk with me."

They left the train station. Dennis trotted happily behind them.

"B as in *back* to Seattle?" Nipper asked.

"Cold. Try again," she said.

"B as in *bus*?"

"Still cold," said Samantha.

She scooped up Dennis and carried him across a busy avenue. When they reached the other side, she dropped him, and they continued on their way.

"*Boat?*" Nipper asked, looking left and right.

Samantha stopped, tilted her head, and stared.

"Really? Do you see a boat anywhere?" she asked.

Soon they were back at the Plaza Mayor.

"B as in *building*?" he asked.

"You're getting warmer," she answered.

They walked to the center of the plaza. Samantha waved her hand at a row of ornate buildings across the street.

"*Balcony!*" Nipper shouted.

"Red hot," she said.

Samantha took out the purple sunglasses and put them on.

"Give me a second to find the special one."

Turning slowly in a circle, she gazed at each building. Nipper watched.

"Aha!" she said.

A small three-story building, sandwiched between a museum and a hotel, faced the plaza. On the second floor, a rectangular balcony stuck out over the sidewalk.

Bright yellow letters flashed in the windows:

P S S T

A glowing arrow pointed to a staircase.

"Can I see?" asked Nipper.

"Not yet," said Samantha. "Pick up the pug, please."

She led Nipper to a crosswalk and across the street.

"Okay, here," she said, and gave him the glasses.

"Cool," said Nipper, staring up at the balcony.

He handed the glasses back. She put them on and led Nipper and Dennis through an arch and up a flight of stairs to the building's second floor.

Samantha saw a wooden door on the far side. It had a pulsing yellow knob. She crossed over to the door.

"In here," she said, holding it open for Nipper and Dennis.

They entered a narrow rectangular room, paneled with dark wood. It had the same dimensions as the balcony on the front of the building, but it faced an alley in the back. Four red velvet chairs faced the windows, looking out onto the alley.

Samantha sat down on the far-right chair. It was soft. She set her backpack and umbrella on the chair beside her. Nipper helped Dennis onto the next chair and took his place on the far left.

They sat in their comfy chairs and stared out the window . . . at nothing. Except for the soft sound of Dennis panting, the room was quiet.

"So," said Nipper. "Not much of a view, eh?"

Samantha noticed a wire cable stretched above the

windows. She stood up, reached out, grabbed the cord, and tugged.

Clang! Clang!

A bell sounded twice.

Samantha sat down again quickly as the door behind them slammed shut. Then the rectangular room dropped like an elevator. They watched the alley rise away as they sank beneath the city street. A layer of asphalt went by, followed by bricks, stones, and dirt. They touched down in darkness.

Small overhead lights switched on. At the same time, the four puffy seats pivoted ninety degrees to the right.

Clang! Clang!

They started moving again. The room had become a narrow train car, with Samantha seated up front. They gathered speed and rolled forward.

It was dark and a little bumpy, but the soft red velvet chairs cushioned the ride.

A bright dot shone ahead of them, and they rolled out into sunlight.

Samantha checked the umbrella in the seat behind her. She double-checked to make sure the glasses were in her purse. Then she sat back and enjoyed the ride.

They rolled up a steep hill and through another long tunnel, and coasted down into a valley.

Samantha couldn't decide if they were riding in a "balcony bus," a "cabin coaster," or maybe a "closet car." She knew it wasn't actually important, but she had fun trying to invent just the right name.

"Yes! Yes! Yes!" Nipper shouted.

"What's going on?" asked Samantha.

"I found snacks under the seats," he said triumphantly.

Samantha turned around and saw him waving a bag of crackers and a small bottle of sparkling water.

The "terrace-train" banked around a mountain lake. The views were breathtaking.

"You did it, Sam," said Nipper, tossing a cracker to Dennis. "We are traveling in style."

Samantha smiled, then sank into her chair again and admired jagged peaks blanketed with trees. Farther in the distance, the snow-capped Andes shook hands with the sky. The "locomotive lounge" rolled on.

"Hey, Sam," Nipper called to her. "Can I tell you something?"

"Sure," she answered.

"Lately, I've been worried you were turning into Buffy," he said. "But it's pretty clear to me you're becoming Uncle Paul."

"What do you mean?" She couldn't tell if it was a compliment or not.

"You're getting better at finding secret ways to travel," he said. "But your instructions to *me* are getting trickier, too."

"Maybe," she replied. "I suppose I got a little carried away with the plan B game."

Her ears popped as they moved higher into the mountains.

"That's all right," said Nipper. "But sooner or later, you're going to have to make a decision."

"What decision?" she asked.

"Will you wear orange flip-flops or big rubber boots all day, every day?"

CHAPTER FORTY-FOUR

HAPPY TRAILS

Clang! Clang!

The bell rang twice. The "super-secret power porch" coasted into a tunnel and stopped. The door creaked open. Samantha jumped out of her chair, grabbed her umbrella and backpack, and headed out the door. Nipper fished the last cracker from the bag and popped it in his mouth.

"On my way," he called, mouth full of cracker. He picked the pug up and followed Samantha into a dusty room.

It was more of a shack than a building, just one small room with a bare wooden floor and a table, but no chairs. A half-closed door to the outside was about ten feet away. Samantha was standing at the table. Nipper crossed the room to take a look.

The table displayed brochures in many languages. Next to them, the label on a glass jar read *"Depósite un nuevo sol."* Colorful Peruvian banknotes filled the jar.

Samantha sorted through the brochures on the table.

"Here's one in English," she said, and held it up for him to see.

PERU'S SKY STRONGHOLD TRAIL
RELAX ON OUR MOUNTAIN

Samantha took a nuevo sol bill from a side pocket of her backpack and stuffed it into the jar. Then she took out the purple sunglasses and stared at the front of the brochure.

"PSST," she said. "Room."

Nipper wasn't sure what his sister meant, but she was doing just fine with the reading and the puzzling.

"You search for clues. I'll search for crackers," he said.

He pushed open the front door and headed outside to look around.

A narrow porch ran the length of the building. They were far from any city now. A dense forest surrounded the small shack. He could hear a river nearby. He leaned left and right and saw green mountain peaks through the foliage. A gravel trail began at the front steps and disappeared into the forest a few yards away.

"Are you still reading, Sam?" he called. "I see a trail out here."

A man wearing a bowler hat and a green T-shirt sat on a stool nearby, reading a book. A few feet away, a llama stood, tethered to a post, in a patch of grass.

Nipper waved to the man.

"Is your llama friendly?" he asked.

The man looked up from his book.

"Oh yes, *señor*," he said, nodding. "Very friendly."

Cautiously, Nipper walked up to the animal. He stroked the side of its snout gently and began to pet its fuzzy neck.

"Howdy, llama. How's your mama?" he said in his best I'm-so-charming voice.

The llama craned its neck back and gave Nipper an evil look. It was chewing something, slowly.

Pfftooie! Pfftooie!

Two slimy globs of spit hit Nipper in the chest.

Nipper looked down at his shirt. "Oh, yuck!" he said. "What kind of gross—"

Wham!

The llama cut Nipper off with a sideways swing of its head, bashing him in the shoulder and knocking him to the ground.

"Ow!" he shouted. "That really hurt!"

Nipper was starting to stand up when the llama bent down and chomped the bottom of his pant leg. Growling and snorting, it lurched left and right, dragging Nipper across the gravel.

"Stop it!" Nipper shouted.

He looked over and saw Samantha exiting the shack. She was still reading the brochure.

"Help!" he yelled.

The llama let go of Nipper's pants and reared back on its hind legs.

"Hrrarr!" it bellowed.

Whomp!

The llama's front hooves struck the ground, narrowly missing Nipper's face. It began to kick. Nipper struggled to shield his face from the shower of rocks and dirt.

The llama made a long, horrible, slurping sound as it worked up another batch of spit. Then, as if chang-

ing its mind, it suddenly bent down and clamped onto the bottom of Nipper's shirt. It growled as it tugged, dragging him farther away from the porch. Jerking its head back, the llama tore Nipper's shirt off completely!

"Sammy!" Nipper shouted.

"Hrrarr!" the llama roared, shaking its head with the shirt in its mouth.

It reared up on its hind legs again.

Dennis scampered out of the building.

"Wruf! Wruf!" he yapped.

The llama stilled and gazed down at the little barking dog. It dropped the shirt, stepped to the other side of the hitching post, bent down, and nibbled on some grass as if nothing had happened.

Samantha rushed over to help Nipper.

"Wait here," he told her.

Trembling, Nipper staggered up to the man on the stool.

"I . . . thought," he panted, "you said . . . your llama . . . was friendly."

"He is, *amigo*," said the man, looking very serious.

He adjusted his bowler hat.

"But *that* is not my llama," he added.

Samantha grabbed Nipper's arm before he could respond. She pointed to the gravel trail.

"That connects with the main road to Machu Picchu," she said.

She pulled Nipper's New York Yankees sweatshirt from her backpack and handed it to him. Nipper put it on. Then he looked back at the man on the stool.

"Here," said Samantha.

She handed him the two remaining granola bars. He paused and put them in the front pocket of the sweatshirt. He looked over at the man in the bowler hat again.

"Hand me the other bag of clown seasoning," he muttered.

She shook her head and pointed to the trail.

"Forget about that guy," she said. "There are too many clowns in this world. You can't season them all."

CHAPTER FORTY-FIVE

ONE OF A KIND

Samantha and Nipper shared the trail to Machu Picchu with visitors of all ages. Her umbrella came in handy as a walking stick. Dennis padded happily behind them. For an hour, they zigzagged across the face of the towering, tree-covered mountain. Up ahead, stone walls and buildings glistened in the sun.

Samantha took out the brochure she'd purchased in the shack.

"'Machu Picchu is an ancient abandoned city in the mountains of Peru,'" she read. "'It was built around the year 1450 and served as a royal estate for the rulers of the Inca Empire.'"

The path up the mountain turned again and Samantha and Nipper followed the hikers, crisscrossing the side of the mountain for the fourth time.

Samantha turned over the brochure. A simple map of Machu Picchu covered the back side. There were a dozen landmarks labeled on the map, with names such as "Royal Tomb," "Funeral Rock," and "Ritual Fountain." Along the side, four additional landmarks were listed. Dotted lines pointed to their locations on the diagram:

> Palace
> Sun Temple
> Sacred Rock
> Terraces

Samantha smiled and stopped walking.

She called to Nipper to join her and they waited until a group of visitors passed them on the trail.

"Read this," she said, pointing to the map.

" 'Palace, Sun Temple, Sacred Rock, Terraces,' " said Nipper. "So what?"

"No," said Samantha. "Read the *first letters*."

" 'P . . . S . . . S . . . T,' " said Nipper. "Coincidence?"

Samantha shook her head. She took out the purple sunglasses and examined the brochure again. In a blank corner of the map, a bright yellow dot blinked.

They let other visitors pass as they made the last two zigzags up the mountain.

"The Lost City," Samantha said, sounding satisfied.

The ruins of Machu Picchu stretched out before them—and above. The ancient citadel was surrounded on three sides by steep mountain peaks. Row upon row of stone terraces formed the mountain city. They looked like giant green staircases. Jagged ruins of stone buildings dotted the wide landings.

Samantha gave one big nod and let the sunglasses drop into place. Along a stretch of the wall, at the edge of a terrace, the letters *PSST* flashed. An arrow pointed to a gap in the wall. Samantha removed the glasses and checked to make sure no one was paying attention to her and her brother. She led Nipper across the grass to the wall. Most visitors wouldn't notice the narrow strip of grass, and if they did, they wouldn't see anything special.

Together, they walked through the gap. To their left, stairs hugged the wall leading down to a small terrace. Samantha and Nipper descended the stairs, where they found another opening, and went inside.

They stood in a square room, four feet across. It was more of a box than a room, really. Light poured in from the entrance behind them, illuminating the dark, pitted stone wall before them. It was covered with small carvings, though they were hard to make out on the stone. Most of the carvings were too old and worn to identify.

"I think this one's an animal head," said Nipper, pointing to a shape.

"Possibly," said Samantha. "This one *might* be a boat."

They spent a few more minutes staring at and touching the wall. They got nowhere.

"Hang on," said Samantha, putting on the glasses once again.

A large yellow arrow appeared on the wall. It pointed to the left.

"Let me see," said Nipper.

She handed him the glasses.

He nodded, turned left, and started examining the blank wall in front of him.

Samantha didn't turn. On a hunch, she put both hands on the old stone wall, applied pressure, and pushed sideways.

The whole wall slid to the left—revealing a new wall!

A *really* new wall. This wall was shiny and smooth, with crisp, clear images carved in neat rows. A tiny silver dot sparkled between every two carvings. Samantha guessed there were more than a thousand pictures covering the wall from ceiling to floor.

"Super-sneaky," said Nipper, handing the glasses back to her.

They stared at the wall and saw fish, birds, monkeys, and spiders. They saw mountains and boats. There were lots of faces and symbols.

"There's a llama," said Samantha, pointing to an animal drawing.

"Did you hear something squeak?" asked Nipper, changing the subject. He turned to another part of the wall and examined it.

They searched the pictures, looking for patterns. They tried to find hidden letters. They tapped on carvings.

And yet, nothing.

Samantha put on the purple glasses again and stared. Still, nothing.

While she was putting the glasses away in her purse, a smell caught her attention. Cumin. She stared at Nipper's ankles. He was still wearing the tube socks from six days ago.

"Seriously?" she asked. "You haven't changed your socks in a whole week?"

"I used up all my other socks," he answered. "What else could I do?"

"Laundry," she said.

Nipper bent down and pulled up his smelly socks. A shiny coin clattered onto the floor.

"My lucky nickel!" he shouted.

Samantha rolled her eyes. She thought again about Uncle Paul's advice when he'd given the nickel to Nipper.

"She's *one of a kind*," he'd said. "Look after her." Then he'd winked at Samantha.

"'One of a kind,'" Samantha repeated. She waved for Nipper to come look at the wall with her.

They studied the stone carvings once more, keeping

track of images that repeated. There were dozens of identical bird carvings, and many matching boats. They found pairs of fish and triplets of lizards and frogs. Samantha counted at least five stars and six monkeys. There was only one llama.

"One of a kind," said Nipper.

"Yep," said Samantha. "Now *look after her.*"

Nipper leaned in and stared at the llama and the tiny silver dot next to its tail.

"Wait," he said, taking out his magnifying lens. "Let me see."

They both peered through the glass at the dot. A woman's head surrounded by stars sparkled in the center of a silver circle.

"Feeling lucky?" Samantha asked, and waved her hand under the circle. "Go ahead."

Nipper pressed the silver dot. They heard a click and a squeak and the dark stone began to slide away, revealing an opening to another room. A round room.

"*PSST,*" said Nipper, pointing up.

A banner hanging from the ceiling read:

PARTNERSHIP
OF
SUPER-SECRET
TRAVELERS

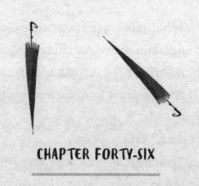

CHAPTER FORTY-SIX

JERK IN THE BOX

"I seeeeee you," said Major Helium in a high, squeaky whisper.

The balloon soldier crouched on the narrow terrace. A pile of colorful deflated balloons lay in the grass by his feet. He adjusted his cap and peeked around the stone doorway to see what the boy and girl were up to now.

They hadn't noticed him all the way from Lima to Machu Picchu. Now he was on the ground and up close. He didn't want to be seen—not before he found out their secrets.

With their backs to him, the kids stood looking through an open doorway. Major Helium adjusted his nose ball. The boy smelled awful.

The clown took a long, skinny gray balloon from his

pocket. He inflated it quickly and held it up to the terrace wall. It matched the color of the stones nicely. He began to rub the balloon against his sleeve.

"Static eeeeeee-lectrici-teeeeee," he sang softly.

He held out the balloon, reached into the room where the kids were now standing, and poked the boy's sweatshirt pocket. He wiggled the balloon and pulled it back carefully.

A rectangular object clung to the balloon. He squinted and saw that it was brown and bumpy. It looked a lot like oats, nuts, and honey. It was very sticky. If all the other clowns of the SUN hadn't warned him, Major Helium would have thought it was a granola bar. But he knew better.

"The super weapon," he snickered to himself, "is mine."

He delicately separated the dangerous, deadly device from his balloon and slipped it into his pocket.

The kids stepped forward into the space beyond.

Major Helium crept into the small square room and continued spying.

"I'm getting read-eeeeee," he squeaked as he took out a new balloon.

This one was narrow and black. He didn't inflate it. Instead, he stretched it way back and aimed through the doorway at the girl.

He waited . . . and listened.

CHAPTER FORTY-SEVEN

THE MIDDLE

The world surrounded Samantha and Nipper.

Charts and diagrams covered the walls. A few maps showed the whole planet. Some world maps included Antarctica and the North Pole, while others did not. Samantha and Nipper did not see a clear pattern. Drawings of continents appeared alongside maps of individual countries or cities. Scattered throughout, there were close-ups of buildings.

Samantha noticed several maps of the United States and a close-up of Seattle.

Drawings of people and objects completely covered the walls around the maps. It reminded her of the treasures in the Seattle magtrain station, but there were many more things to see here. The pictures also reminded

Samantha of the hieroglyphics in the Temple of Horus in Egypt and the carvings on Borobudur in Indonesia. But these pictures featured modern people from all over the world.

Samantha studied the kids and adults, and some pets, too. People worked and played, read and shopped, danced and painted. In one picture, a girl rode a bicycle. In another, a boy kicked a ball. Someone cooked, stirring a pot. Someone played a saxophone. There were too many pictures to count. Together, they described what the world was all about. Nothing seemed out of place or unusual. Nothing seemed strange.

"We are in the middle of everywhere," she said softly.

A pedestal with a shiny metal basin on top sat in the center of the room.

Hundreds of holes and tiny cracks peppered the ceiling. Light trickled in from above, scattering dots and dashes on the stone floor. Most, however, hit the basin on top of the pedestal. The basin shimmered with a thousand tiny pinpricks of light.

"Is that a birdbath?" asked Nipper.

"No," Samantha answered. "Watch."

Without thinking about it, she walked to the sparkling basin and flipped it over. It became a shiny silver dome.

The light filtering in hit the dome and reflected

around the chamber. The maps lit up with lines and squiggles, dots and shapes, spirals, waves, and arrows.

Lines connected countries. Dots highlighted cities. Circles and arrows revealed patterns everywhere. It was like the Super-Secret Plans, but arranged neatly in order, and projected clearly onto maps of the whole world.

"This is it," said Samantha. "All the secrets in one place."

"Holy cow," said Nipper, staring at her.

"What?" Samantha asked. "You're not even looking at the walls."

"You, Sam," he replied. "The way you just figured out how to light up the maps. That was amazing."

Samantha smiled as she and Nipper began to explore super secrets all over the world.

"Look," she said, pointing to Asia. "There's a path that follows the Great Wall of China."

"Look at all the things that connect to Seattle," said Nipper.

He walked to a map of the United States, found the West Coast, and tapped on a twisted line that looked like a crazy straw.

"I wonder what this loop-de-loop means," he said.

Samantha rested her hand on a map of Italy as she peered around the entire room.

"I want to visit every amazing place on planet Earth," she said. "I want to meet people everywhere."

Nipper looked at the East Coast of the United States, searching for New York City.

"Okay, Sam. I'm about to prove something," he said. "You should have helped me push Cleopatra's Needle. I really think there may have been a secret— Hey. Look at this!"

He pointed to a note taped over Manhattan.

"Here," he said, handing the paper to Samantha. "I'm sure you'll think this is interesting."

The drawing showed a pair of big rubber boots.

She frowned. She had forgotten about Uncle Paul for a moment. His mysterious messages and confusing clues. She didn't think it was interesting. It was maddening. From "Watch out for the RAIN" to "I'll see you in June," Uncle Paul had produced endless unhelpful hints. Nothing made sense, and suddenly Samantha felt angry.

"That's it," she said. "This has got to stop."

"Stop what?" asked Nipper. "And did you hear something squeak?"

"Just listen to me for once," said Samantha.

She scrunched the note into a ball and flicked it across the room. She walked over to Nipper, put her hands on his shoulders, and shouted.

"Uncle Paul was in New York City and he's probably still there! Our family's going back in a week, and I'm going to find him! I'm putting my foot down!"

"Foot?" asked Nipper. "Where?"

"Can you stop clowning around for once?" she said.

"No, Sam," he replied. "Foot . . . wear?"

She stared at him blankly.

"Footwear," he repeated. "As in . . . *June footwear.*"

She stared at him, but not blankly.

"Oh . . . my . . . gosh, Nipper," she said at last. "You're right. Uncle Paul is still in Buffy's apartment. He's in the June footwear room. He told her 'See you in June!'"

Ka-snappp!

Something lashed Samantha's leg.

She howled in pain.

CHAPTER FORTY-EIGHT

BAR NONE

"Yow!" Samantha cried, and spun around.

She almost fell down. Her leg felt like it was on fire.

A clown in a checkered body suit stood in the door-way, grinning at her and Nipper. He wore a leather cap and goggles, and the same red nose as all the other SUN clowns. Rainbow suspenders held a silver tank to his back. A long, black, uninflated balloon dangled from his hand.

"So," he said. "New York Ci-teeeeee."

He spoke in a high squeal, like a chipmunk. He stretched the balloon, pulling one end over his shoulder.

"I have your super weapon, boy," he said.

Samantha and Nipper shot each other confused looks.

"And now I know where to find your weeeeeeeeeeird uncle," he squeaked.

He aimed the other end of his balloon at Samantha's face.

"Now hand over your umbrella," he said slowly, "and no one gets hurt."

Samantha stepped between Nipper and the clown.

"Who are you?" she asked. "And why are you bothering us?"

Nipper pulled a granola bar from his sweatshirt pocket. He looked at it longingly, closed his eyes, and dropped it to the floor.

"Wruf! Wruf! Wruf!" barked Dennis from the small square chamber outside the map room. Maybe he saw a moment for greatness. Maybe he wanted to save his friends. Or maybe it was just that he heard the sound of a fresh granola bar hitting the floor.

He bolted through the doorway, ignoring the strange clown who blocked his path, and sped toward Nipper and the dropped snack. The balloon clown blocked the doorway. Dennis aimed straight for the space between the clown's legs, but his plastic cone was too big. Instead of going through the clown's legs, he knocked him off his feet. The clown went flying and landed hard on his rear. The silver tank clanged on the stone floor.

Samantha pulled the umbrella from her shoulder and whacked the man on the hand.

"Eeeeeek!" the clown squealed, and dropped the balloon.

He sneered up at Samantha. Then he tucked his legs in and rolled out of the room.

Nipper started to run after him, but Samantha grabbed him by both shoulders.

She heard a hissing sound—louder than a Komodo dragon but quieter than a water rocket. Cautiously, Samantha stepped forward, Nipper at her back, and peered into the square room. Nothing.

Samantha inched across the little room and peeked beyond to the terrace. The clown was gone!

"Up there!" shouted Nipper, pointing to the sky.

The clown was floating high above them. In each fist, he grasped the strings of a dozen colorful balloons.

"I know your seeeeee-crets," his piercing, squeaky voice rang out.

They watched him rise higher and higher, until he vanished over the Andes Mountains.

Samantha's leg still stung. A lot.

"You are very noble," she told Nipper.

"Huh?" he asked.

"You sacrificed your granola bar to save me."

"Sure," he replied. "Of course, I knew I still had one bar left."

He reached his hands into the front pocket of his Yankees sweatshirt.

"Clowns can hurt you," Nipper added. "But hunger can— Wait. No, no, no!"

He looked at her helplessly.

"Sam! I lost my last granola bar."

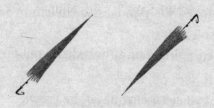

CHAPTER FORTY-NINE

NO PLACE

Samantha gazed around the *PSST* map room again. Cities, countries, and continents twinkled, crisscrossed with dots and lines. She could easily spend months—maybe years—exploring the secrets here. But she didn't have any time for it today.

"That creepy balloon clown knows about this room," she said. "Soon the whole SUN will know. And about Uncle Paul, too. Let's get moving."

Nipper gulped.

"Do we have to go back to that shack?" he asked.

"I guess so," she answered. "But I'll keep you safe."

Nipper rubbed his shoulder where the llama had bashed him with its head.

"I don't know, Sam," said Nipper. "That llama's trouble."

He raised a finger and rubbed the red bruise on his cheek.

"A lot of places are trouble," he growled.

Nipper started pacing around the room, pointing at maps. He stopped under Norway.

"Sure, there are a lot of places to visit," he said pointing upward. "But we keep winding up in strange places in the middle of nowhere."

Samantha took a deep breath. She wasn't mad at her brother—this time. But he still had a lot to learn.

"No place is the middle of nowhere," she said, smiling.

"You're acting like Uncle Paul again," said Nipper.

"Yes. I am," she replied. "Because it's true. A lot of places seem strange before you visit and learn about them. But take a closer look. Those places are never strange to the people who live there—just to you."

She smiled again and added, "Strangers are just people you haven't met."

She looked at the drawings—people around the world living their lives, doing interesting things.

"Everything Uncle Paul said was really true," she mused.

She spotted a drawing of two people. One waved a stick. The other sat by a large string instrument.

She smiled.

"Cello lessons," she said, and pushed.

Something clicked, and a section of the wall slid open. It revealed a small compartment about a foot wide and a foot deep. A glass bottle, filled with pebbles, stood in the center. The word *Lima* was etched on the outside.

Samantha put on the purple glasses. Yellow letters glowed in the compartment behind the bottle.

NO PLACE IS IN THE MIDDLE
OF NOWHERE.

CHAPTER FIFTY

A FINE LINE

Samantha stared at the message for another moment. She took a deep breath and held it. Then she looked at the map of Peru above the compartment and exhaled.

"This is your lucky day, after all," she said. "You get to skip that llama."

On the map was a stone fortress surrounded by three mountain peaks.

"We're here," she said, pointing.

Nipper came closer to investigate.

A dozen straight lines extended from Machu Picchu, fanning out in every direction. Each line had a different number. Samantha pointed to a short line that ended on the coast.

"Lima," she said. "Six."

She picked up the bottle and shook six pebbles out into her hand. Then she put the bottle back in its place and stowed her sunglasses in her purse.

"Follow me," said Samantha.

She took one last look at the map room, knowing she would be back. She flipped over the silver dome and led Nipper out the door, through the square room, and outside to the terrace.

Dennis was already outside. Since the clown had left he'd been searching the area for more snacks. They saw him trotting busily around the narrow, grassy field, scraping the ground with his cone as he sniffed for granola crumbs.

"I hope you enjoyed my snacks, old pal," Nipper muttered.

"Wruf," Dennis replied.

"Come on," said Samantha. "Make yourself useful and help me find six holes."

"Holes?" asked Nipper. "What size?"

Samantha smiled.

"Larger than chocolate chips, but smaller than malted milk balls," she replied. "This big."

She held up one of the pebbles and winked.

They walked up the stairs, through the gap in the wall, and headed across the clearing.

"Aren't you going to use the Plans?" Nipper asked.

She shook her head.

"I checked before we got here. This secret isn't on the umbrella," she answered.

She pointed to a set of stone steps.

"Whatever we're looking for, it's probably on a ledge," she said.

They reached a small, grass-covered landing. A large, flat stone rested in the center.

"Here we go," she said, pointing to the slab.

It had six small holes in a row.

One by one, she dropped a stone into each hole. As she dropped the last pebble, she heard a sound like the crack of a whip, followed by a loud *twang*.

"Take a closer look over there," Nipper said, pointing above a wall at the edge of the landing.

The mountain peak beyond wobbled.

Samantha squinted. In the distance was a wide chair, the kind you'd see on a ski lift. Painted to look like the mountain and sky behind it, it was almost invisible. It rocked ever so gently from a sky-colored cable.

"Double-triple super-sneaky," said Nipper.

They climbed onto the chair. Then Samantha leaned forward and picked up Dennis. She wedged the pug between herself and Nipper and pulled a long seat belt across their laps.

"Get ready," she said, snapping the buckle. "Now, rock."

She and her brother leaned forward and back several times. The chair started swinging. They felt it drop a few inches. The chair moved along the cable.

"Hang on," said Samantha.

The chair eased out over the edge of the terrace—and kept going. Looking down, Samantha saw a sheer cliff plunging hundreds of feet into a ravine. She took a deep breath and stared straight ahead. The chair rolled along, dangling from the cable and rocking gently as it carried them through the sky. Slowly, she let out her breath, relaxed, and started to enjoy the ride.

The ruins of Machu Picchu shrank behind them as they sped through mountain peaks and clusters of pine trees. They raced over lakes. Far below, a locomotive chugged along, hugging a hill. They quickly overtook it.

Faster and faster, they zoomed down the cable. Samantha scanned the sky for clowns or balloons. She didn't see any.

"The SUN is going to know about Uncle Paul and New York City," she said. "And the *PSST* map room."

"They'll use the secrets to launch an all-out rubber pancake and circus peanut attack," said Nipper.

Samantha thought about the ridiculous clowns as she gazed far ahead.

She smiled.

"That clown was too busy bothering us and looking for Uncle Paul," she said. "I don't think he even noticed the map room."

"He didn't take a closer look at things," said Nipper, nodding.

"That's right," she answered. "And we just sent all of the SUN to the same place at the same time. I think Uncle Paul wanted that to happen."

Lima appeared in the distance.

"And you know what else?" she asked.

Nipper shook his head. The breeze blew his hair wildly.

"I don't think these ridiculous clowns are our biggest danger," she said.

"Really?" said Nipper. "But they're so awful!"

"When things get awful, have a waffle!" she said.

"Give it a rest, Sam," said Nipper. "You're trying a little too hard to be like Uncle Paul now."

They zoomed into a tunnel. Their ears popped, and everything went black.

"You there, Sam?" asked Nipper.

"Where else would I be?" she replied.

Overhead, sparks flew from the cable. The tunnel glowed orange. Gradually, a light appeared in the distance, growing larger as they started to slow down.

Poppity-poppity-poppity-poppity-poppity-pow!

They rolled across a long stretch of cable wrapped in plastic packing material. Smoothly, the chair slowed to a crawl.

"Bubble wrap," said Nipper. "Is there any problem it can't solve?"

They glided into the round cement chamber with the scaffolding. They were back beneath the plaza in Lima. Samantha stepped onto the landing. Nipper passed her the pug.

"It's almost time for our family trip to New York City," she told him. "And opening night of *Scarlett Hydrangea's Secret of the Nile*."

"Wait," said Nipper. "Now you're looking forward to seeing Buffy's play?"

"Not really," she replied. "But I think that's where we'll block the SUN."

Together, they slidewalked home.

Lucy the Elephant

"Lucy the Elephant" is a six-story, elephant-shaped building in Margate City, New Jersey, two miles south of Atlantic City.

In 1881, James V. Lafferty built the unusual structure to promote real estate sales and attract tourists.

It is constructed of wood and tin sheeting.

Lucy is the oldest surviving roadside tourist attraction in America.

Do NOT attempt to slide down the inside of Lucy's trunk!

It is a dead end. You will get stuck at the bottom and you'll have to wait for someone to come and fish you out.

The elephant's left front leg, however, conceals a ladder down to a *kogelbaan*, or marble run, station. Enter this secret chamber and climb into a giant marble.

You can roll from here to a dozen locations across the United States, including Seattle, Washington, and Mitchell, South Dakota.

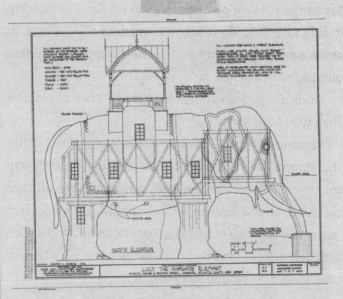

CHAPTER FIFTY-ONE

HUNGRY, HUNGRY HISSES

Samantha had big plans to sleep in on Sunday morning. It didn't happen. There was too much to think about. By seven a.m., she was sitting at her desk, tapping her yellow notepad with a pencil.

"Ridiculous clowns," she muttered. "They're probably already in New York City."

Samantha started to worry about the SUN. Then she stopped and smirked. Maybe the antisocial clowns couldn't travel by airplane. They'd have to take off their big shoes. They'd have to get unbearably close to security guards and squeeze in beside sweaty nervous flyers, babies with full diapers, and thrifty passengers with homemade tuna and onion sandwiches.

She took out a map of the United States.

"Reedsburg . . . Sauk City . . . ," she said, tapping all the towns around Baraboo. "Wisconsin Dells."

A brand-new set of loud noises exploded from Nipper's room. They included snapping, bumping, and furniture-scraping-on-the-floor. She tried to ignore all of it, but the sounds made it hard to concentrate on secrets and clowns. She sighed heavily, picked up volume III of *The World's Deadliest Animals,* and headed into her brother's room.

Nipper was standing on his bed, clutching a pillow. The Komodo dragon stood close to the bed, reared back on its hind legs. Its tail swished wildly and thumped against the floor as it snapped at him.

"Easy, Kym," said Nipper, waving the pillow.

The lizard hissed and snapped again, narrowly missing his feet.

"She seems a little peppier today, don't you think?" asked Nipper.

It snapped again. This time, one of its fangs caught Nipper's pillow. It jerked its head, ripping the fabric and tearing a big chunk of foam from the pillow.

"Uh-oh. I'm going to want that back at bedtime." Nipper leaned over the edge of the mattress and tried to pick up the pieces, but the lizard snapped again. He pulled his arms close to his body and stood back up.

Samantha didn't walk any farther into the room. She waved volume III of *The World's Deadliest Animals* at her brother.

"I read about your stupid lizard," she said. "In captivity, Komodo dragons eat every other day."

Nipper watched her, trying to follow what she was saying.

"As far as I can tell, that horrible lizard is eating a dozen chinchillas over the course of every two days," she continued.

"So?" Nipper asked.

"So!" she fired back at him. "As soon as all the chinchillas are gone, that monster is going to eat Dennis . . . then you . . . then me!"

"Me before you?" asked Nipper. "How come?"

"I was guessing he'd eat from smallest to big— That's not important!" she shouted. "I don't really know how long it takes before it eats us all."

Her brother looked puzzled.

"Hold on!" he said. "I know just the guy who can figure this out."

Before Samantha could stop him, he hopped off the bed, zipped around the Komodo dragon, skipped past her, and sped down the stairs.

She looked at the lizard. It looked back, wiggling its long, forked tongue as it slowly crept toward her.

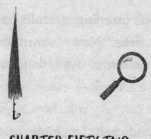

CHAPTER FIFTY-TWO

OF MATH AND MENUS

"Hi, Pop," said Nipper, walking through his father's open office door. He made sure not to step on any stray papers or tools or electrical gadgets.

George Washington Spinner sat at his desk, holding a small, glowing lightbulb in one hand and shining it on several lengths of wire.

"Oh. Hi, son," he said, putting down the gadget and looking up from his work.

"I've got a puzzle I'm trying to solve," said Nipper. "It has numbers in it."

"Ah . . . math," said Mr. Spinner.

"Let's pretend," said Nipper. "Suppose someone sends me eighteen candy bars twelve times. And then I start eating six candy bars every day."

His father was listening carefully and nodding.

"After four weeks," Nipper continued, "how long do I have until I run out of candy bars, and I get hungry and start eating Dennis—I mean, other things in the house?"

"Hmmm. Candy bars," said Mr. Spinner.

"Yeah," said Nipper. "I know you're all about light-bulbs. But maybe some of that science works with chocolate, too."

Mr. Spinner looked at him thoughtfully. Nipper was sure this was not the time to bring giant lizards into the discussion. His dad calculated in his head. He took out a pencil and wrote on a pad of graph paper.

$$STARVING = (CHOCOLATE \times WEEKS / 2) - (EAT \times 3.5)$$

"Eighteen times twelve is two hundred sixteen," said Mr. Spinner. "Subtract thirty-five times five and you'll have almost a week remaining. To be precise, you'll have exactly—"

"Okay. That's what I thought," said Nipper. "Thanks."

"On the other hand," Mr. Spinner said, "if you want a solution based upon the number of calories per hour, then you should multiply—"

"No, we're good," said Nipper, cutting him off. "I've got what I need."

He started to leave.

"Just a minute, son," said Mr. Spinner. "What's gotten you into problem solving? I've always thought you didn't enjoy calculations or analysis."

"I've developed a deep love of math," Nipper said. "I've decided that numbers and equations are almost as interesting as major league baseball."

Mr. Spinner raised his eyebrows. He had a strange expression on his face. Nipper left him in his office and skipped up the stairs.

"Okay, Sam," Nipper called. "I think I've got it figured out."

The door to his sister's room was open.

"You still around?" he asked.

He leaned in through the open door but saw no one. He heard movement across the hall. He headed to his room and pushed the door open. Samantha was standing beside his desk.

"Dad helped me calculate," he told her. "A dozen chinchillas times twelve minus ten times five. Eighteen times ten is one hundred eighty. We have at least a week before we need to worry about—"

Samantha stood motionless, with her hands at her sides. The Komodo dragon slinked slowly around her in a tight circle.

"A dozen is *twelve*," she said through clenched teeth. "Not eighteen."

"Oh. Yeah. Of course," said Nipper. "I haven't seen any chinchillas around for a while. I figured something was up."

"They're all gone," she said softly.

The lizard stared up at Samantha. It swayed its head from side to side with its mouth open, hissing like a big, leaky balloon.

CHAPTER FIFTY-THREE

THE LOST ISLAND OF THE DINOSAURS

The Komodo dragon looked at Nipper and snapped twice. It turned back to Samantha and opened its mouth wider than before. Globs of clear goo dripped from the top row of its razor-sharp teeth.

Samantha reached for volume III of *The World's Deadliest Animals*. She picked it up and held it out in front of her. The lizard eyed the heavy, leather-bound book and shrank back. She opened the book and quickly flipped through the pages.

" 'What to do when a Komodo dragon gets hungry,' " she read.

The lizard sprang forward and clamped its jaws on the open book. It hissed and shook its head, shredding the pages. Bits of cover fell to the floor and strips of paper filled the air.

Samantha knelt, keeping an eye on the lizard as she gathered torn pages. With the book still sandwiched in its mouth, the creature hissed and moved toward her.

"Read the book!" Nipper shouted.

The lizard jerked its head around to look at him. The mangled book slid from its mouth and fell to the floor with a heavy thud. The lizard began to move toward Nipper.

Nipper had backed into the corner and was sitting on the floor. He looked up at the Komodo dragon looming over him. The creature stood on its hind legs. It hissed loud and long. It sounded like someone had turned on a fire hose.

Samantha held a pom-pom of shredded paper in her hands.

"'Talk to it. Say something in a low, calm voice,'" she said, trying to read the ball of torn pages. "Wait! No! That's for Kodiak bears."

Nipper closed his eyes. In a low, calm voice, he began: "In a mist-covered ocean far, far from home, there's a mountainous island where dinosaurs roam. While it sounds like a place to amuse and delight you—watch out! Hungry creatures are waiting to bite you."

The lizard froze. It stared at Nipper with cold black

eyes. It closed its mouth and sank to the floor. It dug its sharp gray claws into the wood and inched closer to Nipper. It rested its head on his lap and began to purr as it slowly closed its eyes and drifted off to sleep.

Samantha stood still, stunned. She listened to the gentle purring of the Komodo dragon in her brother's lap. Was the creature dreaming of a mountainous island far, far away?

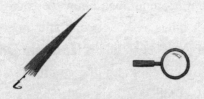

CHAPTER FIFTY-FOUR

NUTRITION

"What on earth is going on in here?" said Dr. Suzette Spinner, Doctor of Veterinary Medicine, as she marched through Nipper's open bedroom door.

The rodent-and-lizard expert looked around. Nipper's chair rested on its side. Cardboard, leather, and paper littered the floor. A chunk of a pillow lay in the corner. A faint smell of cumin hung in the air.

Something colorful caught her eye. It might have been a picture of a cardinal or a starling at one point, but she couldn't be certain.

Samantha stood with her back to a wall, silent and motionless. Across the room, Nipper sat quietly in a corner, petting an adolescent Komodo dragon.

"Come with me," said Dr. Spinner.

"But, Mom," said Nipper, pointing to the huge lizard resting on his lap.

"He'll be fine," she said. "We're just going to the kitchen."

"*He?*" asked Nipper.

Dr. Spinner nodded.

Nipper looked down at the lizard.

"Well, Kym can be a boy's name, too," he said.

The lizard tilted its head sideways and stared up at him with one eye. Its tongue flicked twice before it lowered its head and began purring again.

"Come with me *right now*," Dr. Spinner repeated firmly. She walked out of the room and down the stairs.

Nipper moved the lizard's head gently to the floor and stood up.

Samantha followed her mother quickly. She heard Nipper shuffling down the stairs behind her.

Dr. Spinner went to the kitchen and got to work.

"Hand me the sifter," she told Samantha.

"What are you making, Mom?" Samantha asked.

"Just help, dear," she replied.

Samantha reached into the cabinet beneath the counter, found a metal flour sifter, and handed it up.

Dr. Spinner set it beside an open bag of cornmeal and a jar of wheat germ. She picked up a handful of Dennis's dog food and dropped it into a large mixing bowl.

Dennis sat under the kitchen table, watching her intently as she cracked an egg into the bowl, added the cornmeal and wheat germ, stirred a few times, and poured the mixture onto the waffle iron.

Nipper walked into the room.

"Doesn't anyone remember that I give speeches about *nutrition for very large lizards*?" she asked. "Remember the Exotic Pet Expo? When we left you two alone and drove to Tacoma? On a Saturday three months ago? When those smelly people dressed in black tried to steal my umbrella?"

Samantha and her brother looked at each other. *Now* they remembered!

After two minutes, Dr. Spinner popped open the waffle iron and used Uncle Paul's waffle tongs to lift out a steaming round waffle—bright orange with brown spots.

"Really, Samantha. I thought you took a closer look at things," she said, and tossed the waffle on the floor.

Plastic cone tapped on kitchen tiles.

Dennis crept forward from underneath the table. He pointed his cone at the waffle and sniffed cautiously. He stretched his tongue beyond the edge of the cone and licked twice.

Like a bolt of lightning, the Komodo dragon zipped into the room and hissed at Dennis. The pug jumped back from the waffle and fled. The lizard bit into the orange disc and devoured it ravenously.

Dr. Spinner tossed a second waffle on the floor. The Komodo dragon grabbed it and exited the kitchen. Her children stood beside the table, quietly listening to the *thump-thump-thump* of a very large lizard heading up the stairs, back to Nipper's bedroom.

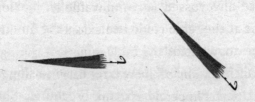

CHAPTER FIFTY-FIVE

STRANGERS ON A TRAIN

"You know, everyone," Nipper announced suddenly during dinner that night, "the United States is chock-full of amazing things between Washington and New York."

"Very true," said their father. "In fact, if you were to draw a line between here and any one of the contiguous states, you'd intersect—"

"That's not my point, Dad," Nipper said, cutting him off. "What I'm *trying* to say is . . ."

He cleared his throat.

"I've always wanted to see the most beautiful treasures of North America from a *train*."

"Really," Samantha said sarcastically. "Since when?"

"Since always," he answered loudly, making sure everyone at the table could hear. "It's the America you can't see anywhere else."

Samantha could tell he was repeating a slogan from one of Uncle Paul's old Amtrak brochures. She shot him a quick I-know-you're-up-to-something glance. But it was okay. She had a plan now, and it included letting her brother convince their parents that he was suddenly interested in a scenic train ride. Buffy's play was set to open on Broadway in ten days. They'd arrive in time to see the show, stop the SUN, and—hopefully—find Uncle Paul.

"Let's see the most from coast to coast," Nipper called out. "There's something about a train that's magic."

After an hour of listening to Nipper recite slogans for train travel, their parents agreed to exchange their plane tickets for seats on the Empire Builder from Seattle to Chicago, and then to New York City on another train—just as Samantha hoped they would. The three-day ride would get them to Buffy's play on opening night.

"Let's take the train and see what we're missing!" Nipper declared triumphantly.

"Stop it, already," she whispered. "That's the motto for British Rail International. Uncle Paul got that brochure from England."

Samantha went to work preparing for the trip to New York. Between finishing the school year and packing for the big trip, the week was going to pass quickly. She decided that the umbrella needed extra security for their train journey. Nipper handed her a trombone case. Uncle Paul had given him an antique trombone last year, but it went missing immediately.

"How does somebody lose a trombone?" asked Samantha, pressing the umbrella into the velvet-lined case.

Nipper shrugged.

"Trust me, it happens," he answered.

Later that evening, Mrs. Spinner saw Samantha lugging the case and gave her a puzzled look.

"It's extra security for our trip to the big city," she said, opening the case to show her mom.

"You carry that red umbrella everywhere you go, dear," said Mrs. Spinner. "Why do you want to lock it up now?"

Samantha closed the trombone case and fiddled with her sunglasses, pretending not to hear her.

"Did you pack Word Whammy!, Mom?" she asked, changing the subject.

The Spinners had arranged to leave Dennis with the Bogden-Looples during their trip. Nipper promised to lock the Komodo dragon in his bedroom, along with two hundred nutrient-rich waffles.

On Saturday, they drove to King Street Station to board the train to Chicago. Mr. Spinner carried the large suitcase that he shared with Mrs. Spinner.

"I threw in an extra flashlight," he told everyone. "Just in case of a lightbulb emergency."

"And I've got three days' worth of snacks and card games for the trip," Mrs. Spinner added, holding up a tote bag.

Samantha saw the letters E-P-E on the side of the tote and tried to place what they meant.

"This is from the Exotic Pet Expo," said Mrs. Spinner. "Remember? Your father and I went to Tacoma a while ago? We left you and Nipper alone and—"

"I remember it now, Mom," she answered quickly.

Samantha brought her own small bag, her purse with her glasses, and the trombone case. Nipper dragged an enormous duffel bag. Samantha didn't say anything as she watched him struggle to stuff the oversized bag in the rack above his seat.

"I decided to plan all of my outfits for the trip this time," he told her.

Samantha didn't respond. She just looked at him—and his ridiculously huge bag.

"Well, maybe *I'm* starting to sound like Buffy," Nipper said.

"I smell a lot of dishwasher detergent," said Samantha.

"There weren't any more spices left in the house for clown seasoning," he answered. "That's all I had."

"How much did you bring?" she asked.

Nipper held up a half-gallon plastic bag of sparkling blue powder.

"Okay," she said. "*That* might actually be helpful."

The train started moving and they took their seats.

The Empire Builder set out through the Cascade Mountains, passed Spokane, Washington, and rolled through northern Idaho into Montana. Everyone agreed that Glacier National Park was one of the most beautiful places in the country.

After western Montana, the land outside their windows flattened. Passing from Havre, Montana, to Fargo, North Dakota, they crossed the Great Plains and miles of wide-open prairies. As they approached Minneapolis–St. Paul, Minnesota, the views became more rugged, and more urban, too. By the time the Empire Builder moved through Wisconsin, cities, farms, and factories rolled by.

"Pay attention," Samantha whispered to Nipper when they stopped at Wisconsin Dells. Suddenly, the train seemed crowded.

"This ride is getting very odd," said Mrs. Spinner. "I keep thinking I hear ducks quacking."

Nipper glanced at Samantha nervously.

"I agree one hundred percent," said Mr. Spinner. "On my way back from the dining car, I heard a man shouting, 'A granola bar is not a super weapon,' over and over again."

Samantha shot Nipper a look, too.

"Then the angry man took off his top hat and pointed it at his friend," their dad continued. "I think I saw a boxing glove come out of the hat and punch his friend in the face."

"How odd," Mrs. Spinner repeated.

"Everything gets odd when you add clowns," Samantha whispered to Nipper.

"Okay, Sam," Nipper replied. "That is *exactly* something Uncle Paul would say."

Samantha smiled. She liked that she was learning from Uncle Paul. Then her smile faded a little. She didn't like the idea of wearing flip-flops or rubber boots all day, every day.

CHAPTER FIFTY-SIX

START SPREADING THE NEWS

Aunt Penny waited for them outside the train station in New York City. She sat behind the wheel of a six-door stretch limo—bright purple, of course.

"How on earth did you find this vehicle, Penelope?" Mrs. Spinner asked.

"It was easy," she answered. "You've just got to practice taking a closer look at things."

"Did you hear what she just said?" Samantha whispered to Nipper in the way, way back of the long car.

Samantha looked way, way forward. Was Aunt Penny staring at Nipper in the rearview mirror? She had a worried expression.

"Don't trust N T," Nipper said to Samantha.

"Shhh," she replied.

Samantha had so many things on her mind. Worrying about Nipper worrying about their worried aunt couldn't be one of them.

When they arrived at Buffy's sky castle, Aunt Penny offered to help Samantha carry her trombone case. Nipper handed her Samantha's suitcase instead.

"Don't trust N T," he whispered to Samantha.

Nathaniel waved for Mr. and Mrs. Spinner to take the main elevator. Samantha could see he was working very hard to force a smile. When she and Nipper tried to follow, he held up a hand and stopped them. As soon as the elevator doors had closed, he scowled and led them down the hall to the loading dock.

Nipper followed him into the freight elevator, dragging his enormous duffel bag behind him. It trapped Nathaniel in the elevator with him, leaving no more room for Samantha.

"Yo . . . I mean, *you* . . . can take the main elevator," Nathaniel called grouchily to Samantha. "Just this once."

As soon as she entered the apartment, Samantha rushed to the June shoe room. The vault door stood wide open. She leaned in and saw at least a thousand pairs of shoes. Other racks were piled high with handbags, hats, and scarves. She saw a tie-dye paint station and a motorized spin art wheel. But there was no sign of Uncle Paul.

"It's nice to see you're finally getting interested in fashion," said Buffy, walking up behind her.

Buffy wore a shiny gold headdress. Samantha thought her sister looked like an Egyptian queen—in a kindergarten Halloween parade.

"But these things are all mine," said Buffy, pulling Samantha back into the hallway.

She slammed the door and led Samantha out to the living room, where everyone was waiting.

"I'm glad you've all demanded that I let you come to my play," said Buffy.

Samantha started to sigh heavily, but her sister snapped her fingers loudly.

"Yes," said Buffy. "It has been quite an adventure, but that licensed theater critic is wrong. *Scarlett Hydrangea's Secret of the Nile* has survived for nine days of previews, and tomorrow is opening night."

"That's wonderful, dear," said Mrs. Spinner.

"For the first night, I sent free tickets and private limos to all the fashion editors and boutique owners within one hundred and six miles of New York City," explained Buffy. "They all got gift bags with glow-in-the-dark lipstick, electric Egyptian earrings, and fluorescent rainbow unicorn necklaces. It was a huge, shiny, sparkly, lit-up success!"

"Interesting," said Mr. Spinner.

"Before the next night, I hosted a thirteen-course

banquet, including steak-stuffed turkey, lobster pot pie, flan, a chocolate waterfall, designer burritos, and a make-your-own deep-fried ice cream sundae bar. Everyone was so stuffed after that enormous meal that they fell asleep during the performance—and they stayed for the whole show!"

"Okay, not bad," said Nipper.

"Then I lined Broadway and Forty-Sixth Street with bouncy houses," Buffy continued. "Everyone who came to play tumbled into theater seats without realizing it. It took six days until the authorities figured it out and hauled away all the inflatables."

Samantha had to admit that was kind of hilarious, but she didn't say anything.

"I made tonight *free surfboard night*," said Buffy. "The theater will be packed, even though most of the audience is going to be wearing hideous wet suits."

"It will be a seaworthy night," Nathaniel said, and nodded in agreement.

"Tomorrow, show number ten, is my big opening night," Buffy announced. "And it's going to be sold out!"

"How did you manage that?" asked Samantha.

"It was easy," said Buffy. "I bought all the tickets to every other play in town. I also reserved seats to every concert, dance recital, museum lecture, and poetry reading. If anyone wants to see a show in New York tomorrow, they have no choice: the only available tickets will be for *Scarlett Hydrangea's Secret of the Nile!*"

"That's wonderful, dear," said Mrs. Spinner. "Now let's get some rest."

Beaming with pride, Buffy led them to their rooms.

It turned out there was a fabulous guest suite on the second level of the apartment. Mr. and Mrs. Spinner moved into the suite, which had a double-triple king-sized bed, a private movie theater, a kitchen, a pool table, ten pinball machines, a swimming pool, a sauna, a steam room, exercise equipment, a robot massage chair, and an old-fashioned movie theater popcorn popper.

"How come we didn't see this amazing room before?" asked Samantha.

"Sorry," said Buffy. "The door was blocked by the Micronesian flag."

"Where did that giant blue thing go?" asked Nipper.

"I ordered Nate to take it to the theater," Buffy answered. "It clashed with several of the $167,000 rugs."

"I . . . I . . . ," said Nathaniel, "couldn't fit it in a cab. I had to go a-carryin' it for twenty blocks."

He made a slightly pained expression and rubbed his lower back.

"A hoist . . . would have been useful," he muttered.

He reached down to touch his knee. Then he noticed Samantha and Nipper watching him and shot them an *extremely* pained expression. Both kids tried to look around, pretending not to notice.

"Walk this way," said Nathaniel, and stumbled to the escalator.

Samantha and Nipper followed him to the stables on the apartment's first level, but they were empty. The beds were gone.

"Your sister used the mattresses to make a mermaid cave for the play," Nathaniel said dryly.

"What are we supposed to sleep on?" asked Nipper.

Nathaniel pushed a stack of old newspapers into the room and began to tear them into strips. He made two huge piles of shredded paper.

"This is a lot more comfortable than it looks," said Nipper, sinking into one of the piles.

Samantha stood watching as her brother shut his eyes and drifted off to sleep. She decided she might as well give it a try, too. She adjusted her pile of newspaper strips and hopped on top.

Deep in the shredded paper, they both slept soundly through the night.

In the morning, Mr. and Mrs. Spinner met them by the stables, ready to leave with them for Yankee Stadium. Even though Nipper wasn't officially the owner of the team anymore, they seemed excited for him. After hearing him talk about it for months, they were all going to see the Yankees play baseball.

"Aren't you going to wear your team shirt and hat, dear?" Mrs. Spinner asked Nipper.

"I forgot to pack them, Mom," he answered.

Samantha looked over at her brother's giant duffel bag. He smiled at her and shrugged.

"What about your matching pants and shoes, son?" Mr. Spinner asked.

"I guess I should have planned my outfits for the trip more carefully," said Nipper. "Whoopsy, look at the time."

He led them all down the hall and into the elevator.

Before the elevator doors could close, Buffy reached in and held them open.

"You'll all be at the show tonight, won't you?" she asked.

The elevator doors beeped, trying to close.

"It's *my* big night, and *you* won't want to miss it," she said.

"That's why we're all here, dear," said Mrs. Spinner.

Samantha didn't say anything. She definitely was not there to see her sister sing, dance, or do whatever secret Nile things she was planning to do.

"Fine," said Buffy. "Don't be late."

She let go of the doors and they slid shut.

The Spinners headed uptown. Samantha kept her sunglasses in her purse and carried the umbrella without the trombone case. Before they entered the subway, she raised the umbrella over her head, opening and closing it several times.

"I'm sure there's a point to what you're doing, dear," said her mother.

They rode the subway uptown. As soon as they exited the station, Samantha raised the umbrella over her head and opened it again.

"Come on, Sam," said Nipper. "My Yankees need me."

She closed the umbrella, looked around, and followed the family to their seats in the stadium to watch the Yankees face the Boston Red Sox.

"I count only thirty-seven people today," said Mr. Spinner as he looked around at the seats. "I think this team could use Buffy's help selling tickets."

"Oh, George," Mrs. Spinner replied. "You'd be sound asleep before you finished half of your deep-fried ice cream sundae and lobster pot pie."

"Well, I *know* this team could use Dennis's help catching some of those balls," said Mr. Spinner.

Nipper sat in his seat and gazed longingly at the owner's box. Samantha sat next to him, opening and closing her umbrella.

"Don't distract my Yankees," he told her.

Samantha closed the umbrella. She looked at Nipper. For a boy with the attention span of a chinchilla, he could certainly focus on a baseball game.

The Yankees set a new major league record with eighty-three errors in a single game. The Red Sox won, 19–0. The Spinners filed out of the stadium with the dozen other people who had stayed until the end.

"I'm sure there must have been a point to that game," said Mrs. Spinner.

Samantha started to open the Super-Secret Plans again.

"And be careful with the point of that umbrella, too, dear," she added.

Samantha stopped. She made eye contact with her mother. Was she onto her plan? She smiled meekly and closed the umbrella.

They rode the subway to Grand Central Station together, before Mr. and Mrs. Spinner announced they were heading to the American Museum of Natural History.

"You really should come with us to see the new pangolin exhibit," said Samantha's mother.

"True," said her father. "There's something very special about those creatures and the way that they defend themselves by rolling into a—"

"Sorry," said Samantha, cutting him off. "I have many places to go and a lot to do!"

They agreed to split up, have dinner separately, and meet at the theater at showtime.

"It would be nice if you didn't open and close your

umbrella during the performance," Mrs. Spinner said to Samantha.

"Don't worry, Mom," she answered. "I'll leave it at Buffy's apartment."

Samantha and Nipper spent the rest of the day wandering around Manhattan. They walked through Midtown and down to Greenwich Village. She kept the sunglasses stowed in her purse, but every four or five blocks, she stopped to open and close the umbrella.

"Don't tell me," said Nipper. "You have a plan."

Samantha thought she heard a duck quack, but she wasn't sure. There were too many buses, cabs, and chattering people.

"Let's keep going," she said.

They reached Buffy's place by six p.m. Nathaniel had prepared a stew with spicy fish, yams, and rice. Once again, it was delicious. And once again, he scowled at them throughout the meal.

After they ate, Samantha changed into nicer clothes for the theater, but she still wore her sneakers. She didn't bother saying anything to Nipper about changing his outfit. She was pretty sure he didn't have any more clothes in his duffel bag. She secured her umbrella in the trombone case and buried it under shredded newspaper in the stables.

It was time to leave for the theater. Nathaniel watched them closely, so they went straight to the freight elevator. Samantha pushed the button for the ground floor and started down.

She smiled.

"Did you have time to digest?" Samantha asked.

"Sure. I guess so," said Nipper. "Why?"

They reached the ground floor.

"Because my plan is to . . ."

The doors slid open and they faced a loading dock full of clowns.

". . . run for it!" she shouted.

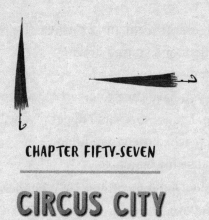

CHAPTER FIFTY-SEVEN

CIRCUS CITY

Samantha and Nipper bolted from the freight elevator. The dozens of clowns were busy juggling and practicing bad jokes, so the breakout took them by surprise. The Spinners ran through the crowd, zipping between stunned pie throwers and shocked pancake flingers. They threaded through the hallway, into the lobby, and onto the street before the first peanut gun fired. They heard screams and a few quacks, but didn't look back.

They ran for fifteen blocks, zigzagging around traffic. Finally, they stopped to catch their breath. Up ahead, the lights of Times Square blazed. Far in the distance, amid the giant video screens and sky-high advertisements, they spotted a neon sign.

"Stick with me," said Samantha, heading toward the sign.

"I'm right behind—waitaminute, waitaminute, waitaminute!" Nipper yelled.

Near them on the sidewalk, a vendor stood next to a colorful food cart. In rainbow letters, the sign above him read:

SUPER

FRUITY

SLUSH

BOMB

Samantha was about to pull her brother away from the cart, but she paused and let him speak.

"Make it super-hot cinnamon," said Nipper.

Samantha smiled

"It's your tongue, buddy," said the vendor.

He picked up a bright red bottle and squirted it three times into a big plastic cup. Then he turned to start his ice grinder. While the man chopped ice into snow, Nipper reached over the counter and grabbed the bottle. Samantha didn't say anything. She just stood and watched as her brother squirted an almost-full bottle of super-hot cinnamon syrup into the cup.

The vendor turned back, mixed in the ice, and snapped on a lid.

Samantha heard ducks quacking in the distance.

"That'll be ten dollars and five cents," said the vendor, sliding a straw through a hole in the lid.

The sound of quacking ducks grew louder.

"Sam," said Nipper, "can I have my ten-dollar bill back?"

Samantha reached in her pocket and found the bill she had been holding since Peru. She handed it to the vendor. The duck sounds were getting close.

"It's five more cents, buddy," said the slush vendor.

Nipper reached into his pocket and took out his lucky nickel. He held it up between his thumb and index finger.

"Hmmm," said the man, staring at the coin. "That looks valuable. I wonder how much it's worth?"

"Hurry up," said Samantha. The quacks were too close. She could hear clown shoes slapping.

"Maybe I should throw in a souvenir crazy straw," said the vendor. "That might make it a fair agreement or trade. Don't you—"

Samantha snatched the coin from Nipper and slapped it on the cart.

"Oh, just take it!" she said, and grabbed the double-triple-cinnamon Super Fruity Slush Bomb. She shoved the drink into Nipper's right hand. Then she grabbed his left hand and began to drag him along the sidewalk.

"No *backsies!*" the vendor shouted behind them.

"What did you do that for?" Nipper asked as they moved through the crowd.

"You were going to lose it anyway," said Samantha.

Nipper didn't have time to answer. He followed her as they ran down Broadway and turned right at Forty-Sixth Street. In the distance, the word *Hydrangea* flashed in neon. They sped up the street and stopped outside the entrance to the theater. People waited in line to enter. Five women in blue dresses with pom-poms, aprons—and bright red nose filters—watched the crowd from across the street.

"Pie clowns," said Nipper. "Yuck."

One pointed at Nipper and grinned.

"Who wants the blue plate special?" she croaked, adjusting her blue wig and raising a pie tin piled with gray goo and squirming blue shapes.

The other four pie clowns smiled, too. They adjusted their frizzy blue wigs and raised their horrible pies.

"This way," said Samantha.

They ran past the theater, sped to the end of the block, and turned south. Halfway down the block, they made another left turn, into an alley. A sign swung from a pole.

SCARLETT HYDRANGEA'S
SECRET OF THE NILE
LOADING DOCK
NO PARKING
EXCEPT FOR UNICORNS

From the other end of the alley, an army of clowns approached.

Samantha and Nipper ran straight for the loading dock behind the theater. Samantha grabbed the handle of the enormous sliding door and pulled, but the door was locked.

"SUN-set!" a voice called out.

She and Nipper turned. One hundred horrible clowns of every ridiculous type surrounded them. Pie clowns, peanut clowns, pancake clowns. The tall woman with the gold crown towered in back.

A clown in a top hat cleared his throat. His immense shoes slapped the street as he stepped forward and adjusted his nose ball.

"Excuse me, young lady," he said, in a creepy, fake-friendly voice. "If you'd be so kind as to tell us where your uncle is vacationing, then I'm sure we could—"

"Watch out!" one of the clowns screamed, as loud as any clown has ever screamed. "The boy has the super weapon!"

Samantha looked over at Nipper. He was sipping his cinnamon slush. His fingers covered two of the words on the cup, which now read:

SUPER

—

—

BOMB

"Stop them," yelled another clown, "before they destroy us all!"

Whap! Wham! Crunch! Crack!

A storm of pancakes and candy peanuts sailed at Samantha and Nipper. A rubber flapjack smacked her ear. Hotcakes flew by and thumped against the door behind her. Steel-rimmed johnnycakes splintered wood.

Clank!

A johnnycake hit the metal roller at the top of the door, snapping it in half. The door wobbled and tipped backward, then fell straight into the building.

"Go!" Samantha shouted to Nipper.

Nipper didn't have to be told twice. He ran through the open doorway, with Samantha on his heels, into the back of the theater.

CHAPTER FIFTY-EIGHT

OPENING NIGHT

"I'm glistening, now start listening!" shouted Buffy Spinner, adjusting a green glow-in-the-dark rhinestone atop her pink Egyptian headdress. "Charles von Bagelhouven is coming to see the show tonight, and we're going to prove him wrong. *Scarlett Hydrangea's Secret of the Nile* will survive!"

She strode up and down before the rows of dancers, musicians, makeup artists, accessory porters, and stagehands. Onstage behind her, a scale replica of Cleopatra's Needle towered over a shiny golden sphinx and two neon-pink pyramids.

She turned to admire the set. It was extremely realistic. Hopefully, the audience wouldn't notice that there weren't any unicorns.

"We are going to make it, everyone," said Buffy, waving a silver scepter in the air triumphantly. "We've encountered obstacles along the way, but we're not going to miss opening night!"

The makeup artists standing closest to Buffy watched the shiny stick nervously. It had an ibis head on the end, with a long, pointy, razor-sharp bird beak.

Like a royal Egyptian warlord, Buffy walked among her subjects and inspected the neon-pink hooves of the bright blue giraffes. No one would know they weren't real animals. The human pyramid of bagpipe players was so stable it could stand forever. The monkey seemed calm.

"Nothing strange will happen," she continued. "The Great Flingo will keep his cool. There will be no surprises. Not tonight."

She slid her dangerously sharp scepter into a scabbard on her belt. Everyone in the cast and crew breathed a sigh of relief.

"Nothing, absolutely nothing, happens tonight without my permission," she ordered.

Suddenly, loud banging and smashing sounds filled the air. Everyone looked around. With a thundering crash, the loading dock door fell forward.

Samantha and Nipper raced inside, chased by a mob of angry clowns.

CHAPTER FIFTY-NINE

BROADWAY SMASH

Samantha and Nipper burst into the building.

"Watch out for the SUN!" Nipper screamed.

Rubber pancakes and candy peanuts rained in behind them.

Buffy stood backstage, surrounded by her cast and crew. She was dressed like a weird combination of a princess, an elf, a lighthouse, and an Egyptian royal court jester. She was busy whining at the cast and crew about unicorns.

"Buffy!" Samantha yelled, as she and Nipper pushed through a line of extremely fake-looking giraffes. "Call the cops!"

Everyone turned to see what was happening, without Buffy's permission.

Clowns poured in through the open door.

"Get the girl!" someone screamed.

"Get that boy, too," shouted someone else. "He's so annoying!"

Everyone was confused. The giraffes craned their necks, as the people inside struggled to see what was going on. A human pyramid of bagpipe players began to play. Confusion turned to panic.

Ka-snappp!

A black balloon whipped one of the fake giraffes on its rump.

From inside the costume, someone howled in pain.

All the fake giraffes started to stampede in a way that was very realistic.

"Call the cops!" Samantha shouted again.

"Breeep!" screeched a monkey.

Swi-thunk!

A johnnycake sailed past Samantha's nose and sliced into a mermaid cave made of mattresses.

Samantha grabbed her brother's hand again and ran for one of the stage wings. Ahead, she saw a narrow spiral staircase leading up to the rigging.

All of the SUN was backstage now. As Samantha and Nipper reached the base of the staircase, several clowns pointed at them.

"SUN-burst!" barked the clown in the top hat. "Round up everyone in this theater and—"

"I said NOT TONIGHT!" Buffy screamed at the top of her lungs.

Everyone froze.

Buffy began pointing at everyone with two fingers. Samantha recognized it as the same two-finger point their mother used to calm down rodents, lizards, and children.

"Musicians. Start your fog machines," her sister shouted. "Grab your instruments. Get in the pit and play!" she yelled. "Mermaids. Turn on the lights on your fins and go . . . to . . . your . . . cave!"

Everyone in the production shuffled away quickly and quietly.

With both hands, Buffy pointed to the crowd of stunned clowns.

"All of you," she said. "Stay out of my way . . . until you get . . . a makeover!"

She walked to the curtain, slipped under it, and disappeared.

The orchestra began to play.

"Did she go to get the cops?" Nipper asked.

"I don't think so," said Samantha.

The drone of bagpipes drifted from beyond the curtain.

"Who saved room for pie?" a chorus of voices rang out.

In a V formation, seven pie clowns skipped toward Samantha and Nipper, pans of goo held high.

"Start climbing," Samantha told Nipper. "I'll catch up."

Nipper raced up the staircase and Samantha reached for a large power switch dangling near the wall.

"Order up!" croaked the seven clowns in unison.

Samantha flipped the switch. An engine roared to life.

The pie clowns let loose their volley of greasy pies.

Samantha aimed the wind machine and a great gust caught the horrible desserts, flinging them back at the clowns and splattering them with oily muck.

Samantha turned up the dial on the mighty fan. The clowns sailed across the floor, tumbling under the curtain and onto the stage.

Over the roar of the machine, Samantha heard screaming clowns and wailing bagpipes. Then: *Smack! Smack! Smack!*

From the opposite side of the theater, a dozen clowns flung rubber pancakes at Samantha. She ducked and dodged to avoid the barrage.

"Batter up!" a clown hollered.

Another swarm of fake flapjacks sailed overhead.

Low to the floor, she noticed smoke seeping under the curtain from the stage.

Fire? Samantha wondered.

She sniffed. It wasn't smoke. It was artificial fog. She spotted one of the big black barrels of fog-machine juice from the loading dock at Buffy's apartment.

Smack! Smack! Smack!

Another storm of pancakes sailed past, inches from her head.

Samantha reached forward and grabbed a thick rope hanging from the ceiling. Hand over hand, she pulled, raising the curtain. A dense fog bank billowed in from the stage. It swirled around Samantha.

The pancakes came again, but this time they were way off target.

"No fair!" a clown shouted.

A loud horn honked. Two beams of light cut through the fog. A clown car! Samantha sprinted for the spiral staircase as the tiny car drew near.

A truck engine roared, and a monster truck appeared, emerging from the fog.

"I said NOT TONIGHT!" Buffy yelled from behind the wheel, aiming straight for the clowns.

There was an incredibly loud *crunch* as she rolled the massive pickup truck over the hood of the tiny car, flattening the engine and pinning it to the floor. The clowns seemed okay, but the squashed front kept the car doors from opening. Trapped inside, they pounded on the windows angrily, shouting.

Buffy hopped out of the cab of the truck, walked over to the screaming clowns, and gave them a double-triple super frown. They all went silent. Then she walked to the side of the stage and tugged the rope. The curtain between Buffy and backstage dropped. She was back in front of the audience and out of sight.

Samantha looked at the tiny car. The clowns—at least five of them—started banging on the windows and screaming again. They were stuck for now. She let out a sigh of relief. Then she started up the staircase to find Nipper.

She climbed the spiral stairs so quickly she felt dizzy. At the top, she looked around as she caught her breath. A catwalk stretched across the theater from where she stood. It was a narrow bridge about two feet wide. A few lights hung from it, along with a massive wooden model of the Temple of Horus.

From her perch, Samantha had a view of Buffy's whole show. The stage set featured a gleaming white three-story obelisk. It would have been a very convincing scaled-down replica of Cleopatra's Needle—if neon-pink pyramids, a glittering gold sphinx, and a trio of mermaids dancing around a glowing cave didn't surround it.

She could also see dozens of SUN clowns running around backstage, yelling at one another and pointing up at her.

Nipper stood at the far end of the catwalk. For the first time in Samantha's life, her brother was the least ridiculous person around her.

"Over here, Sam!" he called.

She looked at the catwalk again—wooden planks separated by two-inch gaps. There were no handrails. Samantha took a deep breath. She was afraid to cross. Then she remembered looking down at the mountains around Machu Picchu and realized in an instant that this was nothing. She let out her breath and started to walk.

Crack! Crack! Crack! Crack!

Four peanut clowns stood below her, firing their guns.

Cra-tack!

A candy peanut hit one of the planks in front of Samantha, blasting it away.

Cra-tack!

Another candy peanut hit the bridge and another plank came loose. It dropped to the stage below and banged against something.

"Hey!" shouted a voice. "I'm getting battered!"

Samantha was sure the person was one of the pancake clowns she'd seen in Mali. She kept moving along the catwalk. She passed the model of the Temple of Horus, dangling from the bridge beneath her.

"You forgot to say *duck!*"

Cra-tack!

"Ouchie!" cried another clown.

Cra-tack!

"Wahoo! That hurt!" cried another.

Cra-tack!

"Wagga Wagga!" wailed another clown. "My noggin!"

As scared as Samantha felt, she still took a moment to reflect on the absurdity of these clowns.

Cra-tack! Cra-tack!

The bridge planks were disappearing, and she was only halfway to the other side. In front of her, Nipper watched with a terrified expression. She gritted her teeth and kept walking, taking extra-long steps to avoid missing-plank spaces. More clowns gathered on the floor, thirty feet below Samantha and the disintegrating catwalk. They grinned up at her as they eagerly awaited her doom.

Cra-tack! Cra-tack!

Planks, splinters, and candy peanuts flew by. Even more clowns came to watch.

"Hey, girl," a clown shouted. "Drop by anytime!"

The clown standing beside him laughed as if this was the funniest joke in the history of the world.

Cra-tack!

Samantha stopped walking. The bridge had become unstable. It wobbled each time a plank flew away.

Samantha thought of the tongue depressor suspension bridge her dad had helped her build. The one that the chinchillas chewed. How many more planks could the catwalk lose before it came crashing down?

She knew the entire SUN stood below wondering the same thing.

Samantha looked over at her brother. And smiled.

"Nipper!" she called. "There's a New York Yankees logo on the bottom of your slush cup!"

"What?" Nipper called back. "There is?"

He flipped over his plastic cup and inspected the bottom.

"Liar!" he shouted.

The top came loose. An almost-full bottle of super-hot cinnamon syrup fell thirty feet into the center of the SUN.

The cinnamon explosion sent bright red droplets in every direction, splattering the clowns. Cinnamon mist mixed with artificial fog, forming a spicy crimson tornado. A hot red cloud rolled across the floor.

No red ball nose filter has ever been invented that can withstand contact with a double-triple super-hot cinnamon cloud.

The clowns wheezed. They sneezed and coughed. Some dropped to their knees. Others fell, face-first, on the floor. They rolled, moaned, and whimpered. None remained standing.

Samantha started moving across the catwalk.

"Turn back, Sam," Nipper yelled. "This is a dead end!"

Samantha stopped. "Seriously?" she replied. "You couldn't tell me that before I walked halfway across this death bridge?"

"Which one of us told a big fat lie about the Yankees logo on a cup?"

Samantha held out her hand. Carefully, Nipper crossed to Samantha. When he got to her side, she helped him step over the gaps in the catwalk and they slowly made their way back to the spiral staircase. Before they reached the end of the bridge, they both stopped and looked down. They took a moment to glance at the SUN, still on the floor below.

Quack-quack!

CHAPTER SIXTY

SQUEAKY CLEAN

Samantha and Nipper were only a few feet from the end of the catwalk. The duck-foot clown blocked their path, towering over them. She looked down, seething with rage. She wheezed heavily. A sticky red drop of super-hot cinnamon syrup dangled from a spike on her crown.

There was no way to get around her. Samantha looked back at the wobbling catwalk and then down to the floor thirty feet below.

"Clown seasoning!" Nipper shouted suddenly.

Samantha watched as Nipper pulled out the plastic bag of blue powder. He threw it on the bridge between them and the huge clown. Then he stuck out his foot and brought it down on the bag with a mighty stomp.

The bag didn't break open. Instead, it slipped through a gap between planks and disappeared. Samantha heard a faint thud as it landed on a clown far below.

She saw the tall woman give Nipper a double-triple super-evil look and raise one of her huge legs, aiming a big yellow webbed foot at his face.

Samantha took a deep breath. She leaned in, grabbed hold of the duck shoe, and yanked it from the woman's foot. It quacked once in her hands.

Standing on one foot, the clown tried to snatch the shoe back, but Samantha dodged to her right. The woman lost her balance and fell forward. She crashed onto the bridge, snapping three planks at once.

Samantha and Nipper dove over her to the top of the staircase as the catwalk gave out.

Boards and duck-foot clown tumbled down, taking lights and the Temple of Horus with them, and crashing backstage on top of the rolling, coughing SUN.

A loud creaking sound filled the theater. Samantha looked at the stage in time to see the model of Cleopatra's Needle begin to wobble. Three mermaids noticed it, too, and dove from their lair in the nick of time. The obelisk toppled onto the foam-mattress mermaid cave, crumbling into a thousand pieces.

A ripping, crackling noise rang out. Samantha watched as the glittering Sphinx split in two and collapsed, crushing a pair of neon-pink pyramids. In a matter of minutes the entire set disintegrated. A new cloud rose above the stage—plaster dust, bits of foam, and flecks of gold paint.

"Hey, Sam," said Nipper, tapping her on the shoulder. "If you're not going to say 'That was to get your attention,' can I?"

"I think the moment's passed," she answered.

Just as she spoke, Samantha spotted a man, center stage, rising from the wreckage. Covered in plaster dust, he was white as a ghost.

Calmly, he began to brush himself off. The mermaid trio shuffled over and fanned him with their light-up tails. Dust swirled away.

The man wore a tuxedo T-shirt.

His pants were plaid.

He wore bright orange flip-flops.

It was Uncle Paul!

Samantha gasped. She turned and raced down the spiral staircase. Halfway to the bottom, she spotted Buffy pulling the curtain rope.

"Wait!" Samantha cried, as she reached the bottom of the staircase.

She hopped over a coughing, cinnamon-covered clown and raced toward the stage—but she wasn't fast enough. The curtain dropped. Uncle Paul was gone again!

Buffy poked her head through an opening in the curtain and pointed her deadly sharp ibis scepter at Samantha.

"Stay away from my stage," she barked, and disappeared behind the curtain again. The orchestra began to play.

Samantha searched for another path to the front of the theater. Then she noticed the floor, covered with groaning clowns.

"We've got to find a way to keep them here until the cops arrive," she told Nipper.

In a corner, on the far side of the building, she spotted the rolled-up flag of the Federated States of Micronesia.

"Help me wrap them up," she said.

Samantha and Nipper ran to the giant spool of fabric and began pushing. They rolled it to the middle of the backstage area and lined it up next to the SUN. Together, they grabbed one corner of the fabric, draped it over two clowns, and tucked it beneath them. The clowns were too incapacitated by the cinnamon to argue. Or even to make bad puns. Within minutes, they had the clowns tied up inside knots of blue fabric and white stars.

"There they are!" someone called.

Samantha recognized the voice immediately. It was their mom.

She looked at the loading dock door and saw twenty-two police officers following her parents to the SUN pile. They began to tug at the fabric.

"We've been tracking these clowns for a long time," one of the officers said to Mrs. Spinner. "How did you know to contact us?"

"We were up in the mezzanine," she answered. "I clearly heard my daughter asking for someone to call the authorities."

"Well . . . good job paying attention and listening, ma'am," he said.

Samantha noticed her mom looking around at her family.

Mr. Spinner stood by the big wind machine, inspecting it closely.

Nipper kicked a little gold crown.

"I sure wish more people paid attention and listened," Mrs. Spinner said to the officer.

"Spectacular," said Mr. Spinner, fiddling with the fan controls. "I'd like to see the specs for this device."

Something squeaked.

"Up there!" Samantha shouted, pointing to the rafters.

The balloon clown hovered close to the ceiling. He dangled from a dozen colorful balloons.

"You can't catch meeeeeeeee!" he squealed.

Nipper picked up the bag of sparkling blue powder.

"Here's detergent, Dad," he called, tossing him the bag. "There's a barrel of glycerol behind you . . . and a great big fan!"

Mr. Spinner caught the bag and looked over his shoulder, and then back to Nipper. He nodded. He turned on the wind machine; then he pulled the lid off the barrel of glycerol. He scooped the clear liquid into the bag, shook it, and poured it in front of the vibrating, roaring fan. Soapy bubbles swirled into the air, rising to the ceiling.

Samantha looked up. Bubbles swirled around the clown. As he tried to bat them away, they popped, coating his hands with goopy foam.

"Eeeeeeeeeeek!" the clown screamed, and the balloon strings slipped through his soapy grip. In a flash, the balloons disappeared into the rafters.

Whomp!

The clown landed on the SUN pile. Before he could move, two police officers stepped forward and quickly pulled a corner of the Micronesian flag over him. They tucked it under and twisted the bundle twice, securing him to the big blue clown collection.

The balloon clown's voice buzzed and squeaked from inside the pile, like a shipment from Chinchillas Direct.

Mr. Spinner turned off the fan and walked over to Nipper.

"I'm proud of you, son," he said, patting him on the shoulder. "Good job paying attention and listening when I used glycerol for the super-bubble science show at your birthday party a little over two years ago."

Samantha saw their father wink at their mother. He kept patting Nipper on the shoulder. Or maybe he was wiping glycerol and dishwasher soap from his hand.

As she headed over to congratulate them, she heard the curtain rustling.

"Uncle Paul?" she asked, excited.

But it wasn't Uncle Paul who poked a plaster-covered, paint-flecked head through the curtain. It was Buffy.

CHAPTER SIXTY-ONE

FASHION DISASTER

"Mom! Dad! Why aren't you in your seats?" Buffy screamed, looking past Samantha.

Buffy shook her head angrily, sprinkling bits of glitter from her Egyptian fairy-tale headdress.

"Hi, dear," said Mrs. Spinner. "We had to call the police and help stop some clowns."

Buffy looked at Samantha and glared. Then she turned back to her parents.

"How much of the show have you seen so far?" she asked suspiciously.

"We'll go up to our seats in a minute," Mrs. Spinner replied. "Your father and Nipper just used bubbles to stop a strange flying clown and—"

"Oh, mother!" Buffy groaned. "You and your Seattle

excuses. You're missing my play. So many things are happening without my permission. I'm trying to make *Scarlett Hydrangea's Secret of the Nile* survive."

"Excuse me," said Samantha. "Where did Uncle Paul go?"

"Uncle Paul?" Buffy shot back. "Uncle Paul? I'm working my fingers to the bone, watching every nickel and dime, herding all the people and animals, and all you care about is Uncle Paul!"

Samantha waited.

"Horribly dressed people are all over my theater and—"

Buffy stopped and inspected Samantha's shirt. Her eyes came to rest on a spot of cinnamon slush.

"It's true," she said. "There are actually people out there who look worse than you do!"

Samantha didn't respond.

Buffy stepped away from her sister and pulled back the curtain, revealing the stage and the audience beyond it, and raised her voice even louder.

"My sets are destroyed! The Great Flingo isn't calm! I'm trying to tell the story of the magical eternal battle between good and evil, nobody can find any unicorns for me to buy, and all you care about is Uncle Paul!"

Samantha listened to her sister breathe heavily for a few seconds.

"So . . . do you know where Uncle Paul went?" she asked again.

"Can't you pay attention to anything ever?" Buffy howled. She pointed at the audience. "Look at that crowd! Everyone came to see my show. Everyone got dressed up to look fabulous and—"

She glanced up at the mezzanine.

"Well, almost everyone. There's a fashion disaster in row HH, seat 115."

Samantha looked out at the theater. Nearly two thousand people sat in the audience. Some wore suits, some wore tuxedos, some wore ball gowns. The man in row HH, seat 115, wore a tuxedo T-shirt.

Samantha let out a loud gasp.

"Okay, so there's Uncle Paul," Buffy said quickly. "Happy?"

Samantha was frozen. She could barely breathe.

Buffy turned to her parents.

"Now . . . are you two finally going to watch my show?" she asked.

"Buffy," said Mrs. Spinner. "Did you just find your missing uncle?"

"He didn't need any *finding*, Mother," Buffy snapped. "He was with me in New York, calling himself Horace Temple. I didn't care what he wanted to call himself until he disappeared and I had to make this whole play survive on my own."

She glanced sideways and brushed a chunk of plaster from her shoulder. Then she turned back to her parents.

"Are you . . . going . . . to watch . . . my show?" she asked forcefully.

"Yes, dear," said Mrs. Spinner.

"Good," Buffy snapped.

She took a quick step backward out toward the audience and yanked the curtain shut in front of her.

Samantha heard the muffled sound of her sister shouting. Music started again.

"I'm going to see Uncle Paul right now," Samantha told her parents.

"Come sit with us for the rest of the performance," said Mrs. Spinner. "I'm sure your uncle can sit through a few more . . . Wait—where's your brother?"

Samantha looked around.

"That's odd," said Mr. Spinner, rubbing his chin thoughtfully. "He was located adjacent to me, and then he just vanished."

Samantha shrugged calmly. "It happens all the time, Dad."

Mrs. Spinner wasn't thoughtful or calm.

"This is New York City, George," she said firmly. "We've got to find him before he does something foolish, reckless, or unwise."

Holding hands, Mr. and Mrs. Spinner walked quickly through the backstage area of the theater and left through the loading dock's smashed doorway.

Samantha sped to the theater's side stairs and raced to the second balcony.

Before she'd caught her breath, she began searching for row HH, seat 115. There sat Paul Spinner. Explorer, billionaire, fashion disaster. Waffle maker, storyteller, sticker collector, fugitive, linguist, Hula-Hoop champ, hieroglyphics forger, note writer, flip-flop aficionado, code crafter, flea market trader, art and architecture enthusiast, flannel maven, dog walker, raccoon inflator/deflator, brochure hoarder, Word Whammy! player, exploding-sandals survivor, invisible-ink scribe. Unexplained vanishing person, lavish gift giver, super-secret traveler, and uncle.

She stood at the end of the row and observed. He sat, leaning back, with his arms behind his head, watching her sister's crazy show.

"*Psst,*" she said finally.

Uncle Paul turned and saw her. He gave her a big smile, stood up, and squeezed his way to the aisle.

"I was just starting to enjoy this show," he said. "It looks much better from out here."

Samantha wanted to yell at her uncle. And ask why he had to be so mysterious. And complicated. She thought she might even tell him that this was the last time she'd ever talk to him. She decided she wanted him to be punched squarely in the face.

She clenched her fists.

No. That was not going to make her feel better.

She unclenched her fists and gave him a big hug instead.

"I've really missed you," she said.

Uncle Paul let the hug go on for a good long time. Then he took her hand and led her downstairs to the lobby, where they didn't have to shout over bagpipes, monkey screams, and explosions.

"You were onstage? Inside Buffy's phony Cleopatra's Needle?" she asked.

"Not by choice," he answered. "That balloon clown caught me and stuffed me inside."

He brushed some plaster from the shoulder of his tuxedo T-shirt.

"When the door opened to the June shoe room, I expected it to be you," he continued. "I don't know how he figured out I was in there."

"Sorry," said Samantha. "He overheard us when we figured it out in Machu Picchu, and he got to New York first."

"That's okay," he replied. "You found a way to make everything right again. You're amazing."

It was Uncle Paul's turn to give a big hug.

"I'm so proud of you, Samantha," he added. "A lot of us are."

"A lot of us?" she asked. "Who is 'a lot of us'?"

"Well," he said, "there's your mom and dad, for starters."

She didn't think that was a complete answer.

"Where are your parents anyway?" he asked.

"They went to look for Nipper," she answered. "He's disappeared . . . again."

Uncle Paul looked worried.

"The SUN can't still be dangerous," said Samantha. "Can it?"

"They were never too dangerous," he answered.

She wrinkled her brow, confused.

"Take a moment and reflect on the absurdity of those clowns," he said.

"Been there, done that," she replied.

"I'll explain on the way to Buffy's apartment," said Uncle Paul. "Your brother's in real danger this time, and we've got to find him right away."

Samantha followed her uncle out through the lobby to the street. A taxi sat waiting with an open rear door.

"Central Park West," Uncle Paul told the driver as he hopped in and slid across the seat.

"Quickly, please," Samantha added, following him in and pulling the door shut.

The cabdriver sniffed three times, two short snorts and a long one, and then hit the gas. They sped away, leaving *Scarlett Hydrangea's Secret of the Nile* behind.

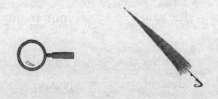

CHAPTER SIXTY-TWO

WEST SIDE, SORRY

Once in a lifetime, a licensed theater critic makes a mistake. A little over a month ago, my mistake was going to East Forty-Sixth Street to see an exclusive one-night preview by Scarlett Hydrangea. I witnessed something atrocious, amateurish, and annoying.

It turns out I had gone to the wrong building.

This evening, I went to the theater on West Forty-Sixth Street. The performance I saw was like no other.

The show began with a parade of animals stampeding onto the stage. They were all unquestionably real, except for the monkey.

Who knew that real live animals could be so good at standing still once a big wind machine got going?

There was an experimental Scottish-Japanese dance number, with flying bagpipes and women in foamy white makeup. They tumbled across the stage as waitress-warriors, holding small silver shields. I couldn't fully understand the meaning of their dance, but it made me hungry for pie.

Then the theater filled with fog. I heard the incredibly loud horn of a huge ocean liner. A loud crunch reverberated through the theater. Without showing or telling us anything, Miss Hydrangea re-created the tragic voyage of the RMS Titanic as it struck an iceberg!

Suddenly, a dramatic explosion of red! A crimson cloud drifted across the theater. An unseen chorus of a hundred voices wailed and moaned in complex harmony. I'm sure it was meant to symbolize the magical eternal battle between good and evil.

Then, boldly defying all theatrical conventions, the sets collapsed! Obelisks and pyramids crashed to the floor, preparing the stage for the stunning, climactic finale.

A colossal blue mummy, as tall as the theater itself, stumbled in from the wings. This was the Secret of the Nile! It moved through the wreckage while twenty-two actors dressed as New York City policemen wrestled the Egyptian behemoth out of sight.

Head, nay, run to this theater, and catch Scarlett Hydrangea's play. I would gladly see it fifty nights in a row, but I am off to the West Coast, where I will secure financing for the big-budget movie version. The world needs more spectacular spectacles such as these.

Charles von Bagelhouven III,
Licensed Theater Critic

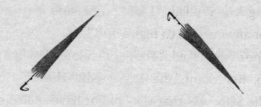

CHAPTER SIXTY-THREE

HEAVEN SCENT

"I didn't doubt you for a second," said Uncle Paul.

The cab turned onto the West Side Highway, heading north.

"I knew you'd find a way to stop the RAIN and the SUN," he said.

"Thanks," said Samantha. "But you left without saying goodbye."

She looked out the cab window, feeling hurt. She watched a few brightly lit skyscrapers pass by. Then she turned back to him.

"And why did you have to make everything so crazy mixed-up, mysterious, and confusing?" she asked.

"I knew that other people might be watching or

listening," he replied. "I had to be sure it wasn't too easy for anyone else to figure out."

"Who?" she asked. "Those ridiculous clowns again?"

"No, not them," he answered. "The only danger from the SUN was that they might have spilled our secrets to someone who is *really* dangerous."

"Really dangerous? Are you worried about Aunt Penny, too?"

Uncle Paul looked confused.

"Aunt Penny?" he replied. "What are you talking about?"

"Nipper thinks 'Don't trust N T' meant our aunt," Samantha said. "I didn't think he was right, but I hid the umbrella in a trombone case just to be safe."

"No," said Uncle Paul. "He's completely wrong. That message meant don't trust—"

Bonk!

A red leather boxing glove shot from the front of the cab and punched Uncle Paul squarely in the face. He fell back against his seat, stunned.

As one, the cab doors clicked locked and tinny circus music began to play from the speakers.

"Thank you for protecting my umbrella until I was able to retrieve it, young lady," the cabdriver said in a creepy, fake-friendly voice.

Samantha was half frozen with fear. She didn't

say anything as she glanced back and forth between the driver and Uncle Paul. She remembered wanting her uncle to get punched squarely in the face when they were in the theater. Seeing it happen definitely did not make her feel better.

They rode the rest of the way to Buffy's apartment building in silence. Samantha noticed Uncle Paul rub his face several times. He looked dazed. That punch must have hurt a lot.

Samantha needed to come up with a new plan.

The cab screeched to a halt in front of the entrance to Buffy's building. Without turning off the engine, the driver got out and opened Samantha's door. He had enormous shoes and wore a red ball nose filter. It was the same horrible top hat clown that spoke to her by Buffy's theater before the play. But now he wasn't wearing his top hat. He was holding it pointed at her face.

"Get out, both of you," he said.

He wasn't using his fake-friendly voice anymore, either.

Samantha and Uncle Paul walked ahead of the clown into the building. There was no sign of Nathaniel, so they went straight to the main elevator. The clown stepped in front of them and pushed the button. The doors opened and he waved them inside, keeping his boxing-glove top hat pointed at them.

Samantha smiled. Nope. She didn't need a new plan.

Samantha and her uncle stood with their backs against the rear elevator wall. The clown aimed his hat at Uncle Paul, then at her, and back at her uncle again.

Samantha glanced at her uncle. He still seemed stunned from the punch in the cab. His face drooped. His arms hung weakly at his sides.

He gave her a quick wink. Then his face drooped again.

Samantha smiled.

She took a half step forward.

"My sister lives up there," she told the clown, and pointed to the penthouse button.

She waved her finger and pointed several times, making sure that she drew his attention to the top button on the panel.

"Yes, yes. I'll handle it," he said, stepping in front of her without taking a closer look at things. He waved his hat a few inches from her nose. "I already know where to find your sister . . . and now my umbrella."

He reached for the elevator control panel with his free hand, not taking his eyes off Samantha. She watched him closely as his hand swept up the vertical panel and hovered. He pressed the top button with his index finger.

Nothing happened.

Keeping his eyes—and his hat—trained on Samantha, he pressed the button again.

But the elevator doors didn't close.

Still not looking, he scratched at the button with his fingernail.

He stopped. His eyes began to turn red and tear up. He sniffed the air three times. A look of horror crept across his face.

He spun to face the elevator panel. His eyes darted quickly up the line of buttons. The top button was labeled "PH." Just above it—where he had pressed twice and scratched—he saw a sticker shaped like a long, thin red fruit.

"A hot chili pepper!" he shouted.

He pried the sticker off the metal panel and turned back to Samantha.

"Did you know about this?" the clown wheezed.

With one hand, he shook the sticker at her.

"She . . . Nose!" said Uncle Paul as he reached out and pulled off the clown's nose ball filter.

With his other hand, Uncle Paul snatched the sticker and stuck it on the clown's real nose. The clown coughed twice and gasped, then fell to the floor, unconscious.

Samantha pushed the real button to Buffy's penthouse.

Uncle Paul picked up the top hat. Using his foot, he rolled Chuckles J. Morningstar out of the elevator just before the doors closed. They started to rise.

"When did you put that sticker there?" Uncle Paul asked.

"Yesterday, as soon as we arrived," Samantha answered.

"Impressive," he said. "How did you know you'd need it?"

"I took a moment to reflect on the absurdity of those clowns," she replied.

The elevator chimed.

"Good one," said Uncle Paul.

The doors opened.

"So," said Uncle Paul. "Where was—"

"Aye!" shouted a raspy voice.

CHAPTER SIXTY-FOUR

WARTS AND ALL

"Scurvy dogs!"—a gruff voice echoed around the glitzy, garish living room.

Nathaniel. He stood near the balcony door, shouting. Instead of a leather coat, he wore a puffy white shirt and a black vest. A red bandana covered his head. With one hand, he waved a sword in the air. With the other, he was gripping Nipper's collar.

"I knew it!" Nipper called. "He's been talking like a pirate the whole time!"

Samantha looked across the room. Mr. and Mrs. Spinner sat on the floor nearby. They were back to back, tied together with colorful yarn. It looked like it must have taken at least a hundred feet of yarn to wrap them so thoroughly.

"Mom?" Samantha called. "What's going on?"

"We're okay, dear," her mother answered. "But I think your sister's assistant is a little unhinged."

"My mind has both oars in the water, ma'am," Nathaniel barked at her. "But my patience . . . has set sail!"

"When we got to the apartment, he said it was time for a *Polynesian surprise*—and he attacked us," said Mr. Spinner.

"Arrrrrr!" Nathaniel shouted.

He swung his sword wildly overhead, scratching the gold ceiling. Flakes of gold drifted onto the $167,000 carpet. Samantha noticed Nipper struggling to get free, but Nathaniel held him tight by his shirt collar.

Samantha had just defeated a hundred clowns and found her missing uncle. A weird pirate did not worry her that much.

"I'm a patient man, am I," Nathaniel growled. "But months of catering to your sister's foolishness . . . has worn me out!"

He swept his hand upward again, banging his cutlass on a nearby statue.

"Now proffer the crimson carapace!" he ordered.

Samantha looked confused.

"I seek the ruby octangulus awning!" he shouted.

Everyone glanced around the room, waiting for someone to interpret.

Nathaniel sighed.

"The umbrella, Samantha. Give me the red umbrella," he said, under his breath.

"Oh. That?" she replied. "No."

"Arrrrr!" he shouted, and waved his sword again. "Hand me the Super-Secret Plans. Then ye shall go free!"

He shook Nipper's collar. "Except for this scallywag," he added. "Far too annoying is he."

Nathaniel pressed the tip of his sword to Nipper's throat.

"Any last words, lad?" he asked.

Samantha held her breath and looked at Nipper. Nipper glanced at her, at the sword, at the piano, and then back at her.

Together, they shouted:

"In a mist-covered ocean far, far from home, there's a mountainous island where dinosaurs roam!"

A scraping, twanging, pounding noise filled the room. It sounded like a guitar tumbling inside a washing machine. The mahogany lid of the grand piano flew open. The Komodo dragon burst out and flopped on the floor next to Nathaniel. It hissed up at him, loudly.

"Bluebeard's bloomers!" Nathaniel exclaimed. "How has this infernal beast found me?"

The giant lizard lurched forward and sank its teeth into the man's leg.

"Avast!" Nathaniel shouted, dropping his cutlass
and falling to the floor.

He flailed his arms, struggling to free his leg from
the mouth of the venomous lizard. But the creature refused to let go.

"Release me!" Nathaniel screamed, slapping at the
lizard's snout.

The Komodo dragon jerked its head mightily and Nathaniel's left leg separated from his body. It was fake!
The rubber leg slid off a wooden stick. The lizard rolled
under the piano with the phony leg in its mouth.

Nathaniel stood up quickly, balancing on the wooden shaft where his left leg used to be.

"He's got a phony leg!" shouted Nipper.

The elevator chimed, and a pair of pink marble doors slid open.

Aunt Penny stepped out with two men in uniform. Samantha read the words *Wild Animal Rescue Team* on their windbreakers. One man held a long pole with a very large net. The other man had a tranquilizer dart gun in each hand.

"There's the monster!" shouted Aunt Penny.

The man with the dart guns fired them both. Two darts hit Nathaniel in his good leg.

"Ahoy!" shouted Nathaniel, collapsing on the floor.

Under the piano, the Komodo dragon chewed furiously on the fake limb.

The other WART agent knelt, reached out his pole, and gently lowered the net over the lizard.

"Yarnnn-nnn," Nathaniel said softly, and then he began to snore.

"I'm so glad you're all safe," Aunt Penny said, helping to untie Mr. and Mrs. Spinner. "I called WART as soon as I saw your suitcase wriggling. But they put me on hold for nineteen hours."

"How did you figure out it was a Komodo dragon?" Nipper asked.

"I didn't," Aunt Penny laughed. "But when your brother is married to a rodent-and-lizard expert, it's always a good idea to be on the lookout for this kind of thing."

Nipper gave Aunt Penny a big hug.

Mrs. Spinner went to check on the Komodo dragon. She took Uncle Paul's waffle tongs from her purse and used them to pull the net away from the spot on the lizard's snout where Nathaniel had slapped it.

"Watch out," Nipper said. "Don't trust . . . net!"

"All right, that's enough," said Uncle Paul, stepping forward. " 'Don't trust N T' was supposed to mean don't trust . . ."

"*Nate,*" finished Samantha.

Everyone looked at the snoring pirate on the floor. Uncle Paul put his hand on Samantha's shoulder.

"You'll have to practice your super-secret codes," he said, "if you're going to become a member of *PSST*."

"I will," she said. "Wait. I mean, I *am*?"

She glanced at her brother, still standing with his arms around Aunt Penny.

"What about Nipper?" she asked.

"I'm not sure he's right for *PSST*," said Uncle Paul. "He seems more like WRUF material to me."

Mr. Spinner stepped forward.

"WRUF! The Worldwide Reciters of Useless Facts," he said excitedly. "I've been a member for years."

He pulled a laminated card from his pocket and held it up.

Samantha squinted at the card. " 'Level Five . . . Master of Minutiae,' " she read.

"Their headquarters is in Llanfairpwllgwyngyllgogery-chwyrndrobwllllantysiliogogogoch," Mr. Spinner added.

"Oh. In Wales," said Nipper.

"This evening keeps getting odder," said Mrs. Spinner.

"Everything gets odd when you add clowns," said Uncle Paul.

Nipper shot Samantha a knowing look. She couldn't agree more.

"We'll take the dragon to the Central Park Zoo, folks," said one of the WART agents.

"Drop the pirate off at the police station on the way, would you, boys?" asked Aunt Penny.

Uncle Paul took out the top hat that used to belong to Chuckles J. Morningstar and adjusted it on his head.

"Oh, no!" Aunt Penny gasped at her brother's new fashion choice. "Please, no. Anything but that."

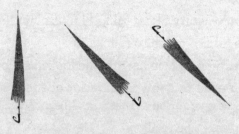

CHAPTER SIXTY-FIVE

CONTRACTS

Samantha and Uncle Paul looked at the city through the panoramic windows of Buffy's living room.

"I knew Nipper would try to talk Mom and Dad into taking the train so he could sneak the lizard to New York," Samantha explained. "And since the train was going past Baraboo, I figured the SUN might sneak on board, too."

Her uncle nodded approvingly.

Samantha put on the purple specs and stared directly at him.

"No clues on me," he said.

"Are you kidding?" she replied. "You're one great big ball of super-secret clues."

"Don't worry," he said. "I'll explain everything. There's just so much to tell."

He turned to face her, and he looked serious.

"You need to know about a lot of super secrets, Samantha," he said. "This goes way beyond you and me and the umbrella."

Samantha noticed that a dark expression had crossed his face. This was the most serious her uncle had ever sounded.

"Okay," she said. "Start with this: Why did you hide in the June footwear room?"

"I didn't hide," he answered. "I got locked in."

"Really?" Samantha asked slowly. "Was it the SUN?"

"No," said Uncle Paul. "When the RAIN showed up in Seattle, I put on big boots and a fake raccoon to make sure the ninjas would see me, and follow me out of town. I also made sure Morgan Bogan saw me, because I knew he'd tell people, and then nobody else would believe it."

Samantha nodded.

"Of course, I knew that you would figure out he was telling the truth," he continued, voice brightening.

Samantha was relieved to see that Uncle Paul was smiling again. He was excited and he waved his hands. He was a great storyteller.

"I took the slidewalk to Indonesia, and I took a hot rocket to New York," he said. "I left stickers behind to help you follow the trail."

"Hot rocket?" asked Samantha.

"Yes," said Uncle Paul. "It's by the Super-Secret Stalagmite. I put the raccoon there so you'd see it."

"Oh," said Samantha, thinking back. "I guess I should have taken a closer look."

"Hmmm," he continued. "I came to New York and made sure that Buffy loaded her show with things that would trip up the SUN. About that time, I realized just how comfortable those big rubber boots were. I only took them off because your sister screamed so much."

Samantha pictured Buffy wailing and whining at her uncle, calling him a fashion disaster.

"So I told her I would fetch different shoes from her June footwear room," he said. "But Nathaniel saw me go in and locked the door."

Uncle Paul glanced up at the ceiling, studying the scratches that Nathaniel had made with his sword. "I warned you about that guy," he said. "I guess I should have kept a closer watch on him myself."

Samantha nodded. "And the A-L-I-M?" she asked.

"You mean L-I-M-A?" he replied.

"I knew you'd be in the hall sooner or later," Uncle Paul went on, "but you wouldn't be able to hear me through the heavy steel door. That's why I used Word Whammy! cards to spell *Lima*. I wanted you to go to Machu Picchu and start learning about *PSST*."

Uncle Paul wiped a bit of plaster from behind his ear.

"That obelisk sure wasn't as nice as the shoe room," he said. "That place has a hot tub and a massage chair, plus a big-screen TV. You wouldn't believe how many shows there are about unicorns."

The elevator chimed again, and pink marble doors slid open. Buffy started wailing before she even stepped into the apartment.

"You're all here!" she howled. "Didn't anyone stay to see the end of my show?"

The room got quiet.

"We had to make a decision, dear," said Mrs. Spinner. "Watch a musical play, or save our children from clowns, pirates, and venomous lizards."

"To some, this might be a difficult, complex decision," said Mr. Spinner.

He walked over to Buffy and put an arm around her.

"To us, the answer was obvious," he went on, and gave her a hug.

Buffy looked at her father and sighed. Then she turned to her mother and sighed again, even more loudly. She gritted her teeth and let out little blasts of air.

"You look like a Komodo dragon," said Samantha.

Buffy walked to the piano in the center of the room.

"Dearest Mother. Clever Father. Won't you stay and see my show?" she pleaded. "I worked so hard to make it survive."

She draped one hand across her forehead and pounded on the piano keys with the other. The musical notes were muted because the piano was full of nutrient-rich waffles for very large lizards.

"Is this still part of the show?" Nipper asked.

"Oh, won't someone watch my great big musical?" Buffy continued.

"Of course we will," said Mrs. Spinner. "We can stay an extra day."

"I wouldn't miss it," said Uncle Paul, and he smiled.

Aunt Penny elbowed him.

Samantha rolled her eyes.

"Hold on a minute," said Mr. Spinner. "You and Samantha can stay, but I've got to fly home with Nipper tomorrow."

He took an envelope out of his pocket, opened it, and removed several folded pages.

"Calculus camp starts Monday morning," he said.

"What?" Nipper shouted.

Mr. Spinner held out the papers.

"You told me you've developed a love of math, so I signed you up for five weeks of computation and problem solving."

Nipper snatched the pages and read out loud.

" 'From its long-division drills to its algebra obstacle course, Camp Pythagoras is an exciting math experience for boys and girls who love computation and problem solving as much as they love major league sports.' "

Nipper handed the papers back to his father.

"I think I'm dying," he said dramatically. "Tell my Yankees I loved them."

"This is better than I thought," said Mr. Spinner, reading. " 'Polynomial equations and square roots come to life through art projects, sing-alongs, and interpretive dance.' "

Nipper looked like his head might explode.

"Mom? Sam?" he pleaded. "Do I have to go?"

Mrs. Spinner didn't answer. Samantha didn't say anything, either, so he turned back to Mr. Spinner.

"I changed my mind, Dad," said Nipper. "I'm kind of over math now."

"Sorry, son," Mr. Spinner told him, examining the pages. "It's an unbreakable contract. You've got to be in Seattle before Monday morning."

He squinted at the fine print.

"Unless . . . you can pass the trigonometry time trials," he added. "Then you can transfer to Pi camp. That starts three-point-one-four days later."

Nipper groaned. His arms fell listlessly to his sides. He knew when he was defeated.

"Little things," Samantha said. "Big consequences."

"Contract," Buffy said suddenly. "I almost forgot."

She walked over to Nipper and held out a manila folder stuffed with papers. Nipper didn't move. He was still stunned by the prospect of five weeks of calculus camp. She tucked the folder under his arm.

Slowly, he opened it and examined the contents.

His eyes grew wide.

"My Yankees!" he gasped.

"You were nice enough to come visit last month," said Buffy. "It really cheered me up. I wanted to do something nice for you."

Nipper hugged the players' contracts and the deed to Yankee Stadium to his chest. It looked like he might cry—tears of pure joy.

"I asked Aunt Penny to buy something special for you without spending too much money," Buffy continued. "She purchased the whole lot of them for three hundred dollars."

Samantha had never seen her brother so happy. Aunt Penny was smiling, too. Samantha had to admit it: her aunt truly was a four-star treasure hunter!

"If you ask me," Buffy added, "I'd rather pass trigonometry time trials then spend a day in a smelly stadium watching a bunch of— Mom? What's wrong, Mom?"

Everyone turned to look at Mrs. Spinner. She stood frozen and pale, with a look on her face like she'd seen a ghost.

Samantha knew exactly what her mother was thinking. It had just dawned on her that she'd promised Buffy she would stay. And if Nipper and Mr. Spinner were going back to Seattle, and Mrs. Spinner wasn't, there could be big trouble. The last five times Mr. Spinner and Nipper spent a weekend alone in the house, there had been destruction, chaos, and—on more than one occasion—explosions.

"Let's make sure no one's careless or forgetful," said Samantha. "Right, Mom?"

Mrs. Spinner smiled at her.

"We don't want any little actions to have big consequences," Samantha continued. "Isn't that correct, Mom?"

Mrs. Spinner nodded.

"We need to make sure everyone takes a closer look at—"

"We all get it, Samantha," Mrs. Spinner said, cutting her off.

She waved to Mr. Spinner.

"Come here, George," said Samantha's mother. "It's time for plan B."

"Ahh," said Mr. Spinner. "B is for *boys* home alone."

All the Spinners, including Penny and Paul, huddled around Samantha's dad and Nipper. They strategized and discussed everything from window repair, to the minimum age for a pilot's license, to farm animal restrictions within Seattle's city limits.

"Don't let anyone play ball in the house," said Mrs. Spinner. "And no paint-filled balloons, either."

"Make the world a better place," Aunt Penny said to Samantha's dad, and she pointed at Uncle Paul's green plaid pajamas. "The two of you could buy some *real pants and shoes* for someone."

For a full hour, they compared lists and grilled Mr. Spinner, prepping him for every possible emergency.

"Do you think some clowns are still out there?" asked Nipper.

Buffy pointed at Samantha's purple octagon sunglasses.

"Well, *she* looks rather clownlike," said Buffy.

"Watch out for the RAIN," said Samantha, ignoring her sister.

"*Psst,*" Uncle Paul whispered to Samantha.

She looked over at him. He had that knowing and worried expression again. It seemed like he was about to say something important.

"Hey!" Mr. Spinner interrupted. "What if there's a lightbulb emergency?"

"I'm sure you can handle that one, dear," said Mrs. Spinner.

George W. Spinner, Senior Lightbulb Tester at the American Institute of Lamps, walked with Nipper to the elevator and pressed the button for the lobby.

The doors opened and the two of them stepped in.

"Wait, Nipper," Uncle Paul called. "Watch out for the WIND."

The elevator doors closed.

Samantha couldn't be sure if Nipper had heard him.

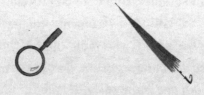

CHAPTER SIXTY-SIX

THE FLYING DUTCHMAN

Nathaniel sat in the back of the Wild Animal Rescue Team van.

He eyed the Komodo dragon beside him. Nestled in a metal cage, it gnawed on a shredded piece of rubber that used to be his leg.

"Just like old times, my fellow nautical dragoon," said Nathaniel.

The creature grunted.

"Have it your way, dragon," he sighed.

Nathaniel reached out to touch the very large lizard's snout. It hissed at him, and he yanked his hand back quickly. The Komodo dragon and the pirate stared at each other for a moment. Then the dragon went back to chewing.

An alarm sounded and a radio crackled.

"Car Nine! We have an urgent primate development in the theater district!" the radio blared. *"A monkey has been spotted fleeing from the police. He is armed with a samurai sword and throwing stars."*

Nathaniel felt the van change direction. A few minutes later, it screeched to a halt. The back doors opened.

"Sorry, captain," a man wearing a WART hat and sweatshirt said. "We don't have time to take you to the police station."

He pointed across the highway to the Hudson River. An aircraft carrier loomed above them.

"That's the USS *Intrepid*," he said. "It belongs to the government. At least it used to."

Nathaniel looked up at the giant ship.

"Go find somebody in charge there," said the WART agent. "Tell them what you've done and turn yourself in."

Nathaniel hopped onto the sidewalk. Behind him, he heard doors slam and the sound of the wagon peeling away. Still woozy from the tranquilizer darts, he looked up at the aircraft carrier. A banner read:

INTREPID SEA, AIR & SPACE MUSEUM

Nathaniel ambled over the bridge above the West Side Highway. It was late at night, and most of the ship was dark, but he saw lights inside the museum lobby. He pushed open the glass doors and entered.

A man in a trench coat and a fedora sat behind the ticket counter. He was reading from a tattered newspaper. A tattered French-language newspaper. The man wore a tin badge shaped like the Eiffel Tower, with the words *Détective Goulot* engraved along the bottom.

"Ahoy!" said Nathaniel. "What's a landlubber like you doing on a vessel like this?"

The man put down his paper and leaned over the counter. He raised his hands and wiggled all ten fingers as he began to speak.

"I was a security guard at the Eiffel Tower," he said slowly, as if telling a ghost story.

"Two American children ran up the stairs without paying for a ticket," he continued, becoming louder and even more dramatic. "I pursued them, but they disappeared. Completely! They left nothing behind . . . except for pieces of a very foul-smelling baguette."

Détective Goulot reached into his coat pocket, pulled out a handful of bread cubes, and waved them under Nathaniel's nose. They smelled like old sneakers, whiteboard markers, sardines, rotting onions, wet paint, and a moldy banana peel left outside for six days.

Nathaniel was a pirate who had lived in a castle on top of a skyscraper until a giant lizard attacked him—but this French guy's story sounded ridiculous!

The peculiar man turned his back to Nathaniel and gazed at a map of the United States taped to the wall. A dozen cities had big Xs drawn through them with a red marker. Circles and question marks surrounded St. Louis, Las Vegas, and Seattle.

"I made a vow to the moon and stars," Goulot continued in his thick accent. "I will bring those young criminals to justice if it takes the rest of my life."

As the Frenchman babbled on about kids, the *Mona Lisa,* and the sewers of Paris, Nathaniel walked through the turnstile and into the Intrepid Sea, Air & Space Museum.

The sound of Nathaniel's wooden peg leg thumping on metal echoed as he walked across the aircraft carrier's flight deck.

Nathaniel reached into the top of his puffy shirt and pulled out his necklace. It was a simple gold chain with a silver charm. The charm was bone-shaped—like a little dog biscuit. The word *Button* was engraved in the center.

Nathaniel pinched it between his thumb and index finger. It clicked. Somewhere nearby, something beeped. He walked on.

He passed several U.S. Navy fighters. Between an F-4N Phantom II and an F-3B Demon, he spotted an old passenger aircraft. With one puffy sleeve, he wiped away dirt on the pilot's side of the plane. The words *Flying Dutchman* appeared on the corrugated metal door.

He opened the door and hopped into the pilot's seat. He scanned the dashboard and flicked the fuel meter with his index finger. The plane had a full tank of gas.

No one in New York City noticed as a 1925 Ford Tri-motor took off from the flight deck of the Intrepid Sea, Air & Space Museum.

The trip from New York to Seattle was long and miserable. The seats in the ninety-year-old aircraft were stiff, and springs poked through the leather upholstery. Nathaniel had to make six refueling stops. Of course, there were no snacks along the way.

If Nathaniel had been able to compare, he would have argued that *his* trip was even worse than flying double-triple super-economy class.

The USS *Intrepid*

The USS *Intrepid* is an aircraft carrier. Commissioned in 1943, it saw action in many battles in the Pacific during World War II, and earned the nickname "The Fighting I."

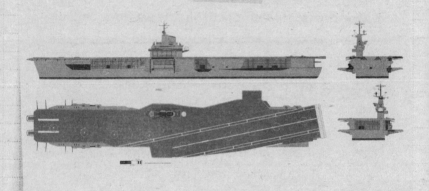

The *Intrepid* was decommissioned in 1974 and anchored off the West Side of Manhattan near Forty-Sixth Street. It is now an air and space museum.

The museum's collection showcases all five branches of the American military and the history of flight. This includes fighter jets, helicopters, a supersonic spy plane, and the space shuttle *Enterprise*.

* * *

Hidden between two fighter jets on the flight deck, you'll find a Ford Trimotor. It's a three-engine transport aircraft, one of those produced by the Ford Motor Company from 1925 to 1933.

You'll need a key to open the door.

The plane is fully operational and has a full tank of gas. There is room for two pilots and eight passengers.

With a flight range of about six hundred miles, you'll have to land and refuel several times to fly from New York City to Seattle.

CHAPTER SIXTY-SEVEN

LIGHTS OUT

"Follow me," said Nipper, walking into his dad's office. "I made an obstacle course. It starts in the kitchen, goes out the window, and—"

Mr. Spinner was on the phone.

"An obstructed potentiometer?" he said. "I'll be there as soon as I can."

Nipper watched him put the phone down and place a duffel bag on his desk.

"Dad," Nipper urged, "I already turned on a hose and primed the booby traps. You've got to come test."

"Sorry, son," said Mr. Spinner. "There's a lightbulb emergency. They need me at the Space Needle."

Mr. Spinner started packing spools of wire and electrical gadgets into his bag. He counted a row of flat, round batteries lined up on the desk table, then swept them into his coat pocket.

Nipper, worried, looked at him.

"It'll be all right, son," Mr. Spinner added as he wound an extension cord around his arm. "I've hired a babysitter for you."

"What? Dad!" Nipper cried. "I'm not a baby!"

"We both promised your mother that we wouldn't set off any explosions," said Mr. Spinner, "and that I wouldn't leave you alone."

Nipper stomped his foot. "I said I'm not a baby."

Mr. Spinner zipped up the duffel bag and slung it over his shoulder.

"Look," he said. "I did some research and hired a woman from the neighborhood."

"What woman? What neighborhood? Who?" Nipper asked, following him into the living room.

"She has a sterling reputation," his father insisted. "I won't be gone very long. Just do everything she tells you to do, and we'll be fine."

He gave a quick thumbs-up and stepped out of the house, pulling the front door closed behind him.

Nipper stood alone in the living room. He crossed his arms. Then he uncrossed his arms. He'd be fine without his dad for a while.

He looked around the room. A professional marker set with 256 colors rested on a high shelf. The vacuum cleaner leaned against the wall. Nipper had always suspected those strange-shaped hose attachments would be good for launching things.

The doorbell rang. Nipper heard the screen door swing. Slowly, the front door creaked open.

"Hello, Jeremy Bernard."

It was Missy Snoddgrass. She grinned menacingly, holding something behind her back with one hand.

"Don't come in, Missy," he said. "There's a sitter on the way, and she's . . . she's . . ."

Missy nodded slowly, still grinning.

His voice trailed off.

"Oh, I *know*," she said.

"You?" Nipper asked, although it really wasn't a question. "You can't be my babysitter."

"Just relax," she said calmly. "I promised your father that nothing would get broken . . . inside this house."

She stepped forward.

"Now you're going to do whatever I tell you."

"Hold on!" said Nipper. "There's no way I'm going to— Hey! Stop it! What are you doing?"

Missy held an industrial cone of brightly colored yarn in one hand. She reached out with her other hand and gave him the end of the yarn. Then she began quickly walking around him.

Nipper looked left and right. Everything was happening so fast. Missy darted back and forth, winding the yarn around his body as she went. Before he knew it, his arms were pinned to his sides.

"Waitaminute, waitaminute, waitaminute!" he yelled.

"Don't struggle," said Missy. "It'll only make it tighter."

She kept going. Skipping now, she went round and round and round. Nipper couldn't move his arms at all. Suddenly, his legs were tied together, too.

"Help!" Nipper cried.

Missy stared into Nipper's eyes for a moment. Then her mouth twisted in a hideous grin. Slowly she turned her head and looked around the living room. Nipper could tell she had spotted the stack of papers resting on the coffee table.

His Yankees!

Missy sneered at him and nodded slowly. Then she scooped up the papers and tucked them into her blouse.

There was nothing Nipper could do about it.

"Oh, you be quiet," said Missy, wrapping yarn across his face.

The room tilted. No. Nipper tilted, trapped inside a big ball of yarn!

"Let's roll," said Missy.

Nipper couldn't see anymore. He rolled, head over heels. He heard a door open and close. He continued rolling.

"Let's roll! Let's roll! *Boo! Boo! Boo!*" a high-pitched voice squawked.

Nipper still couldn't see. He still kept rolling. He tried to think, but he felt really dizzy now.

Nipper tried to remember what Uncle Paul had said, just as the elevator doors closed. What was it? A warning? What did he say?

"Bird brain! Bird brain!" a voice squawked.

"Wait. I got it," Nipper struggled to say. Yarn pressed against his lips. "Watch out for the—"

IT'S TOO BAD NIPPER DIDN'T KNOW ALL THESE
AMAZING FACTS

- John Lennon was a member of the Beatles, one of the most popular rock groups of all time. He was known for wearing glasses with small round lenses. A pair of his sunglasses once sold for $87,000.

- Leo Zimmerman was a trombone player in the early 1900s. He composed many hits in his day and was part of John Phillip Sousa's famous marching band. A trombone owned by Zimmerman once sold for $250,000!

- The 1913 Liberty Head "V" nickel is one of the rarest coins in U.S. history. Only five of them were made. If you find one, it might be worth more than $3 million.

- John James Audubon was a naturalist and artist who specialized in birds. One collection of his illustrations was combined to create a giant book called

Birds of North America. This one-of-a-kind volume sold for $3.77 million.

- Fabergé eggs are sculptures by the artist Peter Carl Fabergé. He created many of them for the rulers of Russia in the nineteenth and twentieth centuries. These highly detailed treasures are covered with precious metal and gems. Some have sold for more than $9 million.

Word Whammy! cards don't cost anything at all. You can go to samanthaspinner.com/wordwhammy and print them out for free.

WHOA, NELLY! THIS BOOK IS FULL OF

SUPER-SECRET SECRETS

You've probably guessed that this book is full of super secrets. So take a closer look at things and find these hidden puzzles and codes:

An Important Message: Do you remember the secret word search from *Samantha Spinner and the Super-Secret Plans*? Try the same trick here! Copy all the ID tags that appear at the top-left corner of Samantha's journal entries. Put them in order by section number, and they will spell out something you should know.

The Snoddgrass Code: Once again, there is a secret message hidden in everything Missy says. Follow the numbers at the bottom of every page where she speaks. There's one digit for each of her words. The number tells you which letter to look at in the word. For example, the number 3 and the word *the* means the letter E. If the number is 0, there's no letter for that word.

The Breakfast Machine: Reread Section 09, about the waffle iron, and make sure you find the secret message. It's too bad Samantha didn't figure it out before they rode the slidewalk to the wrong country!

The Umbrella/Hand Lens Enigma: Each chapter has umbrellas and/or hand lenses at the beginning. It turns out there's a point to them. A *point*. Get it?

Use these super-secret decoders to discover the message.

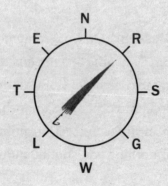

This is *R*, for example. (The handle is pointing to the right and the tip is pointing to *R*.)

This is K. (The handle is pointing to the left and the tip is pointing to K.)

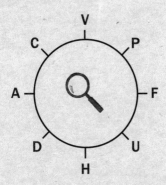

And this is U. (The handle is pointing to U.)

To learn more about all these puzzles, and a whole lot more secrets, go to samanthaspinner.com.

And if you can't get to a computer, or just want some help, keep reading!

SUPER-SECRET ANSWERS

Everyone needs a little help sometimes!

Here are the answers to the puzzles

hidden in this book.

AN IMPORTANT MESSAGE

The Puzzle:

If you put all the journal entry ID tags together in order by section number, they will spell:

TH3R3 1S NO S3CR3T WORD S34RCH H3R3
GO LOOK FOR PUZZL3S SOM3PL4C3 3LS3

Now replace all the numbers with letters:

Change every 4 to an A.
Change every 3 to an E.
Change every 1 to an I.
Change every 0 to an O.

The Answer:

The complete message is:

THERE IS NO SECRET WORD SEARCH HERE
GO LOOK FOR PUZZLES SOMEPLACE ELSE

THE SNODDGRASS CODE

The Puzzle:

At the bottom of any page where Missy speaks, you will find a row of numbers. Each number signifies which letter in each of Missy's words to keep.

For example, when Missy says: **"I'm keeping an eye out for all kinds of suspicious characters,"** the numbers at the bottom of the page are **07001000000**. Each digit coincides with a word Missy says. The number refers to the position of the letter in that word to use to solve the puzzle. For example, **7** means the seventh letter of the word, and **0** means no letter. Thus, the hidden word in this example is **GO**.

The Answer:

The complete message is:

GO TO MY WEBSITE SNODDGRASS DOT COM
TAP THE SKULL

THE BREAKFAST MACHINE

The Puzzle:

Take the letters from Nipper's gibberish on page 88.

```
    D O R P              C H E W
S W I N T Y          S N U L A D
G O R L O N          S T O T S I
S N Y T O T          C H I N S U
M A W E A L          P E N H O O
    U L I A              A R U A
```

Write them into the spaces on the waffle iron diagram.

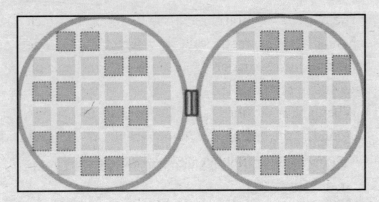

The Answer:

The letters in the shaded squares spell out this message:

    DON'T GO TO MALI

    HEAD TO PERU

THE UMBRELLA/HAND LENS ENIGMA

The Puzzle:

Just like in book one, every chapter in this book begins with an illustration of umbrellas and/or hand lenses. If you can break the code, you'll find that they continue the secret message that started in the first book.

The object's orientation and the direction in which its handle points secretly indicate a letter. (To decode them, use the instructions and the decoder wheels on pages 400 and 401.)

When you're finished, add this message to the one you found in the last book. A double-triple super-secret development in the Spinner saga will be revealed!

The Answer:

NELLY MCPEPPER HAS LEFT THE UNITED STATES AND GONE TO ENGLAND

SHE IS NOW IN LONDON WHERE SHE IS BUSY ASSEMBLING A TEAM OF WARRIORS AND PIRATE HUNTERS AND ART FORGERY EXPERTS

ACKNOWLEDGMENTS

Thank you, **Julian Vecchione,** for telling me this book needed a betrayal, and for all your encouragement and advice along the way.

Of course, this book, just like the first one, happened because of Team Spinner: **Krista Marino, Kevin O'Connor, Kelly Schrum,** and **Dr. Carole Karp.** This book is yours, too!

And what about **Andy Norman, Sean Bond, Mary Travaglini, Nathan Beeler, Peter Sarrett, Mose Milburn,** and **Marta Scully-Bristol?** You all deserve strawberry waffles.

And let me say *gracias, merci, i ni che, spasiba, terima kasi, xie-xie,* and *domo arigato* to **Kathy Dunn** and **Kristin Schulz.** Your support and enthusiasm have helped so much to make sure that Samantha's story isn't super-secret.

Finally, I am way, way overdue for thanking **Mark Levin** and **Jennifer Flackett.** Samantha's story began when you guys encouraged me to be creative long ago!

SAMANTHA'S ON A ROLL, AND NIPPER CAN'T STOP ROLLING!

Turn the page for a sneak peek at the next super-secret adventure.

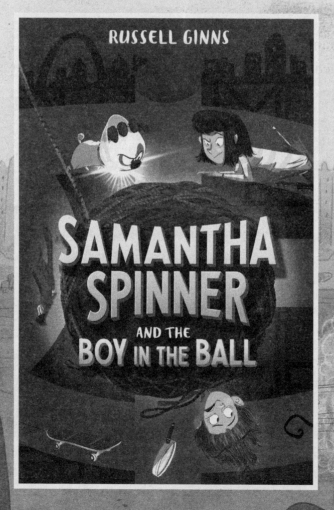

RUSSELL GINNS

SAMANTHA SPINNER

AND THE

BOY IN THE BALL

CHAPTER ONE

THE BAD SEED

"Bird brain! Bird brain!"

Missy Snoddgrass's parrot was still squawking. It never stopped.

"Waitaminute! Waitaminute!"

Nipper had been awake the entire night. Every time he closed his eyes, the horrible bird started talking or squawking or shrieking again.

"Let's roll! Let's roll!"

And, of course, it's hard to fall asleep inside a big ball of yarn.

Everything had happened so fast. One moment he was standing in his living room, talking to Missy. The next moment, she was rolling him head over heels up the Snoddgrass driveway in a massive yarn ball.

"Pajama Paul! Pajama Paul!"

After finally finding Uncle Paul with his sister Samantha, Nipper had had to rush home from New York. His dad had signed him up for calculus camp: Camp Pythagoras. It was an unbreakable contract, and if he didn't show up on time, there would be trouble. Nipper wasn't looking forward to five weeks of calculator karaoke, algebra art projects, and long-division dancing. The trigonometry time trials sounded just awful. But getting trapped in a ball of yarn where you couldn't move your arms or legs was even worse!

He couldn't see anything but yellow wool. And it was really itchy.

"Yankees lose! Yankees lose!"

Nipper was tired, sore, and hungry, and, worst of all, his Yankees really needed him. While she wrapped him up in yarn, Missy had swiped all the New York Yankees player contracts . . . again. She had snatched the deed to Yankee Stadium . . . again. Somewhere out there, beyond the yarn, his Yankees were on a one-hundred-game losing streak, and he was too tied up to do anything to save them.

"Watch out for the —! Watch out for the —! Watch out for the —!"

"Jeremy Bernard Spinner," called a voice. "Stop bothering my bird. You're going to wear her out."

Through a gap in the yarn, Nipper could see the yellow-polka-dot blouse Missy Snoddgrass always wore.

"Come on, Missy," he pleaded. "I've been stuck in here all night. I feel like my head's about to explode."

"Thanks for your words of encouragement," she replied. "I'm trying to set the record for the world's biggest ball of yarn or string or twine."

"Those are three different records," said Nipper.

Through a gap he saw her shadow circling. He figured she was still adding to the ball.

"And you're not even close," he told her. "All three records are more than ten feet in diameter."

"I know, I know," said Missy. "And I'd probably get disqualified anyway because there would be a dead boy inside."

Nipper gulped. He didn't want to find out if Missy was joking or if she really meant it about the dead boy. There had to be a way to escape. He shifted his weight and rocked the ball back and forth a little.

"Stop that," said Missy.

Nipper felt her grab the ball to hold it still. He spotted some fingers through the yarn. On one of them, she wore the emerald scorpion ring he had given her months ago. The green gem flashed.

"Tell you what," she said. "I'll let you go if you give me something I want."

"You already have my baseball team," said Nipper. "Nothing's more precious than that."

"Well . . . your uncle is always giving away interesting presents to you and your sisters," she said.

"I've got two toy cars—and some stickers," Nipper replied, eager to make a deal. "I also have a weird spoon, an old silver dollar, and a really fancy pocket watch."

He struggled to twist his body as he spoke, but the yarn held him in place.

"Let me go and you can have all of it," he pleaded.

Missy's shadow disappeared and reappeared. He hoped she was walking around him, considering his offer. Polka-dot fabric appeared again, very close to him now.

"I'm not interested in stickers, spoons, or watches," said Missy. "But what about that *umbrella* your sister drags around? I'd like to get my hands on that."

"Samantha's not here," said Nipper. "She's still in New York City, and she's with—"

He stopped himself. He was pretty sure Sam wouldn't want him to discuss their adventures. Especially with someone who was double-triple super-evil.

"She'll be back in a few days," he said.

"Fine," said Missy. "I can wait. I'm a very patient person. When your sister comes back, I'll let you go."

"When she comes back?" Nipper cried. "I said *a few days!*"

A strand of yellow dropped in front of his left eye. It reminded him of mustard. That reminded him of hot dogs.

"And I'm getting hungry," he whined.

"Hungry?" she asked. "I can help you with that."

Through the yarn, Nipper could see her reaching into the front pocket of her blouse. She pulled out her hand, reached up to the ball, and slapped the gap in the yarn near his mouth. Little round, dry bits came flying in. He licked his lips. Crunchy . . . but not much flavor. Seeds?

"Hey!" he shouted, spitting them out. "This is . . . this is bird food."

"Oh. So now you're a picky eater?" asked Missy.

"*Picky eater! Picky eater, picky eater!*" squawked the parrot.

In the distance, a doorbell rang. Missy leaned in close.

"You're going *no place*," she whispered through the yarn.

Nipper heard her walk up the side porch and into her house.

He really needed to get out of there. He shifted his weight and tried to make the ball rock again.

"*No place! No place!*" screeched the horrible bird.

He massaged his forehead with his fingers nervously. He hadn't spoken to his wife since yesterday. That was before their son vanished.

"I'm waiting until I find Nipper first," he said.

"That's very smart of you," said Missy. "Very good. Dr. Suzette Spinner would probably be very upset if she found out you lost one of her children."

George nodded. They had spent a lot of time in New York reviewing strategies on how not to lose track of things or let the house get destroyed.

"You don't want your wife to be worried . . . or *really, really mad,* do you?" Missy asked.

George nodded. The odd young woman definitely seemed to understand the situation.

"Do you want everyone in your family to think you're careless, forgetful, and unreliable?"

George shook his head three more times.

"Maybe . . . it's a better idea to call *Samantha*," she said slowly. "Samantha can come home and help you search."

"Excellent suggestion," said George.

Maybe it hadn't been a mistake to hire her as a babysitter. She was definitely a smart young lady.

"Good," said Missy, smiling at him. "Good . . ."

Out of the corner of his eye he could see her reaching for the doorknob. Then . . .

"Bye!" Missy yelled, and she slammed the door.

George stood on the porch for a minute, reviewing everything Missy had told him. Then he turned toward home.

"There's at least one flaw in that young woman's story," he said as he walked to his own front door. "My electric car doesn't make any noise."

CHAPTER THREE

INTERRUPTED VANISHING PERSON

Samantha went looking for Uncle Paul.

He was somewhere in Buffy's apartment.

She had fought off ninjas, traveled from France to Italy to Indonesia to Peru to Mali, tracked her uncle down in New York, and saved him from clowns. Now, finally, she was going to learn *everything*.

Samantha was going to learn all about the Super-Secret Plans. How did all those pictures and diagrams get inside the umbrella? Why did her uncle give it to her? What exactly was PSST, the Partnership of Super-Secret Travelers? What was the story behind that amazing map room she and her brother had found in Peru, under the ruins of Machu Picchu?